T0127211

The VENUS VENDETTA

Rose Pry

Spinsters Ink

2009

In Chapter 24 lines from the song "Snowin' in Brooklyn" by Ferron are reprinted by permission of the composer/artist. "Snowin' in Brooklyn" was copyrighted to Ferron and published by Nemesis Publishing 1983. It is from her album, Shadows on A Dime.

Copyright © 2009 by Rose Pry

Spinsters Ink
P.O. Box 242
Midway, Florida 32343

All rights reserved. No part of this book may be reproduced or transmitted in any form or by any means, electronic or mechanical, including photocopying, without permission in writing from the publisher.

Printed in the United States of America on acid-free paper
First Edition

Editor: Katherine V. Forrest
Cover designer: LA Callaghan

ISBN-10: 1-883523-98-2
ISBN-13: 978-1-883523-98-5

To Linda. You've been the wind in my sails and my safe harbor in life's storms. Twenty-eight years—never ever *dull.*

Acknowledgments

The mystery writer Mary Roberts Rinehart took me for an ice cream cone in her chauffeured limousine when I was seven or so. I was impressed with the writer's lifestyle. Forty-three years later Katherine V. Forrest came to speak at a Women United of Nevada meeting here in Las Vegas. I was not only impressed, but inspired. I went to work writing. Today her divine editing elevates my work. Thank you, pen-sisters.

My firstborn daughter, Kaanii, helped me find my voice and to listen to the sound of my own words. Thank you.

My youngest girl from the first batch, Bobbie, taught me to put the tension and the "Auggggh!" into my stories. Thank you.

My sweetie, Linda, supported me these last ten years as I wrote *The Venus Vendetta,* had it edited and finally published. Thank you, Lindyloo.

My youngest daughter, Roslyn, keeps me young and in touch. Thank you, Rozzie-roo.

My cadre of women has loved me and always told me the truth. Thank you, all.

About the Author

Rose Pry was born in Peekskill, New York, on August 27, 1936, to a first-generation American-Ukrainian mother and a German-born father. Just before the end of the Second World War, after a particularly bitter cold winter, her brave folks pulled up stakes, packed Rose and her sister Evelyn into the backseat of a friend's brand-new 1946 Buick and struck out for the West Coast and a better place to raise a family. She always wrote, even as a child. She kept her scribbles secret but enjoyed reading them to herself.

After a short stint in the air force, a twenty-year marriage to a San Diego cop and having three children, Rose divorced, went back to school, came out, not only of the sexual closet but the housewife closet as well—she became a barber. After a year's apprenticeship in La Jolla, California, she moved to Las Vegas to become one of the first female barbers in Nevada.

She now lives there with her partner of twenty-eight years, a sociology professor, and their sixteen-year-old daughter. The Pry clan now includes five grandchildren and three great-grandchildren.

She was known quite simply as The Rose when she began penning her comedy column in the *Las Vegas Bugle* twenty-two years ago. And again when she did stand-up comedy in her late fifties. Rosie was her byline when she was a columnist for *What's On* magazine.

Now Spinsters Ink is publishing her first novel, *The Venus Vendetta*.

"My life has provided the research and grist for my literary mill," Rose said recently, "now I'm having such a good time putting it all to work."

Prologue
Encinitas, California
October 1998

There was a salty bite to the air. Tracked-in beach sand grated under Jazz's Armani sneakers. The air in the dingy hall, a complex brew of low tide, pine cleaner and hot chicken wings, made his eyes water. He pulled a clean folded handkerchief from his pocket, daubed his eyes and the cold sweat from his brow. He clutched the cloth over his nose and mouth and peered through a bamboo-bead curtain. His ragged breathing was due more to unbridled anxiety than his sprint down the dirt alley behind the bar.

The burly man he had seen get off the Solana Beach train earlier sat at the bar looking half-again as wide and fourteen shades paler than the pub's late afternoon congregation. He hunched over a tall bottle of beer intently fixed on removing its label in narrow strips. A rank of "dead soldiers" stood empty before him, a naked tally of his bar tab.

Jazz sucked a breath through the hanky and swallowed hard. "This guy is a behemoth," he exclaimed and fought the urge to turn and bolt back into the gathering night. Grisly police photos of one of the man's victims flashed unbidden before his eyes. "Oh, God," he gasped and made a conscious attempt to shift his thoughts to Reggie. His big sister needed him. He clenched his eyes shut for a moment and forced his mind back to the task at hand.

After he took a few deep breaths his heartbeat settled down a bit and the whole beachfront bar came into a sharper focus.

A dozen lean and tanned surfer types clustered at tiny tables around a dance floor. A few loners were scattered around the bar. Palm-frond fan blades swirled smoke with snatches of conversation and vintage Beach Boys.

Jazz reached in his jacket pocket to check the time on his cell phone. 4:48. He made sure it was set on silent. After a few more heartbeats and a deep breath, he sliced through the curtain into the convivial atmosphere of the place. The beads chattered in his wake as he walked halfway down the bar and hoisted himself up onto a stool. "Mickey's," he said to the bartender. The man nodded and dropped two stained coasters in front of him.

Three empty stools filled the space between him and the brawny trainman. The stale air felt so thick with his own fear, Jazz was sure the lout could smell it.

He forced himself to count to twenty before he raised his eyes to the angled, overhead mirror that ran the length of the bar. In back of his own reflection, Southern California beachfront bar-life played itself out on this early Saturday evening.

His eyes snapped back when the barman set a frosty mug and a squat green bottle on the coasters in front of him.

"Go, Rebels!" The barkeep smiled and knuckled the UNLV Rebel logo on Jazz's Windbreaker. Jazz raised the bottle to him and waved away the change. His phone vibrated. It was Gillian. He ignored it.

• • •

Three thousand miles away Gillian Waters sat on the floor of a darkened elevator. The door was propped open a couple of inches with a patent leather wingtip. The light from the outer hall cast a narrow beam on a lock of gray hair falling across her strained eyes. "Good grief, Jazz," she rasped. "Pick up. Pick up." His cell went to voicemail again. She took hers from her ear and heaved a sigh.

Jazz tipped his head back to swig directly from the wide-mouth bottle, bringing his gaze back to the mirror. Gradually he eased his eyes to the right. From this angle the huge man's sweaty bald crown, surrounded by a ring of closely cropped hair, seemed to rest directly on his massive shoulders. A fringe of curly back hair crept above his wrinkled collar, and his banana-thick, tattooed fingers were busy stripping his fourth longneck Schlitz. Jazz transposed the mirror images of letters on the man's fingers. The left fist read, ROAR, and the right, RIP 'N'.

A shudder waved through Jazz's body. If he held any doubt about this guy's real identity, Ripley's nickname was . . . Rip.

The hum of casual barroom conversation mimicked a bass line to some circa '70s Creedence Clearwater on the jukebox. In the far corner, a leathery cadaver of a man with a gray ponytail perched his bony butt on an old wind-up piano stool and played along on a tinny upright.

A woman's abrupt shriek of laughter pierced the drone. The big man's startled gray eyes jerked up to search the dusty mirror. His raptor-like gaze swept left and locked onto Jazz's frozen, wide-eyed gape.

Jazz felt the muscles of his inner thighs go weak.

Steady now, he admonished himself as he tore his eyes free and chased the acrid taste of anxiety with a swig of beer. After mustering a degree of nonchalance, he swiveled his head and said, "Have we," his voice cracked, "have we met somewhere?"

The big man looked directly at Jazz with shrewd, suspicious eyes. His expression relaxed visibly once he assessed Jazz's slight frame and the rainbow of six stones piercing the rim of his right ear.

"Could be," the man answered with a smile. "I've been there."

His shaggy, unkempt eyebrows and knobby nose made him look less menacing, but his chilly smile was purely a contraction of facial muscles and did not involve his eyes. After several silent moments he nodded toward the rear exit and said, "What's say we grab some air and see if we can remember?" He dropped a folded bill next to the pile of peeled labels and drained the longneck. He picked up a scruffy suitcase and headed for the back door.

"We could just talk here . . ." Jazz said to the man's retreating back as it disappeared through the swaying beads. ". . . Or not."

His phone vibrated. Once again he ignored it and downed the last of his beer. It slid into his churning stomach like ice-cold thumb-tacks. He gave his option cards one last mental shuffle as he parted the curtain. Everything in his being willed him to avoid the dirty alleyway, but as far as he could see, his options leaned heavily toward . . . none. He wasn't willing to give this randy guy what he seemed to be expecting but at least getting him out the back door was a good start.

Maybe I can convince him to leave the area and avoid Reggie all together. He caught the closing door and started down the five steps to the dimly lit alley.

The last traces of daylight were fading fast. A murky layer of slate-gray fog lowered the sky and muffled the surf. The air was chilled and heavy with the fetid smell of rotting seaweed.

Various scenarios reeled through Jazz's mind as the heavy door clicked shut. The abrupt silence roared in his ears and jarred his equilibrium.

"Sir," he began, feigning a casual air, "I do need to talk to you."

The bruiser dropped his suitcase to the gritty concrete. At the grating sound, Jazz intuitively twisted to vault back up the stairs. The huge man was fast. He grabbed a handful of Jazz's jacket and yanked him around into a jackhammer punch to the left side of his face. R I P 'N' exploded into Jazz's left peripheral vision just before the fireworks burst behind his eyes. He bounced off the metal railing and landed face down on the littered concrete.

"Pervert!" the man spat. "Fuckin' boys upstate don't mean a fuckin' thing, don't give you fuckin' punk pansies the okey dokey to come on to me on the outside," he snarled, "so maybe I'll just teach you not to jump to fuckin' conclusions."

The searing pain in Jazz's head didn't stop him from musing snottily that the jerk managed to use fuckin' four times in one sentence. He struggled to push himself upright with one hand as he held out the other in an ineffective effort to stave off the attack.

"You don't understa—" he began.

The big man sliced off Jazz's protest with a field-goal kick to his ribs that lifted him slightly and rolled him to the murky edge of the puddle of light.

The man threw his arms into the air and did a lumbering jig in mock end-zone triumph. "He kicks! He scores!" he announced skyward and simulated a cheering crowd. "I just love doing that," he gushed.

All Jazz could do was struggle to suck air into his deflating lungs. He knew then he was going to die and couldn't think of a reason why or a single thing he could do to change that fate. He curled into himself like an injured armadillo. Hugging his pain, he felt it . . . the cell phone in his Windbreaker pocket. He peered through thickening webs and managed to press one button and then another. More than anything now, he wanted to sleep.

With the pointed toe of one scruffy boot, the savage flipped Jazz onto his back, his finger hit the speaker button as the little phone scudded from his limp hand into the shadows next to the stairs. Jazz abandoned his body then and let his mind slither like the little phone into its own darkening void.

A doleful foghorn mourned offshore.

The brute unbuckled the young man's belt and yanked his leather pants and white briefs to his knees. He lit a cigarette, dragged deeply and surveyed his work. He bent over and grabbing a fistful of the young man's jacket dragged him toward the stairs.

They didn't hear the whispered, "Jazz?"

The damp, sandy concrete abraded Jazz's naked buttocks and nudged him upward toward wakefulness.

"Oh, God! Reg, the alley!" he sobbed in desperation, before drifting far away to search through his past to find a time and place where he felt true safety.

"Oh, God! Reg, the alley!" the big man mimicked in a prissy falsetto.

Jazz's mind was already far, far afield when the man tossed his cigarette aside, picked up the limp body like a duffel of dirty laundry and threw it onto its belly halfway up the steps to the bar.

Part One

Chapter 1
Indian Summer
1972

Jazz sprawled on his belly in the fine dirt under the scarf-draped plywood shelves that formed The Family's booth. His left cheek rested on one outstretched arm as he dropped small polished stones into little piles in the dirt. The pebbles landed with a click and a teeny puff of dust.

Today, he decided, this was his *very* special place and the silky smooth stones were his *very* best things. *Very* was his new word. He liked the way his teeth bit his bottom lip when he said the word.

"*Very, very, very* good," he whispered. "Star's here. I wonder where Kali and Reggie are—or if that *very* teeny ant can see me."

Vestiges of summer warmed the late afternoon air. Gleeful voices of children at play wafted from an adjacent meadow. A garland of makeshift booths fringed a clearing in a small, roadside forest. Dingy lengths of clothesline anchored The Family's booth to nearby trees. From these anchor ropes a colorful chorus line of shirts and dresses danced and fluttered in the autumn breeze.

People ebbed and flowed around the circle of booths. Most of them wore tattered jeans or bellbottoms, variegated shirts or peasant dresses. There was lots of laughter and music. The weekend hippies had turned in their platform shoes for suede moccasins or leather sandals. Upwind, charcoal stoves grilling assorted foods threaded on sticks sent up fragrant smoke.

Jazz liked to let the silky stones slip from his fingers as he counted, "One, two, seven, nine, twenty-two." He liked silk.

He was a slight boy with skin tanned almost the same color as his faded shorts. A sprinkle of freckles dusted his perpetually peeling nose, and tousled white-blond curls framed his face.

He fingered the hammered silver charm that dangled from a supple, knotted hemp cord tied around his neck and listened to some of The Family making music down by the food booths. He mouthed some words about a peace train. *Trains with whistles and engineers are . . . groovy.* He snickered at the word. He could hear the *V* sound. Reggie had shown him how to pump his fist up and down so the engineer would toot his whistle. "Groovy," he said and laughed.

He liked it here under the counters of the booth hidden by the scarves and stuff that draped down. It felt familiar, like a secret cave that never changed much no matter how far The Family drove in the old flowered bus.

He remembered Reggie, his sort of sister, telling him the story about how they became The Family—at the very beginning.

"*Very,*" he chanted in a whisper.

"The times were too-mul-chew-us," he crooned to himself in Reggie's creepy story voice. That word meant bumpy she had told him. Jazz didn't mind bumpy. He even liked it.

In The Family everybody loved everybody but Star and Kali cared for Jazz and his best friend Reggie most of the time. Reggie was Jazz's special person. He wasn't her "bellybutton" brother. She said he was her "Bonus Brother."

He closed his eyes and heard Reggie's voice reciting from memory word for word.

In spring and summer the commune in upstate New York is home. But, before the onset of the coldest months, like birds, they migrate toward a warmer winter. Never later than September, they gather their motley collection of brightly flowered vehicles to form a caravan and wend as far south as local tolerance will permit.

He always forgot to ask her what motley and tolerance meant.

The grownups make music, cast candles in the sand and roll fat sticks of incense, Reggie recited in his head. *Some make beadwork jewelry and guitar straps. Kali and Star sew filmy dresses and shirts with random bursts of brilliant colors. They call all these things "wares" and sell them at "Happenings" like fairs and flea markets, Love-Ins and sometimes music festivals,* she had explained.

They had joined this fair a week ago on Reggie's sixth birthday.

Jazz thought the powdery dirt smelled like sunshine and old leaves today. His smooth stones were like the magic beans in that story about the giant that Star read him a bunch of times.

"Virginia," Jazz said just over his breath. "We are in Virginia . . . Ver-gin-ya."

This morning he heard some Ver-gin-ya people call The Family flower children and hippies. He would ask Reggie about that.

Sometimes he and Reggie stretched out on their backs in a field or on the beach and peeked at the sky through his translucent stones. But, he remembered he mustn't ever look right at the sun, even with the stones because Reggie told him he might get "eyeclipses" and never see ever, ever again. He promised her he would never do that— not even a little squint.

Jazz rolled over on his back and looked up at Star. With short stubby fingers she lifted her long, dark hair from her soft shoulders and bent to one side to shake it loose. She spotted Jazz under the counter and gave him a sleepy smile. Her eyes looked soft and drowsy.

"Hi, Jazzyboy," she said.

"Hi, Star," he answered.

• • •

Star straightened and tilted her head toward a gust of wind as it rustled through the trees. A flurry of yellow and orange leaves released their grip on the branches and drifted down to herald the fall. She turned her face to the confetti shower and Jazz laughed at the sight.

"It hasn't rained once since we got here," she said, and turned slowly, her face upturned and her arms outstretched, "What's it been, a week?" she asked of no one in particular. She drew a deep breath of sweet autumn air. It carried the scent of decomposing leaves and the freshening hint of an Indian summer storm. "I think maybe today."

The old school bus was parked between the trees a few yards away. Bright flowers, vines and peace signs covered most of the original yellow paint.

"I'm glad we parked the bus close by," Star thought out loud. "If it rains, I can get most of the dresses under cover in two trips."

She was deep in detailed thoughts of how she would sweep the things off the counter into boxes underneath when a tall, thin, bearded man emerged from the crowd and sliced into her fuzzy periphery. He wore a stark, ill-fitting black suit with a skinny black tie.

"Look at that guy," she said, annoyance creeping into her reverie. "He looks like an Amish hit man," she chuckled, amusing herself.

The stranger's dark angular looks seemed out of place here amid the colorful booths and the casual dress of the crowd, but her little inside joke left a broad smile on her lips when she greeted him.

He glanced at the wares on the counter and picked up a gritty, gray ball. "This feels like sand," he said and indicated the round ball of a candle in his hands. He lifted his ice-blue eyes to hers. Star felt little snapping synapses scamper up her neck and prickle her scalp.

It only took a moment for her to shrug off her weedy paranoia. "Yes, sir," she said in a pleasant, friendly voice. "The gritty sides of the candle come from the beach."

He looked at her, his eyes void of understanding.

"We cast the candles in the beach sand," she elaborated, "at the beach . . ." she trailed off redundantly.

She remained aware of him as he fingered the soft, cotton scarves, the shiny pebbles and beadwork. He picked up a small ceramic smoking stone, set it down and drew a fat, fragrant hand-rolled stick of incense from a bunch sprouting out of an empty peanut butter jar on the counter. He passed the pungent stick under his nose.

Jazz listened to the voices as he fingered little bits of subtly tinted, translucent sea-glass worn smooth in the ocean. These were the most magic.

When the dark stranger made his selection Star placed the gray, sand-cast candle in a small brown paper bag and took his money. She dropped the incense stick into the bag and waved off further payment with another smile.

Jazz clenched a piece of smooth, yellow sea-glass in the socket of each eye. He scooted out a bit from his hiding place and peered skyward. The startled man looked down at the tousle-haired, yellow-eyed boy.

"That's just Jazz," Star assured him noting his surprise.

Jazz looked directly into the stranger's gaunt, yellow face. His own eyes shot wide and the pieces of glass fell to the dirt. He felt creepy-crawlies in his chest. It looked as though there were two holes in the man's head and he could peer clean through those holes into the pale blue sky. A brief smile escaped the man's somber face and Jazz ducked back under the shelves.

The man looked back at Star, held her gaze a moment too long then turned away. She shuddered and felt her tiny neck hairs bristle. *Weird.*

A girl had been watching the whole scene unfold from the lowest branch of a tree behind the booth. She wore a dress like the ones swaying from the booth moorings. Under it was a pair of tattered, olive drab and moss-green camouflage pants. Her crinkled reddish-blond curls flipped and twined around her serious face and her two bottom front teeth were missing. She slipped down to the ground with a thud and scuttled under the counter beside Jazz.

"Hi, Reg," he greeted her. She grunted a response. Together they peeked out between the colorful scarves and watched the tall stranger as he left with two other dark-clad men.

Star squinted her eyes and tilted her head. The suits' retreating legs looked like angular, black birds crisscrossing into a sunset.

"Jeez," Star commented as she, too, dropped down cross-legged into the dust. She held the sputtering flame of a wooden match to the twisted cigarette she pulled from behind one ear. The paper burned unevenly and smelled like home. Gripping the doobie with her lips and squinting her eyes against the rising smoke she held a fat incense in the flame before she shook out the match and ground the charred remains into the dirt. After the incense burned a few moments she waved it in circles until the flame died and the tip glowed burnished orange. Wisps of patchouli and tangy THC spiraled into the air joining the fragrance of impending rain and roasting food.

A tall, slender woman with a tangle of shoulder-length auburn spirals stepped into the booth and dropped to the dirt beside them.

"Hey, Kali, girl," Star greeted her.

Both women wore gossamer dresses. Kali's tawny hair was dotted with tiny, purple wildflowers. Six-year-old Reggie's face mirrored the slender woman's but the child's bore a more serious expression.

Each woman in turn sucked on the doobie through pursed lips. They made loud hisses when they drew the heady smoke deep into their lungs and smiled at the children with half-closed eyes. They held their breath for several seconds before the pent-up smoke expanded and whooshed out amid coughs and sputters. Soon they started to giggle. The children giggled, too.

A gust of wind swept through the clearing. More leaves rained down. Star felt a chill. She pulled down a little tie-dye shirt and slipped it over Jazz's bony, suntanned shoulders.

The boy scooped up his polished stones and funneled them into a soft drawstring bag tied to a belt loop on his shorts. He shoved the bag deep into his pocket.

Kali reached up on the counter and got a small brown paper bag of dried apricots. She popped one into her mouth and gave one to Star and each of the children to chew. Syrupy sweet drool dripped down their chins. She pushed a few more of the wrinkled orange discs into the children's pockets.

"Share," she said as she cupped Jazz's little upturned face in her hand. Then with kisses on their foreheads, she shooed them toward the meadow and the other children.

Chapter 2

Stolen Wildflowers

Just before twilight the three tall men in suits backed up their large black sedan to the meadow. The children ran down to see what that was about.

"I'm Preacher Hawk, I'm looking for Jazz," one man said.

"Why, mister?" Reggie asked.

"There's been an emergency. The lady in the booth asked us to bring him to meet her in town," he answered. His eyes fell upon Jazz holding her hand. "Come, Jazz, we will give you a ride."

"He won't go without me," Reggie said.

The man hesitated then said, "That's all right, child, we will take you both to her."

He offered chocolates and the youngsters smiled and climbed up into the rear seat of the big sedan to eat the sweet candy. The car drove away.

Solemnly, the rest of the children stood on the dirt trail and watched as the square black sedan kicked up dust and disappeared around a bend in the road. They wondered why they didn't get any of the brown chocolate and a ride in the big black car . . . and what an e-mer-gi-cy was.

Soon the sedative in the candy took effect. The children lay intertwined on the backseat like two little puppies and fell into a deep sleep. The three men sat abreast on the wide front seat. It was almost dark when one of the men reached back and covered the children with a threadbare green blanket. The car traveled through the night.

When a full bladder awakened Reggie the old sedan was laboring up a steep grade among tall pines. The sky through the oval rear window was steely gray.

Reggie reached up and tugged on the driver's sleeve. The startled man reacted with a jerk.

"Hey, mister," she whispered, "Jazz needs to tinkle."

The men conferred and the driver brought the sedan to a halt. They stood watch as the children peed unabashedly by the roadside.

As the little ones settled back in the car each man slipped discreetly, one at a time, into the brush to relieve himself.

Back on the road again, Jazz dozed. Reggie listened to the strange men's voices for a while and wondered how far town was. The men talked about somebody called gawd and demons and the need to rescue children. They called the children in the backseat the rescued ones. They said things like, "Prazegawd," and "Aw-men!" a lot. She slept.

Later that morning tummy grumbles reminded Reggie about the apricots. She and Jazz dug the linty remains from their pockets and chewed them. One man poured cool water into a heavy, white mug for them to sip and offered them a hunk of crusty brown bread wrapped in a large square of white cloth.

One more shared piece of chocolate, the drone of the motor and the sameness of the woods lulled the little passengers back to sleep.

• • •

"Now, now," a stout man attempted, in his soft Virginia accent, to mollify the agitated crowd in the storefront sheriff's office, "just settle down." In a few moments he tried again. "People!" he entreated, "I cannot understand you when y'all talk at once!"

Despite his extra girth, Doc Crouter's regular army training was still apparent. He stood ramrod straight behind his desk. Crisp parallel creases ran down his starched khaki uniform shirt from the shoulder seam, through his clavicles, over his rounded belly and into his belt. The town's main law enforcement officer/water commissioner/ road maintenance supervisor viewed the band of wild-haired, tie-dyed hippies that stood in front of his desk with a nervous smile as though the alien creatures had arrived in a flower-painted flying saucer instead of the dilapidated old converted school bus parked out front. "One at a time!"

The women were obviously battling hysteria. He feared it would surge up and burst out in a maniacal wail. He hated when that happened. It put him in mind of those screeching women standing knee-deep in the 'Nam rice paddies while their hootches burned. He could take all the other stuff, but the keening women made him want to smash the butt of his M-16 into faces—any faces.

Doc pulled a folded handkerchief from his back pocket and wiped some sweat from his brow and upper lip. His ears were ringing again. He pointed at Gordo who stood beside Kali. "You, young man."

Kali placed her hand on Gordo's huge forearm, gave him a frightened smile and said to the officer, with forced calm, "Someone has stolen our children!"

Doc adjusted his voice to deal with the pretty young woman who spoke out. "Well, now, that's pure awful! Tell me about the children and what happened."

Doc's nose seined through the atmosphere of patchouli, sweat and panic that engulfed the whole band, trying to detect the odor of marijuana. He couldn't quite tell if it was hidden there, but felt sure that it was. On a pocket-sized field interrogation pad he wrote:

. . . *two children three and six, multicolored clothes, peace sign medallions, long hair—check adults for dope and draft cards.*

"They were playing in the meadow," Kali explained, "thirteen kids, when a car just drove up and took our two children away."

"My little boy is three! Oh, my God!" Star's eyes widened, her legs grew weak, "Only three," she repeated. She breathed deeply to drive away the terror and the dreadful pictures that flooded into her mind.

Kali pushed up beside her and looped her arm through hers to steady her. "We were right there—fifty feet away! The other children said it was a big, black sedan—and men in black clothes," she said. "We think we saw them earlier in the day. They looked sort of Amish—you know, beards and black suits and hats."

"So, they didn't take all the kids?" asked Doc as he made more notes.

"No." She looked at Star, swallowed and squeezed her arm. "Only our two."

Doc had dealt with hippies before. Some were real trouble. Some were worthless sons-a-bitches, for sure. Most were just young folk—kind of sleepy-eyed and harmless. They made the townsfolk skittish, though, what with their free love, not bathing and all.

"So, which of you is the daddy?" he asked looking over the unkempt crew.

Kali and Star looked at each other and said in unison,

"Dead."

"Divorced."

Star said, "My old man is dead, and hers is divorced, er, she is divorced—from him," she added.

They all looked at each other—fighting the urge to run into the streets screaming in frustration. They knew they must remain calm, stay level to get through to this guy—to make him care.

Doc looked at them over little round reading glasses perched halfway down his nose and said, "Hmmmm. Do you have a picture of the children?"

Kali dug into the drawstring bag she wore tied around her waist and pulled out a strip of carnival pictures that had been taken by a machine. The first three shots were all the same. The last frame showed Jazz with a wide smile that shined up his face.

"Well, we will do our best," Doc said using the strip of photos to mark the page in the little pad.

Star and Kali were not convinced.

Chapter 3

The Enclave

A weaving, jouncing sensation edged into Reggie's fitful sleep. "I wonder where we're going today," she yawned, and nestled in for a few more winks.

Warm, intermittent rays of sunlight zigzagged over her eyelids. She kept them closed. She became aware of Jazz sleeping beside her and realized that the fabric under her cheek wasn't the cool leather seat of the family bus. Reality oozed into her chest and she let her eyes open a slit.

Rats, it wasn't just a yucky dream.

The trail grew steeper. Reggie pulled herself up to look beyond the men in the front seat. The car was climbing up a rough, dirt track. She opened her mouth wide a couple of times and swallowed to make her ears pop. Twin ruts wound up the incline toward another pine forest. Brambles were in the process of reclaiming the path from both sides and the middle.

The car labored on. Where to? What to?

Deep in her camouflaged pants pocket she squeezed her little paisley bag of treasures. She sat back and rocked a little bit. She felt the acorn. She had picked it up from that man's grave where the little fire burns all the time. The sign said not to. The sharp edge thing was a guitar pick. A tall black man with a headband around his 'fro gave it to Star at that Wood-place where they set up their booth and slept in the bus. There were whole bunches of people. She was just a little kid then. Jazz was a baby.

Reggie smiled when she remembered the tie-dye diaper he wore, and that his pee-pee made it stain his skin. From then on they'd just let him be naked.

"He was still the best-dressed baby at the happening." Star always laughed when she told that part of the story.

Reggie screwed up her courage and said, "Please, sirs, we would like to go home now."

After a minute of silence, she tried again, "Sirs?"

The man on the passenger side looked back and said, "You are with us now, girl. Gawd sent us for you. We will be to a new home soon."

Reggie swallowed again even though her ears were fine. She was thinking of Star and Kali . . . and home. She was scared—more scared than she wanted to let on. She should do something, but what? She had to protect Jazz. She had to do something brave.

She couldn't bite and kick and run and still protect Jazz. She pulled her goodie bag out of her pocket. She could at least make sure they didn't steal their treasures.

The sedan pulled into another forest. The smell of overheated water filled the car. The engine was panting and hissing as the car climbed higher into the rarified altitude. The men talked of stopping but decided they were very close now. Plumes of steam condensed on the windshield.

Reggie nudged Jazz awake and showed him her little drawstring bag. He looked at it, then up to her face with sleepy, puzzled eyes.

He yawned. She nodded and squinted her eyes toward his pocket. He looked down and pulled out his bag of polished stones and glass. Reggie helped him undo it from his belt loop. She shoved her little bag into the deep crack where the seat and the back came together and gestured for Jazz to do the same. He hesitated. Reggie gave him a sweet smile and he shoved his bag of precious bits and pieces down next to hers. He felt a little shivery chill as he pulled his empty hand from the deep crevice. Reggie spit on the pad of her right thumb. Jazz followed suit. They pressed their damp thumbs together and, without speaking, agreed to never tell a soul where their treasures were hidden.

The steaming car pulled through a wide, open wooden gate and into a big compound.

The encircling buildings looked as though they were made of the same kind of trees that surrounded the clearing. A network of split-log walkways connected all the structures. The roofs were fashioned of wavy metal, the dips of which were filled with brown pine needles. Reggie peeked up at a huge, round, wooden thing on tall legs that loomed above it all.

The car stopped. Someone raised the hood. The radiator hissed and clicked and enveloped the car in a cloud of steam. The car door opened. Reggie held Jazz's hand in one tight fist. Fear roared in her ears. A peachy-cheeked woman in a long black dress leaned out of the cloud of steam and into the car door. A vast, white apron covered the front of her black dress from the top of her sizable bosom to the hem. Her hair was pulled back and wound into a fat bun just above her neck. A square of plain white cloth was bobby-pinned on the top of her head. There were other women in the same uniforms, peeking into the car. Jazz huddled behind Reggie.

The first woman took Reggie's face between a firm but gentle thumb and forefinger. She looked into her eyes and smiled. Reggie liked the woman better than the men in the car. She didn't let go of Jazz's hand but she let the women lead them out of the steam cloud and toward a cabin. Some sort of machine made a 'ca-pi-ta-ca-pi-ta' sound and everywhere, underfoot, squawking chickens fussed to protest the invasion of the black sedan. The wind played castanets in the colorful aspen trees and wide-eyed faces gaped in silence from the windows and the yard.

The woman led them past two rooms with cots lined up along the walls and into a bigger room with a zinc tub in the center. An old wringer-washing machine's black drain hose, with a dingy white sock attached, was hooked over the rim of a big gray soapstone sink. It stood next to a black stove against one wall. She saw two toilets in stalls in one corner.

A hose ran from a sink faucet to one of the tubs. Two women lugged big kettles of steaming water from the stove to pour into the tub. The kettles were then refilled and put back on the stove.

The women took all the clothes off the two children and removed the peace sign medallions from around their necks.

Reggie's feet always got cold when she was scared. They were icy cold now.

A plump young woman helped her climb into the large zinc tub of sudsy warm water as another lifted Jazz into the other end. The women scrubbed them from hair to toes with rough washcloths and a gritty, pungent soap. Reggie's feet took guilty pleasure in the warm water.

After they were briskly dried, each child stood, wrapped in a towel as an old, old woman, with gnarly fingers and chin hairs, cut off a lot of their hair. Another woman handed each child a few articles of black and white clothing, a blanket, a comb and a toothbrush.

"What is your name, child?" another woman asked Reggie.

"Reggie," she whispered.

With a heavy black laundry pen the woman marked Reggie on each of her few new possessions and put the stack back in Reggie's arms. With a gentle smile she said, "Put these things on a bed in the girls' room, get dressed, brush your teeth and comb your hair."

Reggie lagged around until Jazz was ready. She took him to the boys' room and told him what to do. The room was stark with four neatly made beds along each wall. He was reluctant to let go of her hand.

"I'll be right back, Jazz," she promised.

The girls' room was the same—clean and cold.

When she came back Jazz was sitting on the floor looking at the leather shoes on his feet, a puzzled look on his little face. She showed him how to tie a bow—she had learned how when Kali taught her to macramé.

The chinked-log walls of the dining hall were painted white. The room was warm. The benches on each side of the long tables were made of wood worn golden and smooth by a history of behinds and elbow grease. The fragrance of baking bread and cooking food filled the hall and their tummies responded with gurgles and growls.

There was another squat black stove on a brick platform next to a raised dais. The dining tables formed a horseshoe around the little stage. The freshly scrubbed newcomers sat in the center of the first row of tables. No one sat on the bench on the side toward the platform. Reggie held Jazz's hand, as much for herself as for him.

The older people sat to the right of the platform. About twenty other children sneaked peeks at the newcomers from the left. The grownups were murmuring and rocking slightly. Something was brewing. Reggie could feel it like a whirring vibration in her chest.

Then, in one fluid motion, like a large, stealthy cat, a man in black leaped from a seated position amongst the elders to the raised platform. Shock rendered the newcomers dumb. It was the Hawk guy.

"Heh!" Hawk snorted as he began pacing back and forth. Every fourth step or so he did a little skip.

He held a smallish, soft black book in his hand. He held it against his head. He waved it in the air.

"Heh!" he uttered again and once again. He clutched a big white handkerchief in his other fist. He banged the book like a tambourine. "Heh!" he exploded. His feet did a little dance step.

"Gaaawd is in this house! Heh! Tonight! Raise your hands and praise Him! Heh! Hallelujah!"

Hands shot up all over the room.

Reggie looked at Jazz. He looked at her. They each raised their hands halfway.

The pacing man clapped the book a couple of times and mopped his brow. "This world is coming to an end! Heh! Bless Gawd! Heh! Gee-zus is goin' ta split the eastern skies! Praaaize Gawd!! Heh!" He was shouting now. "He's gonna come down in glory!"

"Praaaize Gawd!" the assembly responded.

Every time he exploded a Heh, he did the little dance, lifted up his knee and pressed the white hankie to his sweating face and throat.

"He's gonna take the righteous home! Praaaize Gawd! Heh! Satan can haaaave this world! Heh!" Hawk shook the book in the air. "Praaaize Gawd! Have it! Gee-zus is coming! In the twinkling of an eye! To gather his bride! And take his bride home! To Glory!"

"Praaaaize Gawd!" People were on their feet—moving and moaning, waving their hands.

"Praaaize Gawd!"

"Let me hear an Amen!"

"Ah-men!" echoed the crowd.

"Let me hear an Amen!" Hawk boomed.

"Ah-men!" shouted the crowd.

Hawk drew from his coat pocket one of the peace medallions. Reggie touched the empty spot at her throat. She felt Jazz look up at her but she couldn't wrench her gaze from the peace sign.

"This trinket, Heh!" He raised the medallion for all to see. "Yes, this trinket is a symbol of eeee-vil!" He threw the offending medal on the floor and stomped on it with both feet. "Heh!" He scooped it up again. "This is one sign of the devil, that has possessed our young people! Heh!" His voice grew louder. "They have broken, Heh, and corrupted the cross to their use!" His shouts vibrated the windowpanes. "We have rescued these heathen children—" He spread his arms to indicate the two new children at the center table. "Heh! Rescued them to be forged in the fire, Heh! To be cleansed in the fire! So they may do Gawd's work!" He opened the double door on the black iron stove. The orange and yellow flames twisted and writhed.

Jazz felt the heat on his face and thought they meant to put them in that fire. He began to whimper. Reggie squeezed his shoulder and pushed his head down to hide his face in her lap. She did not know he could still see the man's legs and the tortuous flames from under the table. Nor did she know that he was unable to stop looking. Seeing the black legs against the color of the flames was more than just horrifying—it was reminiscent of yesterday with the mothers.

The flames danced a devilish fandango in the black stove. The faces that encircled the open fire were rapt and ruddy in its glow.

"Heh! We will drive you out, Devil!" Hawk raised a skimpy, limp bouquet of the two peace medallions. He held them by their supple hemp cords high above his head for all to see. "We rebuke you, Satan!" His voice grew even more intense.

He began to twirl the clutch of medals by their thongs round and round above his head until they reached a sustained whirring sound. *Mwa-mwa-mwa, mwa-mwa-mwa, mwa-mwa-mwa!*

"Beware the forces of evil," *mwa-mwa-mwa, mwa-mwa-mwa!* "for they are legion!" *Mwa-mwa-mwa, mwa-mwa-mwa!*

Hawk fixed each of the onlookers with a furious gaze, as though they were the legion. *Mwa-mwa-mwa, mwa-mwa-mwa!* "Heh! Ah-men," he snarled and in one unconstrained motion threw the tangle of medallions into the fire.

In unison, thirty-two sharp intakes of breath replaced the Amen. Sparks flew up the chimney and out into the room.

"Be gone! Heh!"

The hemp thongs burned. An acrid smell filled the room.

"Smell Him? Smell the evil?"

The assembly was gnashing its teeth and stomping the hall's floorboards.

"We will drive the dee-mons from these tiny unclean souls! Heh! We will do it with whatever action we must take!"

The frenzy in the room was palpable. The grownups moaned and swayed, alternately wringing their hands and raising them, outstretched to the ceiling. Hawk began to run in one spot. He pumped his knees up and down and flailed the air with his book and his sweat-soaked handkerchief and continued his tirade in strange words. "*Aganan symtergona! Gorayah su hoda conna!*"

Reggie thought maybe it was French.

A woman jumped up and began twirling, her head thrown back. She emitted a gargling scream in the back of her throat.

The new children stared in wide-eyed amazement at the show. The other children looked scared and some imitated the grownups, raising their little hands.

Finally, Hawk slammed the stove door, shutting the colors away. The twirling woman fell backward. Two men caught her before she dashed her head on the floor. Hawk sighed, swiped the big damp handkerchief across his brow a final time and said, "Ah-men." Reggie watched in awe as he flipped headfirst off the stage, rotated in the air and landed on his feet. A quick blessing and dinner was served.

Fragrant steam rose from the bowls and platters that were conveyed from the kitchen. Reggie felt her mouth water. A plate was set before her and one in front of Jazz. His eyes looked like Christmas morning and he set to eating with both hands. There was fried chicken, crispy little fried chunks that had sticky green vegetables inside, sweet smooth applesauce, mashed potatoes, gravy and thick slices of crusty bread with blackberry preserves. The milk tasted a little odd but it was cold. She fell on her food with zest. She was miserable but her fickle stomach was as happy as Jazz's eyes.

Chapter 4
Same Old Same Old

The Enclave was an abandoned CCC camp, perched some five thousand feet above the Tennessee/Kentucky border. Hawk had converted it for a small but fervid congregation calling itself The Rescuers. He interpreted scripture, made the rules and claimed divine revelation. The spirit of The Enclave was almost always grim and spare or loud and punishing. Demons could be found everywhere. There were thrice-daily doses of the eternal blazing hellfire and excruciating damnation—one preceding every meal. Besides those three daily tirades there were lengthy meetings on Sundays and Wednesdays.

One day faded into the next.

Three or four mornings a week the delicious fragrance of bread baking filled the encampment. That aroma became Jazz's haven in the limbo of The Enclave. On those days he would sit on the night-chilled ground, close his eyes, hug his knees and let the warm fragrance embrace him and keep him safe. Sometimes Josepha, a big girl, would plop down beside him and put an arm around his shoulders.

Reggie liked the big girl. She was kind to Jazz.

"I think I can feel a nervousness in the meetings," Reggie told Jazz and Josepha. "I think it makes the people jerk around and holler in strange words. I don't think it is French."

Josepha told them, "They call it speaking in tongues. I don't understand the words exactly, but I think you're right. The way Hawk preaches gets them riled up and causes some of them to act and rant the way they do."

The rescued children were housed by age in cabins divided into boys' rooms and girls' rooms. Reggie and Jazz were assigned to the little children's cabin. School was held from breakfast to lunch.

The colors of the past faded and visited only occasionally, in dreams. Life, like the clotheslines on Enclave washdays, became black and white, fraught with threats of the demonic fate that awaited the unrescued souls. The prayer meetings were full of fear and dread.

When Reggie heard rumors that one night soon there would be live snakes at the meeting, she taught Jazz to sing "Itsy Bitsy Spider" to himself when he got too scared. "If you move your lips," she said, "the elders will just think you are praying."

Much about life here she taught herself. She watched and listened. She discovered the *tap-a-ca-tap-a-ca* sound was a machine that made electricity. They used it on laundry days to run the old wringer washers.

Brother Uding and the Bountiful Sisters and three or four no-name others each had one gnarled and shriveled leathery hand that was useless to do hand things.

"I figure they must be related," she said to Jazz that same night when she recounted the day's stories.

Early one evening, Josepha watched out while Reggie climbed a rickety ladder to the huge wooden vat on stilts. From there she could see the rays of the setting sun skimming over mist-filled hollows and tingeing the mounds of tree-covered hills a soft purple. She peeked over the rim of the vat and saw it was full of water. She figured out that the pipes running down the legs carried rainwater to the compound faucets.

Once, for whatever reason, a very old stooped over woman pointed her gnarly finger up at the water tank then leaned close to Reggie's ear and said, "I got a lickin' once for takin' a swim in a tank like that one when I was your age." She cackled under her breath as she walked away.

One day while the three children were sitting cross-legged on the ground enjoying the fragrance of baking bread, a group of men walked into the kitchen. One man turned and smiled at Josepha.

"He wants to marry me," she said. "He likes to put his hands all over my body then sobs and begs God to forgive him." She shuddered. "He never asks me to forgive him. It's my body."

"Brother Billy Ray? He's so old," Reggie said, "and you're only a kid."

"Yeah," she whispered.

At night Reggie told Jazz about his life. She lulled him to sleep weaving stories of The Family. In an eerie voice she always ended, "The time it all changed was Indian Summer of nineteen seventy-two."

One winter night after he drifted off, she confided in a whisper, "I can't remember their faces anymore. I only remember—remembering."

Chapter 5
The Blue Lady

One sultry September afternoon, Preacher Hawk's sweet-faced son, Clovis, drove into The Enclave with his father. He was fourteen but looked much younger. He tended to be peevish and cranky with the elders. "Tetchy," Sister Lola Faye used to call it. But he seemed drawn to the children—especially to the younger children. He held them in rapt awe with his vivid word-picture Bible stories. His voice was smooth yet animated. Reggie liked the stories well enough. But, true to her nature, she held back and sized up the newcomer. Some days she could almost see the darkness fall over him. When that happened he took to his own little cabin—and stayed there by himself for a week, sometimes longer.

When the gnarled apple trees outside the compound began to bud again, there was a big ruckus. Reggie heard someone yelling about "likker" and Clovis stalked out the gate and down the hill dragging an old, brown duffel bag and raising his middle finger in a farewell salute.

The one time Reggie and Jazz could escape the tedium of day-to-day life and be alone was when they were fetching the mail. The letters and packages arrived in a battered silver mailbox that stood amid a haphazard row of rusted, silver boxes a little over a mile down the grade. Sometimes they carried things down the hill to put into the box, too. They never saw any cars or people on the grade or on the road below.

When they first got the task, Sister Sue admonished them often, "You duck down in the brambles if ever you young 'uns see a car, you hear? Hide if you see a single soul!"

The old woman liked them. But more and more often a confused look replaced the smile in her eyes. She didn't much talk to them or anyone else anymore.

A few paths branched off the main Enclave road and meandered into the woods but Reggie never saw the houses that must have been nearby, sheltering the people who used those other mailboxes.

If they didn't have to carry stuff to put into the silver mailbox, the two would laugh and do awkward cartwheels on their outing. Afterward they checked each other's heads and pulled out any burrs tangled in their hair before they walked back to The Enclave.

One sunny day they left the dining hall early—right after lunch. They got out of scouring dishes that day since one of the Original girls had to do some extra chores as a punishment.

As the two children rounded the last bend, they stopped mid-step. Ducking down, they saw a tall, bile-green truck stopped by the mailboxes. There was a door on the side but no seat. This was curious. They had only seen one automobile before in these parts and that was Preacher Hawk's big black sedan. Jazz wanted to sit down and stay hidden. But he followed along when Reggie hunched over and circled wide to their right. Their hearts pounded in their little chests and their bright eyes widened. They looked both ways, darted across the macadam and trotted back in a roadside ditch.

When they peeked over the edge, still hidden by the weeds that fringed the road, the mystery was solved. A door on the other side was open and framed a driver's seat that was like a high stool, not like the old sedan seats.

"Look," Reggie nudged Jazz, "the driver's wheel is on a different side. This must be a very special car."

They held their breath when a short, robust woman dressed in blue suddenly appeared from behind the truck. She dragged a huge leather pouch and appeared to invoke more power with each grunt. Pudgy white legs laced with bumpy blue veins bulged out of her knee-high pants.

They were close but the Blue Lady didn't seem to see them. Even her hair was bluish. Two small, round, black discs covered her ears. Reggie squinted and saw that two wires trailed down from the discs into the shadow above her ample bosom.

They gaped in awe and stood upright.

The woman was singing, loud and off-key, ". . . me and lalalalala Mageeeeeeeee . . . nah, nah, nah, nananananaa aaaa, nah, nah . . ."

She was dragging the leather bag backward toward the bank of silver boxes. "AUGH! My stars!" she uttered, falling back a step when she saw them. Her face turned a rich, ruddy red.

Oh, no, they both thought, frozen in place. Now she's gonna yell at us.

The Blue Lady with the red face and blue hair sputtered and fanned herself briskly with a fistful of letters and started to laugh. "Oh, my stars and garters," she gasped. "You gave me such a start! Who are you sweet things? Where do you come from?" When they remained silent, she asked, "Aren't you two of the cutest things?"

She pulled the discs off her ears and a tiny musical sound leaked out. She saw they were intrigued. "Would you like to hear?" She looked both ways then tempted the children with the earphones. "You know, my sonny-boy in the navy sent me these clear from Japan! He knows the inventor. They don't even sell 'em over there yet. I'll bet I am the onlyest person in the USofA that has one!"

She slipped the earphones over Reggie's head. The girl's eyes grew wider.

"He even made me a bunch of these little tapes his-very-own-self!" She held up a small black rectangle with two holes. Reggie could see her pride and hear it in her voice.

The wire still disappeared down the crevice between the blue lady's generous breasts. Reggie felt lit from within as the music filled her head. She wanted to share the experience with Jazz but she did not want to stop hearing the music. She pulled his head close and turned one earpiece to his ear. Jazz clutched the disc to his ear and his little face burst into a gleeful grin. They both nodded to the beat.

The Blue Lady fished in her bodice and pulled out a small black box the size of Preacher Hawk's Bible. Reggie flinched at the thought. The lady placed the black box by their feet as they sat in the dirt. They shared the music while she placed letters and packages in the proper boxes.

"Well, you two." She raised her voice so they could hear her. "Neither sleet nor snow . . ." She laughed heartily at her own little joke. Her face was normal now and only her lips and cheeks remained bright pink. She picked up the black box and accepted the earphones from the reluctant children. "So, really, where do you all hail from?" she asked.

Jazz watched her face as he pointed up the hill. Her face turned paler still and her eyes darted up the hill and back. A strange cloud dulled her eyes.

Jazz walked to the battered mailbox, flipped down the little red metal flag and pulled out the handful of papers. He took Reggie's hand and they walked back up the hill. They could feel the Blue Lady's eyes on their backs till they went around the bend.

Reggie and Jazz each spat on one plump thumb pad pressed them one to the other's and swore never to tell anyone about the Blue Lady.

Jazz looked at his moist thumb. A memory tickled the back of his mind.

Chapter 6

Original Sin

Flashes of crimson and gold bigtooth aspens quivered amid the evergreens when Clovis came back up the mountain. There was a cool nip and a buzz of excitement in the air that autumn afternoon.

The very next day, Reggie and Jazz joined the elders and the other children as they queued down a meandering path to the stream that ran behind the compound. The sheer cliff of pine and aspen across the narrow stream provided a colorful backdrop to the scene. There was clapping and singing of praise. Sister Florissa clanged the old silver dinner triangle with such glee that it broke free of its frayed leather tether and flew into the dust beside the kitchen steps.

Clovis was wearing a long white nightshirt. There was a soft smile on his clean-shaven face. Reggie thought he looked like an angel.

Preacher Hawk led him into the waist-high water. Clovis lifted his open hands to the sky and said in a pure sweet voice, "I been a sinner, Lord! I got me in a bunch of trouble down there in the city. I been drinking and gambling. I been having impure thoughts and doing impure deeds, been womanizing and stealing, but I've seen the pure, sweet light of truth. I've seen the beacon that called me back up into these hills. I am powerful sorry I wasted the seventeen years of my life so far and I am ready to accept the Lord into my heart!"

Tears of gratitude streamed into Preacher Hawk's graying beard. He plunged his only son down into the frigid water and into salvation. Great whoops and hallelujahs rose from the congregation. Father and son strode to the shore with legs bright red and lips blue from the icy, baptismal bath. The celebrants gathered them into warm blankets and a jubilant fellowship. The prodigal son . . . rescued at last.

Rapturous singing filled the compound that day. The bustling women roasted two wild turkeys that had wandered into the compound for a free meal of chicken scratch the day before.

Reggie watched with interest as Brother Jake refastened the flyaway dinner triangle to a beam that supported the eaves outside the kitchen door. He used a doubled loop of silver-gray tape. He pulled strips of the tough tape from a wide roll with a loud tearing sound. Brother Jake was so tall he didn't even need a ladder. When he was through with the job he grasped the triangle and lifted his feet off the ground. The tape held his considerable weight. Reggie watched him return the silver roll of amazing tape to a high cabinet in the kitchen.

Reggie heard whispers about some trouble in Louisville. She saw Clovis saved. He was one of The Rescuers now. He was almost grown and spoke softly when he read to the children. Reggie watched and studied him intently.

During the months since they had met the Blue Lady, Reggie and Jazz often found little treats in the mailbox—a tiny carved bird, a shiny coin or a sweet chocolate. They savored the candy and kept the trinkets hidden in a black sock behind the stove in the bathing room.

Reggie was nine-and-a-half years old that spring. The buds on the crab apple trees were fat and ready to burst when Clovis paid his first night visit to her. He smiled down at her in the moonlight and with tender care lifted the little boy from her arms.

As he carried Jazz back to the boy's own little bed he signaled Reggie not to make a sound. She was grateful that he didn't just tell the elders that Jazz was in her bed. There would have been big trouble.

Clovis came back and silently slipped into bed behind her.

Oh, it feels so good. Someone is holding me. Feelings of Kali and Star flooded her being. Someone comforted her again.

He murmured into her ear. Kali used to whisper songs in her ear like that. Tears were running over the bridge of her nose and down her cheek, but she was smiling—a big goofy smile. Reggie soon deciphered the whispers. He was reciting scriptures as he held her against him. His breath smelled like kerosene and his skin had an acrid odor. That was yucky, not like Kali. She always smelled of frangipani shampoo and Dial soap. They bathed together a lot.

Clovis's murmurs degraded into a snarl and he grated in her ear, "Don't scream, don't scream, don't scream!" He clapped one hand over her mouth!

"What did I do," she pleaded into his hand. "I'm sorry! I won't do it any more!" He clamped the hand tighter over her mouth. It hurt. This was wrong. He rubbed his other hand all over her body, inside and outside until she thought she would pee. He rocked her against his body. The cot springs squeaked until, with a strangled moan, he slumped behind her.

After a few minutes he whispered in his soft, sweet voice, "If you tell on me, little sister—I will kill that boy."

He left. This stank.

She waited until she was certain he was gone. She went into the bathroom and spat the sour taste from her mouth. She shuddered and couldn't seem to stop. She felt smothered in the pungent reek of his salty slime. She scrubbed her teeth and her body until her gums and skin were raw and flushed from the gritty soap. She almost cried out loud when she tried to pee. It hurt so badly. This was just one more crummy, wicked thing to endure for Gawd.

After a few nightly visits, Clovis started coming to her bed less often. Soon it was only once or twice a month. She was grateful. She wondered if there were other girls that Clovis visited.

Something felt dead inside her. Life grew grayer and grayer. The only reason she didn't lay down and sleep forever was Jazz. When she did sleep the colors came back—slowly at first. The recollected Family was just wisps of smoke and muffled voices but the flowered bus got brighter and clearer and more tangible every night.

One cold, stark winter day, when the stream was crusted with ice and the sun didn't shine, she closed her eyes and climbed up into that bus. She could smell the cracked leather and feel the corrugated metal floors. She watched out the windows—safe from The Enclave. She spoke only to Jazz or Josepha that year, and only when they were alone. She grew thin and dark smudges underscored her eyes.

Chapter 7
Signs Following

Reggie sat three pews behind and to the left of Clovis during Monday and Wednesday meetings. Sometimes she took her mind away from the repetitious animation of Hawk's tirades by staring at the spots on Clovis's head where all the hair had fallen out. Other times she focused on the four small moles on his neck just above his collar. The imaginary lines she drew connecting the dots formed a diamond. Mentally she drew smaller and smaller circles inside the diamond. Then she pictured herself slowly pushing a large, hollow needle deep into that last tiny circle and letting his sorry life drain out of him all over the pew and the faded pine floor.

Her favorite escape happened when she allowed her focus to slide around the curve of his sweaty neck and spiral into the nothingness where she always found the family bus parked among the trees.

She raised her hands in praise when all the others did but she knew in her heart that gawd was just pretend and started with a little 'g.'

Today her attention snapped back to the meeting room when she heard an unfamiliar sound. It was a bit like the dry fall aspen leaves vibrating in a brisk breeze. Or maybe the seeds in a dozen dried gourds being agitated.

Behind the podium, Hawk held aloft a box. The rustling sounds came from that box. Hawk seemed more impassioned than usual—almost giddy.

When she tuned Hawk back in, he was proclaiming, ". . . last words after his resurrection were: And these signs shall follow them that believe! Heh!" He set the box down on a table. "In my name, he said, in my name shall they cast out devils! Heh!"

"Praise be," responded the congregation.

"They shall speak with new tongues! Heh! They shall take up serpents; and if they drink any deadly thing, it shall not hurt them; they shall lay hands on the sick, and they shall recover. Mark 16:17-18." He lifted the lid from the box. The rattling intensified.

The Brothers and Sisters were on their feet. A few ran up front and drank little cups of liquid.

Josepha whispered in Reggie's ear, "That is a poison called strictnine."

Sister Suzie Belle began strumming a thin, driving melody on her zither.

Reggie gaped as the poison drinkers began gyrating and leaping. One thin woman wailed, "I feel it! It has my body!" She fell to the floor and sprawled on her back arching and twitching and yelling, "Praise be!" The hem of her black dress crept up her thighs but she didn't notice.

"She is saved!" Hawk yelled. "She is in the Spirit!" He lapsed into tongues, twirled and even flipped backward once.

"The Holy Ghost is in this house tonight," Hawk announced in regular English. "The Spirit is here to cast out fear and dread. Are you in the spirit?"

The music grew faster and faster. The congregation began to twirl and dance. They picked up their knees and stomped in circles. They twisted and whirled and raised their arms in praise. Sister Suzie Belle strummed faster yet.

"This body is gonna die one day," shouted Hawk.

"Amen," the chorus responded.

"Rot away!"

"Halleluiah!"

"But the last promises of our Lord will live on forever! Are you saved tonight? If God is moving on your soul, come forward, brothers and sisters. But be sure! Be certain! Bear witness to His last promises before he rose to heaven!" Hawk turned and dipped into the box and hefted a huge, writhing rattlesnake above his head.

The children gasped. And simultaneously Reggie and Jazz drew their legs up onto the pew and sat mesmerized with ankles crossed out of danger.

Hawk held the long serpent in both hands. The creature's head extended a full foot and a half beyond his right hand. It swayed and fixed its beady eyes on the handlers. Hawk held the bulk of its weight in his left hand. The serpent wrapped its tail around the preacher's meaty fist and arm. Hawk lifted his feet and stomped and danced as he weaved and bobbed in and out among the others.

"Praise Him," one woman yelled and ran up and pulled a snake from the box. She was babbling and dancing holding the snake to her face.

Brother Billy Ray grabbed Josepha by the arm pulled her up from the pew and dragged her to the front. "Show us your faith, little sister. We cannot marry until you are sanctified." He grabbed a snake and pulled her into a dance step with him.

"But I am only eleven," she screamed.

He didn't seem to hear her but dipped and wove the snake between them. He stroked the head of the bobbing snake across her face then over her forearms when she held them up to shield her face.

Josepha threw back her head and let loose an agonized scream.

The snake struck not once but twice. She slipped from Billy Ray's grip and fainted to the floor. The bedlam went on around her.

Reggie jumped from the pew and ran to the front to drag Josepha from the frenzy. Blood was running from puncture wounds on both forearms. One old lady helped drag Josepha to the side of the hall and never stopped clogging.

"We need medicine! A doctor!" Reggie yelled over the din.

"No. No!" she shouted. "If she is pure she will recover." And the old lady danced back into the throng of snake-draped dervishes.

Two men lifted a hysterical Josepha, writhing and screaming, and carried her out the door. Another man kept Reggie from following.

"Praise the Lord," rang the chorus.

Later Reggie sneaked out and peeked in windows until she found Josepha. A sheet bound her face down to a narrow cot. Her black and swollen arms dangled over either side. She whimpered. Fluid drained down her arms to rags on the floor. Women and men stood around her and held outstretched hands to her body.

Reggie squeezed back hot, enraged tears. If it were Jazz, she would carry him on her back no matter how far, to get help. But Josepha was a big girl.

Three weeks later when Josepha came back into the community, everyone celebrated her being alive. But all Reggie could see were her twisted and discolored arms hanging limply at her sides. Her spirit seemed as wounded as her snake-bit limbs. The one good thing for Josepha—Billy Ray was looking elsewhere for a child-bride.

Chapter 8

Seduction of the Innocent

One cool, late summer night as Jazz cuddled fast asleep in her arms, Clovis came, wrapped him in one of her blankets and carried him back into the boy's room.

Earlier today when they picked up the mail, she had noticed a familiar date on an envelope. It only then occurred to her that the letter had been mailed on her birthday. She was finally, as she heard Kali once say, "a two-digit midget!"

Reggie stared at the moon just peeping at the edge of her window. She willed herself away from The Enclave—to her safe place. She snuggled far away from harm in a cool leather seat on her flowered bus. "Happy birthday to me," she crooned until she dozed.

When she awoke it was with a start. The moon had traveled clean across the window behind her bed. She felt her body. It was dry. She smiled to herself and snuggled down to dream some more. Just before slipping into the deepest of sleeps, her eyes flew open. Jazz! She had to see that he was all right.

She found the little guy on his cot whimpering in a fretful sleep on her blanket. The roaring of the blood pounding in her ears was so loud she was afraid it would awaken the whole compound. The blanket and his little back were sticky and the foul, fetid smell was far too familiar.

She shook inside as she carried his slim body to the bathroom in both their blankets. Adrenaline-charged anguish shook her body. Cold tears of rage dripped from her chin and a crimson wrath tinged her vision. She grabbed a stump of a candle and a stick match from the stove. Her hands shook violently when she held the flame to the wick. Her huge shadow danced on the bathroom wall.

She tenderly bathed Jazz's frail, seven-year-old body with cool water in the little pool of candlelight. He whimpered but didn't open his eyes. She rocked and chanted curses under her breath but managed to keep her hands gentle. With caution she peeked at his little bottom. The pucker of his anus was torn and battered. The flesh around it was turning blue. A cold calm came over her and she got down to the business of nursing her dear, sweet brother.

She dug out the tube of white stuff from a box on the shelf. Sister Amelia used it on the little ones when they had the diaper rash. She applied a dollop directly to a tiny anal tear and ever so gently spread the soothing ointment all around the area. When she had finished she slipped the tube into her pocket.

She wrapped Jazz in his own blanket. It was dry. She stuffed her own soiled bedding under the other dirty laundry and carried her little Jazz back to her bed and cuddled him.

She would have to kill Clovis. But first she had to get Jazz and herself away. If they had to live in the woods and eat berries and nuts, so be it. Any other life would be better than this. She wished he could dream of the flowered bus.

Chapter 9
The Gathering Storm

With a short series of stuttered sighs, Jazz slipped into a deep sleep. When Reggie felt him go limp she rolled him onto his side, bundled the blanket around him and waited a few minutes before she eased out of the bed and crept like a shadow from the cabin.

The gathering clouds were brewing up an Indian summer storm. The wind whipped through the trees in fitful gusts. She slouched along the wooden pathway to the kitchen. This was not the first time she imagined herself a panther prowling around the compound when all the others were asleep. Over the years she had learned what was in every drawer and cabinet. She knew where every person slept. She was angry with them all for stealing her life and could stab each and every one of them in their sleep if she took a notion to. But, for stealing Jazz's innocence, Clovis needed killing.

Clearly, a line existed over which Clovis would cross at his own peril. Earlier tonight the wretched young man had slithered across that line.

She undid the bottom buttons of her pajama top and tied the loose ends in a knot around her slim waist. A soft night breeze caressed her bare midriff and her tiny sensitive nipples grew uncomfortably erect. She shifted her pajama top away from them. She stopped at the water pump and dipped two fingers in the muddy dirt and dragged them across each cheekbone in turn. She rinsed her fingers in the standing water and listened to the night. She felt her war paint drying on her cheeks. The tree frogs fell still and the silence was profound. Her ears searched the quiet for any sound from her cabin. She willed Jazz into a deep, dreamless sleep. The forest critter chorus struck up again.

At the kitchen door she dropped to her knees and pulled the door firmly toward her. Using a pilfered butter knife she kept in her pocket, she forced the throw back a fraction of an inch at a time. She maintained her progress by keeping pressure on the throw in the doorjamb. After a minute or so the throw slid clear and the door opened.

Her calloused feet barely felt the difference between the worn black-and-white checkered linoleum kitchen floor and the rough-hewn wood of the walkways or, for that matter, the soft compound dirt.

She took a large key from a hook beside the kitchen entrance and locked the door and hung the key back on the hook. The last, low, full moon of summer provided enough cool white light for Reggie to see her way around the kitchen—except when it slid behind the billowing thunderheads in the western sky.

She found the flour sacks the cooks used for dishcloths. The small hunting knife in its scabbard was still in a drawer of odds and ends. Holding the leather sheath, she grasped the bone and metal handle and drew the glinting silver blade from its cocoon. She hefted the knife a few times. The weight made her feel not merely good—more like powerful. She tested the blade's keenness on the flour sack. It sliced through the cloth without a sound. She put all the items except one sack on the counter and pulled a stump of candle from her pajama pocket. She drew several blue-tipped wooden matches from a cluster in a cracked teacup on the big black stove and pocketed all but one.

The hatch to the root cellar lay flat, forming most of the floor of a small alcove. Shallow shelves lined the three walls. Jars of preserved vegetables from The Enclave garden filled most of them. Jams and jellies from the forest vines and applesauce from the old gnarled orchard outside the gate filled the rest. She pulled up on the recessed handle and a counterweight lowered the stairs as the hatch opened fully.

She went down a few steps before she scraped a match across the wooden handrail. Keeping her eyes squeezed shut she listened as the match crackled into life. She didn't open her eyes until she heard the flame settle down. She touched the flickering fire to the wick of the stubby candle and shook it out. She held the charred stick until it cooled, wiped the crusty soot into dust on the wall then slipped the stub into her pocket. The only sound now was the whooshing of the blood in her ears.

She went the rest of the way down the steep steps and found the little crab apples spread apart on a slatted, waist-high wooden shelf. She put six crisp ones in the flour sack and moved the rest around so no one would notice some were gone. As an afterthought she picked up one more and bit into the crisp, tart fruit. She chewed and let the juice run down her face and onto her pajama top. She bit into the apple again and held it in her teeth while she slipped the sack of apples into the pouch formed between her skin and her tied pajama top. She headed back up the stairs and took the apple from her mouth long enough to blow out the candle. She allowed it to cool, then put it in the breast pocket with the charred match, and climbed the stairs.

Her eyes rose even with the floor and reflex stiffened her body. She saw two silhouettes hovering outside the kitchen window. Two sets of cupped hands framed eyes peering in.

"I was so sure I saw a light in there," a muffled, female voice said.

"Ah come on, girl, it must've been your imagination," a male voice answered, "or maybe the stars in your eyes," he purred with a suggestive hint. She giggled. He played a flashlight beam around the kitchen interior.

"Put that out, Seth, before someone sees us! I was the last one out of the kitchen. I have to check."

Reggie heard a big key scraping in the lock. Her heart hammered in her ears. It was too late to lower the cellar door. With as stealthy a maneuver as she could muster, she backed down the stairs and scrambled to the top storage shelf. She pressed herself hard against the cold, earthen wall, squeezed her eyes shut and willed her body as small as possible.

"Well, will you look at this?" the girl asked.

Reggie held her breath. Her ears pricked. She remembered the knife.

"I must have left the root cellar open. Oh, this is awful. What if Sister Joanna stumbled down there in the dark? I'm just glad I was the one to find . . ." She trailed off as she started down the stairs.

"Wait, Becca," the man said, "I will bring the light." They went down the stairs together, his arm protectively around her waist. He swept the light around the room. "Wow, those apples sure smell fine. But . . . mmmm," he said with a small chuckle, "what have we here?"

Reggie stiffened and opened her eyes a slit, hoping their whites would not glow in the darkness. The boy slipped his hand up from Becca's waist and cupped her breast from behind.

"Ahh," she uttered and drew a startled breath. He laid the flashlight on the stair and turned her around slowly and kissed her full on the mouth. With his body he pushed her back onto the stairs. She moaned.

Reggie's eyes shot open. Oh, geez, I'm stuck here. Jazz, please, please don't wake up, she sent the pleading thought.

Everyone's breathing grew labored as Seth began to grind himself against Becca. She writhed in response. The man reached down and began to lift her skirt.

Drawing a deep breath, Becca pulled her face free. "Ah, Seth, it's late," she giggled.

"Aw, Becca, baby, I'm so hungry," he pleaded. She squirmed away and darted up the stairs. He reached for her retreating ankle with a ferocious look on his face. He held it a moment, then thought better of it and let her slip through his fingers. "Shit," he muttered under his breath. He straightened his clothes and ran fingers through his hair before he scuttled up the steps.

"Becca, sweetie, I'm sorry," he whined as he lowered the cellar door.

"Shit, is right," Reggie uttered under her breath. The blackness was the most complete she had ever known. She felt the tiny, earthen room shrink to the size of a grave. The rich dirt smell overpowered the apples and she felt faint.

She nipped a budding panic when moments later she heard the muffled voices fade and a door open and close. She forced herself to count to two hundred but rushed the last forty numbers. Then she reached over from her shelf, grasped the bottom step and pushed herself off into the blackness. Counterbalanced by the opening hatch, she eased to the floor. She took the steps two at a time, lowered the cellar door and swallowed hard.

She pulled herself up on the counter to reach the high cupboard where the wide roll of amazing silver-colored tape was kept. Even after all this time there was still a lot of tape left on the roll. She slid it into her pajama pouch, and dropped without a sound to the floor. The tape felt cool against her skin.

She took a hunk of cheese wrapped in a wet cloth from the big ice box, slipped it in the last flour sack and slid it into the opposite side of her pajama top. The cold dampness made her feel alert.

She had opened a window and started to slip out when she remembered the chief purpose of her raid. She turned and found the knife, apparently unnoticed by the lovebird security guards. She sheathed it and slipped it in her pajama top.

The lowering moon cast her shadow on the ground. She laughed at her bulging bosom filled out by the booty of her night raid.

Galloping giant steps took Reggie down the hill. She dangled the sack of apples and half the cheese from an old tree limb by a strip of tape. She hoped that would keep the small critters out.

There was one more job to do before she dealt with Clovis. She squeaked open the rear door of Preacher Hawk's old car. She reached deep into the dark crease where the seat met the back. She slid her hand back and forth. Then she felt them—the treasure bags.

She taped the treasures and the rest of the cheese to the back of the old soapstone laundry tub. She fashioned a belt from a length of clothesline pilfered from the supply closet she'd found unlocked one day. She threaded the scabbard on the rope and tied it around her waist.

She made sure Jazz was covered and asleep. She was ready.

She became aware of the thrum of her own pulse in her ears over the songs of the tree frogs and crickets declaring their night territory.

Reggie pricked her ears but sensed more than heard the whoosh of feathers on air. A stealthy ol' mama owl swooped down to pluck some unsuspecting critter from its nightly rounds. Her babies' dinner departed with nary a squeak.

Reggie felt good to slink and plot on this moonlit night. Tonight for the first time she felt more akin to the owl than to the critter.

Chapter 10
Wresting Power

Making no more noise than a python slipping from a tree, Reggie slithered through the cabin window and to the floor. The knife, at the ready, was gripped in her teeth. Like some feral Peter Pan, she crouched, sweeping the room with flinty eyes that soon came to rest on its loathsome inhabitant.

Clovis sprawled face down across dingy, rumpled bed sheets, a limp hand dangled over either side of the narrow bed.

Reggie slipped the knife into its sheath. The wide roll of silver tape, like an oversized bracelet, encircled her wrist.

She squatted beside Clovis and peered at his patchy hair. A sticky string of drool dangled from his slack lips.

The gray-blue ceramic jug that lay by his limp right hand smelled like Clovis's night breath. It made her eyes water. Her huntress heart knew that she was smarter than this pathetic excuse for a human being. Solid determination and confidence burned in her belly. This cruel, dark varmint would know pain and fear—tonight.

She kept noise to a minimum by peeling the tape from its roll one slow inch at a time.

She dangled a couple of twelve-inch lengths from the headboard. She anchored the free end of the tape to the far side of the bed frame and inch by inch unwound enough to pass across the back of his knees and anchor on the near side. Now, if her boogieman awakened, he could not give immediate chase. Next, she anchored each wrist to a bedpost. Last, with the silent patience of an industrious spider, she spun her silver web in earnest.

Clovis sputtered and snorted a few times but nothing more.

In her growing zeal, she pulled the tape faster and faster. The sound ripping through the room produced no reaction. When she realized that the ripping and tearing *scritch* wasn't going to awaken him, she began passing the roll across his body with determined glee. When she was satisfied that the job was done, she stepped back and admired her handiwork. Clovis's legs, rump, neck and upper torso were bound to the narrow bed like a spider's prey in the web—ready to be sucked dry. His hands were immobilized.

But Reggie was no fool. This was no innocent, harmless water bug. This was a bloodthirsty creature—sneaky and dangerous.

She pressed a length of tape from the headboard across his mouth and back around the nape of his neck.

Sitting on the floor she cut several strips of tape and hung them from the bottom edge of the footboard.

A loud splutter broke her concentration. She froze. The restrained pariah moaned and flailed a bit. Then there was only his labored breathing.

Sitting cross-legged, she laid the hilt of the knife across her right palm and rolled her fingers around it in a tight fist. She lashed her fist with the strips of tape. The deadly blade sprouting from her silver fist glittered in the intermittent beams of the cloud-bound moon. There was no chance of losing her weapon now.

Reggie stood beside her prey. Excitement and fear throbbed

through her veins. She climbed with caution a-straddle the prone man, grabbed a handful of his ratty hair in her left hand and settled in for a wild ride.

With the butt of her knife she pressed the edges of the tape tighter over his mouth. She felt him flinch when she nicked his cheek and ear with the tip of the honed blade. Her inner thighs sensed his drunken soul reentering his silver-bound body. A muffled scream struggled through the tape when his startled right eye focused on the shiny blade.

The hank of hair in Reggie's hand pulled clean out of his scalp. She threw the offensive clump aside and grabbed another. Clovis thrashed his head back and forth. She stabbed the pillow once right by his nose. He settled down a bit. She pulled another length of tape from the headboard and reinforced the gag. It was awkward but she checked to be sure the tape stuck to his skin. All the while she chanted in a low hiss, "Don't scream, don't scream, don't scream, or I'll cut your neck!"

He jerked against the tape. True to her word, she nicked his neck—just a little. His right eye bulged and looked really scared. With the tip of the knife she dripped his own blood on his face. The knife caught the skin around his ear and cheek a few times and more blood trickled onto the sheets. His frantic hands worked against the tape. Reggie jammed his head into the pillow and lifted her right hand. She better get this done before he wriggled free. *Oh, no! The moles are on the other side!*

He was thrashing now like a pissed off cat trying to avoid a bath. She turned her fist over and with a wide swing clouted him on his bony temple with the butt end of the knife. She whispered, "Don't scream, or I will kill you right now!"

She shoved his face deeper into the pillow to muffle his whimpers.

She laid the heel of her hand on his right buttock, took another deep breath to relieve the pent-up tension and braced herself for the increased struggle she knew would come. She dragged the keen blade across the fleshy mound of Clovis's rump—deep. It sliced clear through the silver tape, his dingy shorts and into the fat meat of his butt. The flesh parted, blood flooded the wound and spilled over the silver tape and onto the bed. She felt his body go rigid between her thighs.

She used her knife-fist to push his face into the pillow. She dipped two free fingers into the blood and dragged them across her cheek. War paint.

She nicked him again. He arched and jerked. The blood-spattered pillow caught most of the scream. It was the kind of noise that would awaken you enough to say, "What was that?" then, not hearing it again, you would fall back to sleep.

She pulled her right hand free and hit him in the head again. A dark stain was spreading on the sheet. She wanted to kill him but found her fury spent.

"Stay clean away from me and Jazz," she warned right into his ear. She leaned across his body to cut the tape holding his left hand. "You best go save your life," she snarled as she sliced through some of the silver-gray bonds around his body. He was panting and keening.

"I will be around to kill you one day," she promised as she backed toward the window and slipped soundlessly into the night.

By the cistern she tugged and unwrapped the silver tape from her hand and rinsed off the blood and the war paint. She shoved the crumpled tape into the gravel under the wooden slats that covered the sump.

Clovis crashed around and squalled in a rampage. Lamps were flickering in a few of the other houses. She started back to whisk Jazz away but fell to the ground when she heard the car door slam. After a moment there was a grinding noise and the old black sedan thundered to life. Headlights stabbed through the blackness. The gears scraped and ground. When they found a mesh, the old whale of a car leapt forward tossing gravel into the air. For a fraction of a second, by the glow of the dashboard lights, she saw a wild-eyed Clovis at the wheel, a strip of silver tape hanging from his right jaw. She noticed with a smile that his body was leaning far to the left. The car crashed through the gate and careened down the rutted road. The twin headlights parried and thrust at the demons of the night.

Lamps were coming to life all over The Enclave.

A man's voice yelled, "Clovis is gone! And there's a lot of blood."

"The sedan's gone, too," someone else piped up.

Half a dozen women clutching coats over their nightclothes hurried into Clovis's cabin. Reggie thought there probably was a goodly amount of blood. She saw one woman carrying the stinky jug to Preacher Hawk.

Reggie was so exhausted. Clovis was gone. He would not be coming back tonight. She crept into her cottage, shoved her bloodstained pajamas under the laundry and crawled naked under the sheet on Jazz's empty bed. It was easier than carrying him back. She could escape with Jazz tomorrow. This panther could prowl no more tonight. She didn't need to feign sleep when a body counter's flashlight cast a beam across the beds and was gone.

Chapter 11
Escape to Oblivion

Clovis clenched his teeth on the blood-drenched sheet and kept tension on the makeshift tourniquet that was his only garment. Salty, pink-tinged spittle and guttural rage oozed between his teeth. He forced himself to lean into the pain and the agony spiked with each bump and rut in the primitive road. He pushed the sedan with as much haste as the heavy old tank would tolerate. He felt something flapping around his face, reached up and pulled a length of tape from his cheek. He tried to throw it on the floor. It stuck to his fingers.

The hospital is less than an hour away, he thought. I gotta stop this bleeding.

He braked the car and pulled a folded map out of the glove box. He wadded it up, shoved it in his mouth and, biting on it as hard as he could, released the sheet.

"Hang on!" he ordered himself around his gag. He drew a deep breath and peeled the bloody linen from the wound and shoved down the tattered shorts.

The scream was there, just behind the wad of paper.

With a dry section of sheet he wiped the skin as well as he could and stuck one end of the silver tape scrap to the bottom side of the wound. He pulled the gap shut and almost fainted. He secured the tape on the other side. It held.

He spat out the crumpled, saliva-soaked map and let one wrenching scream echo into the empty night.

Up the hill, Reggie smiled in her sleep.

Clovis pulled the sheet tight again, gripped it in his teeth and shoved the car back in gear.

"I'll make it," he vowed into the clenched sheet. *Gotta keep my head clear.* He cranked down the window and let the speed-chilled air dry his tears of rage and pain. "Bitch! Bitch! Bitch!" he howled into the wind—only it sounded more like an impotent, "Bith! Bith! Bith!"

At the bottom of the hill the old sedan skidded in a wavering arc as he cranked it south on the asphalt county road.

I can do this. Shock and hemorrhage were draining the color from his face. The pain dulled somewhat and he felt oddly detached from the situation. A shadowy wave of dissociation rose like a blush up his torso and enveloped his head. His ears rang and his eyes frosted over.

Oh, no. No. No. No. Hang on!

Up ahead, he remembered, just over the pass, a spring flowed right out of the rocks beside the road. He could pull into the turn-out, have a drink and splash some cold water on his face. He pictured the icy mountain water driving the wooziness away. He shook his head and stretched his eyelids to their max.

He crested the pass and after several hundred yards turned the car off the road and brought it to a halt. He stumbled out the door and rounded the car to the gurgling flow of water. He held his head in the frigid rivulet and felt the cobwebs recede to the outer edges of his vision. A sixteen-wheeler whizzed by on the downgrade and he felt the strong surge of its passage. The open door of the old car caught the gust like a sail. Under the right front tire a clod of dirt began to give way under the pressure. Clovis heard it first as merely a sigh, then a crunch. Out of the corner of his eye he saw the old car begin to roll.

Clovis turned and gaped in disbelief at the great lumbering sedan's inevitable downgrade glide.

His anguished wail reverberated in the cloudy night as he lunged for the receding bumper. His fingers grasped the heavy, cold chrome. He pulled himself up and tried to dig his toes into the compacted dirt and gravel. The sheet, like a bloody shroud, unraveled in a gory trail behind him. Weakness flooded his arms and he felt his grip slipping from the bumper. In a final act of desperation all ten fingers grabbed for a final purchase on the escaping vehicle. They found the searing exhaust pipe. The air filled with the smell of burning flesh and another primal scream as the metal fused to his skin. The car was picking up speed and the fingers of his right hand relinquished their hold, one at a time. The fingers of his left hand held the scorching pipe in a death grip as his shoulder dislocated and he spiraled toward a merciful oblivion. With exhausted resignation he released the charred-skin glove and slipped out of the bondage of his body.

He watched the drama in ultraslow motion from a spot a few feet above. He saw his face lower to the hard-packed, abrasive, pea gravel. The tiny rocks obliterated his nose, his cheekbones and forehead. His body tumbled after the car for several feet. With gathering momentum the car parted the greenery at the end of the turnout, hesitated, and then plunged noisily into a deep ravine. Clovis didn't observe it, but heard a low-hanging limb slam the sedan's driver-side door shut.

The lush vegetation sprang upright all along the trail behind the receding car as though it had never passed that way at all. The headlights went out when the car impacted the gorge floor. The horn wavered for some time. Then all was quiet.

The sky began to drizzle.

Chapter 12
Serendipity

E. J. Duffy wore a faded orange baseball cap and his long dirty-blond ponytail was held firmly in the driver's side window of his mud-encrusted truck. Pursuing exhaustion and monotony were gaining on him. His eyelids drooped as he reached the pass. His truck began a slow drift toward the roadside ditch. Sleep overwhelmed him and his head snapped forward, yanked his captive hair and jolted him awake.

"Geez, Louise!" he uttered and jerked the truck back on course. He shook his head, rolled down the window to release his hair and drew a few deep gulps of crisp, cold air.

He peered beyond the reach of his headlights for the turnoff he remembered up ahead. There was a spring there where he often stopped for a drink and to relieve himself when he traveled this road. There it was. He stood on the brakes and skidded into the turnoff, pulling up close to the rocky spring.

He drank deeply from the flow of icy water and splashed cupped handfuls over his freckled-face and on the back of his neck.

A faint smell of barbecue lingered in the air. He smiled. A roadside picnic, no doubt. He dried his hands on his wool shirt, filched a twisted doobie from a pocket and placed it between his lips. He flipped open the lid of a shiny silver lighter with a snap of his wrist. It rang like a shot in the stillness. He swiped the wheel of the Zippo down the taut denim of his right pant leg. The acrid tang of lighter fluid crowded out the smell of grilled meat and the wick burst to flame. He held it to the doob and drew a deep appreciative lungful of THC and sweet, fresh, mountain air. The sound of the flowing water stirred his bladder and he moved several feet downgrade and sighed as he relieved himself into the thick kudzu.

A long trail of flotsam floating on a bit of starlight caught the corner of his eye. He shook one leg as he repositioned himself, zipped his fly and strolled over to what proved to be a filthy trail of rags.

"People are so damn inconsiderate," he muttered. "Shit!" he said aloud with a snort, "I sound like my old man!" He grinned and let the pot lighten his mood. He ran in place for a moment then soccer-kicked the rags with alternating feet, driving the growing bundle to the end. He planned to shove the whole mess in the trash barrel chained near the spring.

With his booted toe he nudged the sodden heap at the end of the trail and recoiled from a raspy, bubbling sound. He stumbled backward, regained his balance and fumbled for his lighter again. Blood gleamed black in the matted hair on the back of a head. In the island of light from the Zippo he could make out a distinct diamond pattern of moles on the left side of the neck. Gingerly he rolled the body over. Blood and tissue caked like tar over a mutilated face in the flickering light. Two eyes bore, out of the gore, into his own, until the branding-iron-hot Zippo slipped from his trembling fingers and extinguished. Sounds issuing from the torn and crusted mouth gave witness to life.

Duffy opened the rear doors of his truck, clenched the cold doobie in his teeth and gathered up the whole bloody bundle. He strained his head away but felt the whispered breath in his left ear. He could make out a word or two. It sounded like scripture. He placed the mangled man on a bed of furniture-moving blankets between the doors and his load of old dressers, beds and sofas. A crisscross of ropes secured the load to cleats on the walls of the truck. He slept here himself sometimes when he got too tired to drive. He latched the double doors.

He started to pull out of the turnoff. He stopped the truck short of the road and pulled the hand brake on with a loud, ratcheting sound. He grabbed a small flashlight and trotted back to the end of the turnoff. He looked around until he spotted his silvery Zippo. He picked it up, tossed it in the air and snatched it as it fell. It was his lucky lighter.

He shoved his ponytail up under his baseball cap. "Can't let The Man think I'm a hippie," he said out loud with a grin. He lit the joint again and climbed back into the truck.

He started leaning on the horn before the truck came to a complete halt several feet from the emergency entrance. He jumped out, flung open the double truck doors.

A uniformed guard pushed open the emergency room door a few seconds later and saw the bloody, disheveled man lifting something from the back of a truck.

Duffy yelled, ". . . got an injured man here!"

The guard yelled back into the building.

Duffy cradled the man in his arms and was walking toward the emergency door when the guard and two women in green scrubs converged on him with a gurney to whisk the faceless hulk into the building. The guard helped push the gurney. He shouted back for Duffy to join them. Duffy nodded, started to flash him a peace sign, thought better of it and turned that gesture toward the open doors of his truck.

He slammed the cargo doors shut, glanced toward the hospital and whispered into the night, "Peace, brother preacher man, I hope you've got enough blood left in you to make it."

He climbed back up into the cab. No sense getting more involved. He didn't want to be kicking the inside walls of some Kentucky jail cell 'cause he couldn't explain the pungent green plastic-wrapped bales behind the old furniture in his truck. And besides, he thought, time is money on this interstate run.

"I can't talk any louder!" whispered the furtive young man in the surgical greens. His hand was cupped over the mouthpiece. "I got another one."

"Very good. More details, please."

"Well, we got a veg here with pretty much the upper half of his face missing and severely burned fingers. We sewed up a seven-inch slash on his butt. No ID. There don't seem to be no one in-nerested. They been keeping the wound covered with some pig skin or such."

"A male?"

"Yeah."

"How old?"

". . . About nineteen—twenty . . . ah . . . another hundred bucks?"

". . . As soon as I get the J.D."

"Oh, okay. John Doe, er, J.D. 14768."

"Blood type?"

"Ah, it says here A negative."

"Damn."

"The nurses call him The Sleeping Preacher."

"What?"

"You know, 'cause he mumbles scripture all the time."

Very interesting, the man thought. Not totally brain-dead. This could be a rare opportunity for Dr. Sam. He will be so pleased. "Hmmmm. Any identifying marks? You know, scars? Moles?"

"Yeah, he has four distinct moles in a sideways diamond on the left of his neck."

"Okay, I'll send a relative right away to start the transfer pro-ceedings to our facility for reconstructive surgery. You'll get the hundred."

"Thank you, sir."

"You bet." The older man hung up and dialed another number in Louisville. "Doc, I got one. A really good one. Yeah," he answered. "Martha will go claim him. He has some distinct, identifying moles."

Dr. Sam grinned as he hung up. His heart was doing a little tango. He pulled a cigarette from a silver case and lit up. He drew the smoke deep into his lungs and felt the calm returning. He was over-trained, having done hundreds of partial transplants on cadavers over the last seven months. A breathing patient with a beating heart was at once long overdue and more than he dared hope for, this soon. It would give him a chance to observe the healing, test the anti-rejection drugs, and even test the innervation with electrical stimulation as well as the effects of his new hyperbaric chamber. And, not even brain dead. Who knows? He knew he was already the best plastic surgeon in the South. "Move over Dr. DeBakey, there's a new kid in town!" he gloated.

From his bottom desk drawer he pulled out a bottle of scotch and a white coffee mug, poured himself an inch or two and leaned back in his chair. He lifted his cup and toasted, "Here's to our new collaboration, Mr. Sleeping Preacher." He savored the warmth as the liquor slid down his throat. Propping his crossed ankles on the oak desk he said with a sigh, "Alllll right!"

Chapter 13

A Rescuer Unaware

Most of the community didn't catch wind of the incident and were as puzzled as the children by Preacher Hawk's red-faced rant about stealing and ingratitude that he launched into before breakfast. There was no school that day.

Four teaching sisters scrubbed Clovis's cabin but for all the rest, life went on as usual. When a laundry sister found blood on the blanket and sleep clothes with Reggie's name in big, black letters amongst the dirty clothes, a gaggle of pinch-faced women came, bundled Reggie's scant belongings into a pillowcase and moved her to the big girls' cottage. One younger woman thrust a bag of dingy rags into her hands and told her to use them for the bleeding.

Reggie understood only one thing—they wanted to separate her from Jazz.

Jazz wanted to sleep. Reggie insisted he get up and stay by her.

She used most of the stolen cheese to bribe one of the Original children to do the lunch dishes. She retrieved the knife and scabbard from the back of the old wringer washing machine and tied it under her blouse. She resolved to cut anyone who tried to stop them.

They headed down the hill early, snagging the sack of apples out of the tree as they passed through the orchard. As soon as they were out of sight of The Enclave they broke into a full run. Their feet barely touched the ground.

As they staggered around the last bend they could see that none of the little flags on the mailboxes poked up. The Blue Lady hadn't arrived yet. They darted across the county road and gave the weed-clogged ditch a perfunctory, midair check for snakes before landing in the soggy thatch.

For several minutes they just collapsed against the sides of the ditch and waited for their breath to catch up with them. Reggie decided to share an apple to quench their thirst but not two unless Jazz complained. She used the fresh-scrubbed, pilfered knife to split the stolen apple and started to giggle. Jazz joined her. Soon they were rolling in giddy mirth on the mossy floor of the ditch. The moment was sweet.

To pass the time they played Mancala with Jazz's treasure stones and hollows scooped in the damp earth of the roadside ditch. It was a game one of the older girls, called Bridey, had taught Reggie to play. Mancala meant planting the seeds in Swahili. Bridey told her that was what they spoke in Africa. She'd learned the game from her father. She hardly remembered the man but the memory of the story and the game was vivid. Reggie recited the familiar story to Jazz in that ditch. He liked it when she told the story exactly the same every time. Sometimes his mouth would form the next word.

She began, "In Kenya, Africa, a land far away, Bridey's father made friends with a native black boy. In spite of the value others put upon her father's white skin, that barefoot black boy became her daddy's best friend. Each boy taught the other the best of his culture. The girl's father taught his friend Jomoto to play the noble game of chess. Chess had been a part of the British culture for hundreds of years. Jomoto taught her daddy the three-thousand-year-old African game of Mancala.

"A war of rebellion fomented by the Mau Mau tore the two friends apart. Fear of reprisal by the Mau Mau—" Her voice became menacing with that name and Jazz's eyes grew wide, "drove many of the colonists from the continent. Time and distance separated the friends. But the girl's father taught his daughters Mancala."

That girl had taught Reggie and Reggie taught Jazz. He was pretty good.

After what felt like a very long time they heard the mail truck coming down the county road. The Blue Lady managed to pull the dusty vehicle to a skidding stop at the far end of the haphazard line of rusting mailboxes to the dissonant tune of metal against metal. "Goldernflippinbrakes," she exclaimed, then again lapsed into song, ". . . lalala the world needs now lala lala sweet love . . . not lala lala some lalalalallala everyone."

Her singing was interspersed with grunts and sighs as she tugged and woman-handled a canvas pouch out of the truck. It fell to the dusty ground. "Somebody must be getting an anvil today." She laughed at her own old joke. Minutes later she appeared at the near end of the bank of boxes with a fistful of mail. With her other hand she shaded her eyes against the noonday sun, ". . . la la la la, lalala, lalala . . ." Her distracted off-key song drifted across the road. She stared up the grade toward The Enclave.

Reggie's heart stalled. *What was she looking at? Was Preacher Hawk coming down the hill?*

"Oh, li'l chill-drun, li'l chill-drun . . ." She spoke in a voice slightly louder than normal.

They realized she had not spotted someone up the hill—she was looking up there for them.

". . . lalalala lala rivers and mountains . . ." Her voice rose in full gusto.

The two escapees darted across the road and crept up into the truck. The Blue Lady put each letter and paper into its proper box. The two stowaways worked their way as far into the back corner as possible and settled down under a disheveled pile of empty canvas mailbags.

The Blue Lady whistled her way back into the truck and tossed the empty sack toward the back. She started up the noisy motor. Both of the pint-sized stowaways released their pent-up breath and shared a big smile. Even if there were a window, they would not have looked back.

Chapter 14

Back to the World

An ear-grating screech announced the arrival of the Blue Lady jouncing the dingy green mail truck into the Post Office vehicle yard. Raucous music came from the repair bay at the far end of the fenced area. An orange-vested worker waved her directly there. The music grew louder. It filled the air—a heavy bass beat and a man yelling: ". . . sure dig on rock 'n' roll! When you're rockin' and a . . ."

Jazz clapped his hands over his ears.

The Blue Lady stood on the brakes, skidded into the open front of a big building where she managed to bring the truck to a reluctant halt but not before allowing the truck's bumper to nudge the one and only mechanic working there.

"Gee-zus-Ma-ag-gie-and-Joseph! Take it easy, Shug-gar!" groused the ruddy-faced bald man over the din of the music.

Maggie Ann Joseph must be the Blue Lady's name. Reggie smiled with that fresh information. She just didn't know what Jesus had to do with it. The music faded to medium and Maggie jumped down to the concrete floor.

Reggie peeked as the grease-smudged man wiped his grimy hands on an even grimier oil-stained rag that probably used to be red. His rough comments didn't quite cover the laughter in his voice. He made many more syllables of the words he uttered than they deserved . . . just like Sister Lola Faye, Reggie recalled. It had taken Reggie weeks to understand her.

"Her name must be Maggie," Reggie translated in a whisper to Jazz.

"Oh, Hap, honey, Ahm so everlastin' sorry," answered the Blue Lady—Maggie. "These dern brakes . . ."

The two old friends commiserated over the aging equipment but that didn't negate the need for a written request and work order. They groused about the endless paperwork as they filled out forms.

The little stowaways stretched their stiff legs and made ready to dash. They did not have any idea to where or in which direction. When Maggie walked away the music was cranked up.

Jazz covered his ears again, but Reggie liked it.

HapHoney drove the truck a little ways, jockeyed it a bit and climbed down.

A moment later, a vibration began with a loud metallic grind. The children grabbed anything to steady themselves as their whole world lurched and the dingy truck, creaking in protest, lifted off the ground. The wide-eyed children held on and clutched each other.

Over the sound of the lifting thing and the blaring music, they heard a clang.

dream yon

dream yon

dream yon

The heavy grind diminished and the levitation came to a stop. The clanging bell sounded again. "Goll-durn timin'," HapHoney grumbled.

The children heard his footsteps scuff across the floor and a heavy door whoosh shut. Reggie scooted to the driver's door and peeked over the edge. The old truck hovered above the ground four or five feet.

Jazz crawled up beside her. He watched in awe as she got on her belly and backed out the door. She lowered herself as far as she could and then . . . let go.

Jazz gasped.

He heard Reggie's harsh voice whisper, "Jump!"

Jazz was scared. But he jumped. Reggie cushioned his fall and they both collapsed on that greasy old concrete floor and started to giggle. They jumped up and dashed out. They skirted the Post Office yard sticking close to the fence. They looked back from the gate when the grating sound started up again. HapHoney was watching the truck rise higher yet. Reggie loved when the young man screamed:

Dream Yon Dream Yon

Dream Yon Dream Yon

The music followed them into their first real-world adventure in over four years.

Chapter 15
Searching for Sanctuary

They avoided people and munched apples. Who could they trust? Who wouldn't force them back to The Enclave? They were particularly wary of the white building with the tall pointy roof. Reggie showed Jazz that there was a cross on top.

The cautious escapees watched people from a distance. Not a one wore black and white like they did. Fences were a rarity in this little town so all the yards around the houses could be seen from the street. Reggie solved what she called their "sore thumb" problem when she spotted a working clothesline behind one of the houses.

Jazz thought that clothesline was the most colorful thing he had ever seen. The clothes flapped like a joyous rainbow on the late afternoon breeze. It tugged like a happy memory just out of reach.

Reggie searched for the words to express the overwhelming flood of emotion she felt. "Victory," she whispered.

Jazz looked up to her eyes.

We're coming like settlers to a new land. This colorful clothesline is our flag. She squeezed Jazz's hand. This one multicolored vision and the memory of raucous singing kindled a warmth inside her and let loose the idea of possibilities.

The green and blue shirts they pulled free from the line were slightly damp and felt cool on their skin. They left their neatly folded white shirts in exchange.

They scurried to some nearby woods. They lay on the soft leaves, ate some cheese and, for a bit, just looked up through the trees.

"The radioman said the young man who sang was named Arrow Smith," Reggie announced. "When I grow up and have a son I will name him Arrow after Mister Smith."

"Dream Yon! Dream Yon!" Reggie sang in a high-pitched screech and wriggled her bare feet in the air.

They felt a little less conspicuous when they strolled away on that early summer evening in their purloined shirts, searching for a refuge.

Most all the cars sported license plates with Kentucky and a bunch of numbers on them just like the old, dingy mail truck and Preacher Hawk's sedan. Some plates said Tennessee and the numbers. They walked the streets of the little town not knowing what or who they were looking for.

She didn't know how she knew; she just knew that the cars with flowers and decorations on them were safe. They found only one vehicle with writing and pictures on it. It was an old, decrepit van with flat tires and broken windows. It was tilted and melting into the weeds beside a house. They stood and stared at it for a while. The van wasn't quite right. It was rotting away. They walked farther.

As they were going down a street they had already walked down once, a shiny silver-gray car pulled in front of a house up the way. They watched a slim young woman step from the car and stretch her arms over her head. She was wearing tight blue pants and a long-sleeved, silky peach and blue shirt with pictures of women on it. The license on the silver car said, Washington, D.C. She took a small suitcase from the trunk.

The children were beside her now and caught her eye as she turned toward the house. She stopped and looked at their solemn little faces. Their faded shirts looked odd with their black shorts and skirt and the laced-up black oxfords.

"Where did you come from?" she asked. Jazz watched her face as he pointed in the direction where he thought The Enclave would lie. "Ah, down the block. You must be visiting, too. Best you get home. It's late," she said. She gave them a big smile and only a moment's thought as she walked across the tiny front yard and into the house.

Both Reggie and Jazz felt her warm smile in their chests as they followed her with their eyes. The woman did not seem afraid.

They stared at each other. Reggie's focus slid past Jazz's curly head and fell on a silver emblem standing upright on the front of the shiny gray car. Jazz noticed the discovery in Reggie's eyes. That made him turn and look, too. Jazz shuddered and closed his eyes. A vision of Hawk holding up an object in his meaty fist burned into his eyelids.

"The evil thing!" he rasped and remembered fire. He started to cry. He was tired and scared and now this evil thing . . .

"No, Jazz," Reggie cooed and cradled him in her arms. "This is not evil, this is the sign of The Family." Her words were reverent.

When Reggie walked to the front of the car to touch the emblem, she noticed some letters below the sign. "Maybe that's the pretty woman's name. Mercy-daze," she said aloud as they walked up to the front door of the little house.

Chapter 16
The End of the Beginning

On the cover of this journal I wrote my name. It is Reggie. I do not have a last name yet. This is my journal and no one may read it unless I say so.

The lady I thought was Mercy-daze is really Allyson McAlester. Mercy-daze is the name of the car. The pretty woman is a lawyer-lady from Washington, D.C. Her momma and papa live in the little house where we found the peace sign and all of them. Allyson gave Jazz and me each two thin books with no words in them. One book is to write about now and the other is to put in stuff we remember. Jazz mostly draws pictures, but some words, too. I will try to write most nights.

September 24, 1976

After all the grownups listened to our story, they got real mad—but not at us. I love my new way to make sevens.

A man with a star pinned on his shirt came and talked to us, too.

We went to see a doctor. He said he was sorry he had to poke and prod us. Allyson held our hand, and the doctor was gentle. Boy-oh-boy was he mad, too.

Maggie, the Blue Lady, laughed when we told her the trick we pulled on her. We got to play with some children. That was real fun. We gave back the borrowed shirts and got to buy some new clothes.

9/27/76

I learned this new way to write the date. We went to a big theater and saw our first movie ever. It was about three men in big hats and fancy pants with long hair and mustaches. They talked and laughed when they acted out lots of fights with pointy sticks. Jazz and I made some pointy sticks and pretended to fight until Allyson told us we could put someone's eye out. She doesn't know how I almost did that to Clovis—on purpose. I didn't tell anyone that.

9/28/76

Today we listened to music—rode a real horse and saw the school we will go to. Allyson says it will be more fun than The Enclave School. Tomorrow she is taking her two nieces and us to a big theme park in Georgia where we can go on rides and eat fluffy pink candy.

Chapter 17
The Kentucky Cult Raid
October 1976, 12:00 noon

The uniformed Kentucky State Trooper was hunkered down in a thicket of aspens above The Enclave, a microphone curving in front of his mouth. He clutched high-powered binoculars to his eyes watching what the FBI was calling The Kentucky Cult Raid. He was in radio contact with the FBI agents and officers on the ground.

The agents wore blue flak vests with FBI stenciled on the front and back. The watcher's fellow troopers wore red plaid hunting jackets and red hunting caps. From his angle the red-capped officers looked like corpuscles circulating around the compound in a brisk, even manner.

FBI personnel surrounded the dining hall where The Enclave members were eating lunch. The windows being high up on the walls made their approach relatively easy. Each agent kept a low profile, stooped over and loping into position with a drawn gun held in two hands.

The men of local law enforcement would have preferred to be running this operation, but, as usual, when the FBI was brought into a case because of the interstate nature of the crime, they wanted absolute control and any favorable publicity to be theirs alone. To the watcher it was a prickly old bureaucratic story.

The lead agent held up her free, open hand. The watcher radioed that fact to all the people on the ground. "Mark!"

The troopers all stopped and turned, as one, toward the dining hall.

Several agents were gathered around the front door and several around the back door, out of the watcher's sight.

As the lead agent folded down one finger at a time starting with her thumb, the watcher counted into the microphone, "Five, four, three, two, one."

All the agents burst into the dining hall. Orders shouted into a megaphone and women's screams echoed and bounced around the hillsides. The troopers closed in on the dining hall and the watcher stepped out of the aspen thicket.

Next to the brook below The Enclave five men, each loaded down with arms full of windfall kindling, stood stark still and wide-eyed at the racket from above.

"FBI!" bellowed a bullhorn.

Then, from a flurry of airborne firewood, the brothers bolted up the slope and scattered into the woods. The clatter of flying kindling caught the watcher's attention and he scanned the tree line in time to see the five men disappearing into the forest.

He relayed the news of the escaping men and their approximate directions to the officers in The Enclave compound. He scrambled around the rocky hilltop to see if he could get another glimpse of the fleeing men.

Several troopers in The Enclave broke away from the throng, jumped the fence and slipped and slid down to the brook then clambered on all fours up the steep slope and ran into the woods in as hot a pursuit as they could muster.

The runners had a hefty head start, knew the woods and how to get down to the truck route. By the time the Feds brought in the dogs, they were long gone . . . hightailing and hitching rides.

Chapter 18
Reggie's Journal Continued

9/31/76

I forgot my books when we went to Georgia. So, I am back. I rode a roller coaster fourteen times. It was so good. It stirred up my stomach but didn't make me sick. It made me happy. When I grow up I will get a job riding on roller coasters with children who are afraid.

10/2/76

Allyson told us that The Big Police FBI swooped down on The Enclave and arrested Hawk, most of the men and all the women. She said some of the men scattered into the woods like a stirred-up flock of red chickens! Jazz and I laughed at that story.

10/29/76

I am sorry I have not written for a long time. I have been having fun.

11/30/76

Today we told our story again, this time to a big, old, fat man in a black dress—in front of a lot of people. He was sweet and kind. The worst part was, Preacher Hawk and lots of the Sisters and Brothers were in the big room, too. They sat at a table and the men sent mean looks our way, even when they did not look at us. Some of the Sisters cried and even smiled at us sometimes. Jazz and I got to sit with Josepha and her mommy and daddy. Guess what? The Doctors in Atlantic City, Georgia, are going to take off her ugly, twisted, black, snake-bit arms and make her new ones. I hope she will be able to hug again. She said that dirty rat Billy Ray Ripley got clean away.

12/5/76

A whole lot of people talked a whole lot to that nice fat man. People showed pictures and some even drew pictures on a big tablet on legs. An old wrinkly-faced sheriff from Virginia remembered our mothers. They'd reported us stolen. He dug out his old notepads.

He looked up at the judge and said, "I have kept a Field Interrogation note on every case I've worked on before I went to 'Nam and then again when I came back."

"Excuse me, your honor, what is a Field Interrogation note?" the District Attorney man asked.

"Sheriff Crouter?" the judge asked the sheriff.

"My mistake, Your Honor. Before I went to 'Nam that's what we called them. After the Mary Andy decision by the Supreme Court in the mid-sixties, I think it was, they were renamed Field Interviews."

The judge and the D.A. both nodded.

I forgot to ask Allyson what a Mary Andy decision was.

The sheriff said the boys did have draft cards with an address in New York State. He wrote down their names but not the women's.

That was how some of The Family got found. Family people remembered that in 1972 they were so scared and heartbroken and didn't get much help from the Virginia police. For a while they tried to find us on their own, but people called them hippies in the South at that time and didn't like them much. The Family finally went back up North and split up—at least as far as anyone could remember.

12/8/76

After they all talked again, Your Honor, that is the fat man's name, well, he sent Hawk, whose real name is Randolph Ransom, the Brothers and some of the Sisters far away where they would never, ever hurt children again. But, Clovis was never there. They talked about him, but no one knew where he was. He just drove off in that old sedan and he and it both vanished. The judge convicted Clovis and Billy Ray Ripley in absentia and if they ever find them they will go to jail, too. Allyson said that absentia word means they were gone, but they are still guilty.

Sometimes I wonder how many stitches it took to sew up Clovis's rump. Ha, Ha! That last little sign is an ex-pli-ma-tion mark. It means I really, really mean what I wrote!!!!!!!

12/20/76

The original children and the babies at The Enclave all have found their families. They were mostly from Kentucky. One momma even flew in from Africa for the carving girl, Bridey.

The Family Moms are harder to find. No one knows Kali's or Star's real names.

12/25/76

What a Christmas! Life is really fun.

12/30/76

Allyson told me The FBI, a big American police department, is working on The Enclave case now because state lines were crossed. She says missing children's stories are not shared between states. I don't know why.

1/3/77

Television and newspaper told the stories all around the world. Eventually all the other Family members were located—all, that is, except Kali and Star. The common story was that Star and Kali had gone to school together to be nurses before they joined The Family. When The Family scattered they joined up with a group of nuns and medical people to go to Chile. There were a couple of letters. No one kept the letters and no one could remember the women's last names or even the city in Chile where the letters came from. No one remembered where Star and Kali came from originally or where they went to nurses' school. Jazz and I are very sad about that. Our daddies were never part of the Family.

Allyson told us that Chile was changing in 1972. Food was hard to come by. American companies were taken over by the soldiers. The next year someone took over the government. It was just awful. She said the first four years mostly regular people died. Protestors just disappeared. Folks said Star and Kali were definitely protestors. Jazz and I are very sad about that, too.

1/12/77

We were the unclaimed children. Our story was in the news all over the United States. People sent money—a whole lot of money. The property of The Enclave was divided among all of us kidnapped children. Allyson McAlester, that is her lawyer name, made sure that some of our money be used for a talking doctor for us so we could be not so sad. She suggested the rest be invested in what they call a trust until we were grown.

1/13/77

We will go to school now and do homework. Allyson says we can write in our journals if we want to but we will be very busy.

6/20/77

Big news! Flora and Red Cowels, the founders of the original Family, own a small music store in San Jose, California now and don't have any kids of their own. They asked the court if they could raise us. Now we have a last name. It is Cowels. They are very nice. We will move to California. We will miss our friends here and we will write them and maybe visit.

Chapter 19

The Hunt

Join The Navy and See the World and All You Do
Is See The Sea

Fall 1978

"Yes, ma'am," the burly teddy bear of a sailor drawled, "I am a long way from my Kentucky home." He reached up and swept the crisp white sailor hat from his head, twisted it in on itself and folded it over his waistband. The small bartender with the fine-boned hands freshened his drink.

He took a sip and flashed her a shy smile, "Thank you, ma'am."

She asked, "What's your name, sailor?"

"My given name is Billy Ray, ma'am." He rose and swept her a bow. "Billy Ray Ripley of Buford, Kentucky, U. S. of A. at your service."

Like most bars he'd cruised around the world, it was dark. There were no windows or clocks to make time a reality. He peered into the shadows beside the register. *Bingo!* There they were, the smallish silver framed pictures of two children.

"I sure do like kids. Boys or girls." He indicated the framed pictures. "I was the oldest of seven." He moistened his lips. This part of the hunt was always intoxicating. "So . . . are those sweet darlings your kids?"

Part Two
Ten Years Later

Chapter 20
The Experimental Wing
The Dr. Samuel J. Avery Plastic Surgery Complex
Louisville, 1988

Dr. Sam Avery looked at patient J. Smith's official chart. Vitals right on the money, he noted. Twisting the comatose Mr. Smith's face from side to side, he studied the hairline scar traversing the back of his head at the occipital bone, curling over each ear and tracing just under his jawline. Avery's chest swelled with pride. This was facial transplant number twelve on this male patient, from as many cadavers in as many years—and this one was by far the best. The barely visible scarring was in part due to protection from sunlight, perfect nutrition and Avery's patented anti-scarring ointment slathered on the fading surgical seams daily. There was no sign of tissue rejection. Muscle tone was excellent, exercised by ten minutes of electrical stimulation to every set of muscles daily, full body massages and physical therapy, each three times a week.

He checked the working chart that hung on the back of the headboard. The latest donor had been an unidentified, comatose, homeless white female, a gunshot victim. She'd been brought in by one of his team's contacts in a Paducah hospital. She was 19-22 years of age, blood type A negative and suffering from Alopecia Totalis, as Mr. Smith did. A perfect match! She'd died here in the complex after a month.

During that month, although she was brain-dead, Dr. Sam's handpicked team was able to cleanse her system of drugs and restore complete physical health before they pulled the plug. Smith's surgery had begun within minutes. Her face draped on his bone structure presented an aesthetically pleasing, almost angelic-appearing young man. Never one to waste an opportunity to practice his craft, Dr. Sam sutured Smith's eleventh face on her bone structure. Her new face, of course, never had a chance to heal and become her own.

Dr. Sam leaned his silvery head down to place his ear to the patient's barely moving lips. The almost constant whispered babble had been issuing from deep inside the coma victim they had called The Preacher Man for twelve years.

"And these signs will follow those who believe: In My name they will cast out demons; they will speak with new tongues; they will take up serpents; and if they drink anything deadly, it will by no means hurt them; they will lay hands on the sick, and they will recover."

Dr. Sam's fingers counted the patient's heartbeats. As he started to turn away, the patient clutched at his wrist.

The good doctor's knees sagged in an instant panic followed by a rush of excited curiosity. *What's this—purely an involuntary action?*

He lifted the lids and shone a light into each of the man's eyes. There was something, a flicker, a stirring of—something new.

The tiny, inside voice said, "Thirsty."

Dr. Sam called in The Team.

• • •

The Team got a tip about a local death before the authorities were notified. They brought in the body of a recluse who died when a six-foot stack of newspapers collapsed and smothered him. The stacks totally filled his home except for narrow pathways from one room to the next. When Dr. Sam heard that story, he had his people go back and bring the years and years of unread newspapers to the Experimental/Resident wing of the complex. What a wonderful way for their re-emerging Mr. Smith to catch up with what had been going on in the world while he slept and provided a canvas for Dr. Sam to adorn, again and again.

Clovis didn't tell Dr. Sam or The Team that memory was flooding back and he knew his name wasn't Smith. He remembered everything up until twelve years ago, except how he got here. He didn't know the man in the mirror but he loved what he saw and realized that this exact face fit right in with the life plan he'd devised while lying comatose for endless days in his hospital bed and now walking the corridors learning to use his body again. He read and read.

Since Marcus Hollister survived The Enclave Cult in Kentucky it was news of interest locally in 1987 when he became an Eagle Scout. The story included the fact that Hollister's family owned a small residential hotel in Gurdon, Arkansas. That news was an epiphany for Clovis and he knew what he must do.

It was two a.m. and Dr. Sam and his Team were all in a drug-induced sleep in the Experimental/Resident wing of the complex. Clovis killed the power in the refrigerated morgue room, opened all the body drawers, deactivated the fire alarms in the wing and left all interior doors open. He dumped all the files from the file cabinet in the experimental records room and set them on fire.

He sat in Dr. Sam's gray SUV packed with all the clothes that would fit him and any money he could find. He watched the raging blaze. When the wing was engulfed, the greasy stench of rotting flesh roasting on a spit saturated the billowing plumes of gray-black smoke surging into the moonless sky. He felt quite sure there would be no record of his years as a guest of Dr. Sam outside this wing. Before the flames spread any further, Clovis dialed 911 on a cell phone he'd found at a nurse's station. Then he drove into the shrouded streets heading out of the city. He threw that cell into a river when he crossed a bridge heading south—to Arkansas.

Chapter 21
Any Old Port in a Storm
Amsterdam, Fall of 1988

Professor J. D. Sterling couldn't believe her eyes. Of all the squares in all the towns in all the world, here he was, in her town square, in her adopted city. And, here she was, at this very spot, taking an unprecedented evening off from teaching—being the "Wunderkind" Chair of the Herpetology Department at the University of The Hague, she'd had her choice of classes and chosen evenings.

It's not as though I forgot his face or that he's changed. He was a grown man in 1976. I was only eleven.

It was just that today was the occasional rare day in the last thirteen years when she hadn't thought of him. She and her life had changed a great deal but that man had always been an insidious presence.

She was cozy in her forest green cable-knit winter gear, sitting at a sidewalk table at The Bulldog. She was savoring a conical cigarette of the finest Purple Haze grown in the upper stories of that "coffeehouse." The reefer was clipped to a slender, silver rod that held it suspended six inches above one of her gloved hands. In the other hand was a bottle of Guinness.

The street performers were delighting the semicircular clutch of cross-legged children sitting wide-eyed and thrilled not twenty feet away. JoDee watched her precious niece Katrina as she smeared ChapStick on her perfect, rosebud lips. After capping the tube the child slipped it back into the shoulder bag slung over JoDee's chair, wrapped a gleeful hug around her aunt's neck and scampered back to sit among her friends.

Here, in the real world of family and friends, Professor J.D. Sterling was Jo or JoDee. Her old name, Josepha, had been relegated to her troubled past.

He was checking her out. Why not? She was presentable. She had grown casual with her handicap and hid it well. And, she was the only single woman with a child who was sitting in the front row of tables.

"Ma'am." It was a polite approach. "May I sit and buy you a drink?"

She looked up into his face until he grew uncomfortable and started to turn away. "Wait, sailor," she stopped him. "Sit down. I will buy you a drink." She flagged a waiter.

"You're American. How fine," he stammered. "I'm Bill." His guileless smile was only half-formed when a perplexed shadow passed over his eyes. He studied her face. "Do I know you?" he asked.

"JoDee," she informed him, "and, no, I'm quite sure you don't know me." She indicated the dead doobie she had scraped off in the ashtray. "Go ahead and light that up. I've had enough."

He picked up the oddly shaped number, lit it and took a deep toke. His attention returned to the children.

"One moment, I have to use my handy," she said.

"Handy?"

"Oh. You call it a cell."

He nodded and turned his attention to the children.

She pushed one button on the phone laying on the table, then another and activated the speaker.

Her sister Emily's husband Kurt answered in Dutch. She explained the situation in Flemish. He said they would be right there.

"Anything in particular?" she asked the sailor when the waiter stood beside her.

"Whatever you're having."

She knew the waiter well. He dipped his head and she spoke to him in Flemish. He snapped his eyes to hers with a barely perceptible shake of his head. She said something else and he sighed. With a reluctant nod, he left.

The man watched the magician entertaining the children. He mostly watched Jo's niece.

"That was a very strange language," he noted. "What was it?"

"Flemish. I don't often have a chance to practice it and Gooter indulges me."

Gooter set two beers and two shots in front of Bill and waved off payment by Josepha. "On da howse," he said, sounding as though he squeezed his words out through a mouth full of oily marbles.

The sailor lifted the shot glass in a salute to her, tossed it back and chugged the first beer in two long drafts. The second he nursed a bit. They watched the children.

"You're a long way from home aren't you, sailor?"

Her question seemed to come from a distance and sounded like a record playing at a slower speed than it was recorded.

"Yes, ma'am," the burly teddy bear of a sailor drawled. "I am a long, long way from my Kentucky home." He reached up and swept the crisp white sailor hat from his head and reached for her hand. He felt the hard plastic just under the resilient surface layer. He looked at the posed fingers curved in a slight, receptive grip. He lifted his puzzled eyes to her cold, vindictive smile.

He'd forgotten. *What was it, what did he forget?* He looked back at the children through a dreamy, mauve haze.

"I see you like kids," she baited him.

"Yeah, I like kids." His answer was slurred. "I was the oldest of seven." He moistened his lips. *Was I hunting?* He couldn't remember. He felt intoxicated. "So . . . do you have kids?" There was no answer, only the grayish violet Rohypnol twilight and forgetting.

Jo's brother-in-law pulled his sedan close by The Bulldog and rang Jo's handy once.

She took the signal and coaxed Bill to his feet. She guided him like a tipsy boyfriend toward the car. Kurt hopped out and opened the back door. Jo's sister Emily had parked her car a half a block away. She trotted up and helped them put Bill in the backseat. As they coaxed the very relaxed Bill into the car, Emily slid Bill's wallet from his pocket and handed it to Jo.

Emily clasped her sister in a warm hug. Then, holding her at arm's length she gave her a stern, knowing smile. "You've got him, Jo. You've got him." She waved after them as they pulled into traffic.

She sat down at The Bulldog to watch Katrina. She ordered a hot chocolate.

Kurt drove to Museumplein nineteen. Jo got out of the car.

She stood at the big iron gate of the American Embassy and spoke to the burly, uniformed guard. She showed him Bill's wallet, pulled out his ID and handed it through the bars. Kurt was bringing the stumbling Bill to the gate.

"This man's name is Billy Ray Ripley. He is a wanted criminal in the U.S. He is quite drunk. He told us he is wanted on several counts of child molestation. He saw himself on *America's Most Wanted* and is tired of running. He wants to turn himself over to the law."

She gestured to the glassy-eyed Bill. "We're afraid to take him home with us tonight in order to bring him in during business hours." She gave the guard her card and Bill's wallet.

The guard opened the gate and took Bill inside. "We'll hold him in protective custody tonight." He looked at her card. "Thank you, Professor. Bring your passport when you come to sign the papers tomorrow."

"I will be here tomorrow at ten," she promised.

She fairly skipped back to the sedan.

January 1989

"Billy Ray Ripley," the muscular, dark-haired FBI agent said at the Customs gate, "Welcome back to the United States of America. You are under arrest for child molestation, child pornography and evading arrest. Anything you do or say . . ."

Billy Ray winced when the agent whirled him around and began to frog-march him through the airport.

"Gentlepeople of the Jury." The gray-haired, black-robed judge peered over her tiny reading glasses to address the twelve people in the jury box. "How find you on the seventh count of participating in the making and distribution of child pornography?"

The short, bespectacled foreman said, without even glancing at the big, gentle-looking monster standing next to his attorney, "We find the defendant guilty."

"Guilty on all counts," pronounced the judge with finality.

Billy Ray sucked it up. He felt a twinge of gratitude that the hundreds of other boys and girls hadn't been found to bring charges and testify.

I'm a big guy, I work out. I can do ten years. I toughen up real good. Adaptation! That's the name of the game.

Another Ten
Years Later

Chapter 22
Sharing Poetic Justice
Early Spring 1998

It was evening when Bridget Clemens, driving an unremarkable white rental car with a silver and blue Texas-U-Tote trailer in tow, parked at the top of a tree-lined circular driveway. She tilted her head and peered through large, heavy-rimmed glasses up the seven steps to the Long Island portico. The large house with its opulent entrance belonged to her sister, Belle McCreedy.

I wonder if I should park in the rear with my tacky little caravan. She swallowed two of her little blue "coping" pills with the last swig of a flat, tepid cola she had bought at a New Jersey drive-through.

"Too late," she said aloud when she saw Belle, a dervish in hunter green and russet, practically skipping down the stairs.

Belle tore open the car door and dragged Bridget to her weary feet and into a monumental bear hug.

The strain of the drive from Houston to New York felt etched around Bridget's eyes. She collapsed small and spent into Belle's warm embrace. Within minutes of settling on Belle's elegant chambray couch she was fast asleep leaving her steaming mug of fresh-brewed coffee untasted. She was slumped, half-sitting, half-reclining. Her bag had slipped to the floor.

"Oh, dear, sweet Bridey," Belle murmured. She didn't have the heart to rouse her so she tugged off her shoes and helped her stretch out. She lifted the glasses from her nose and set them on the table beside the coffee and covered her with a fleecy yellow throw she kept handy for just such chilly evenings.

Belle studied her big sister's face. Bridget favored their mother's dark aquiline features. Her severe brunette bangs and the scar that divided her upper lip made her look stern even in repose. Belle and her twin sister Haley Baxter looked more like their dad. The one feature they all shared was Mum's clear, hazel eyes.

Bridget awoke the next day to the chatter of her twin sisters trying to talk softly in the kitchen. She fumbled in her purse for her pill case and washed down two pills with the cold coffee she found on the end table. She slipped from the room and into a downstairs bathroom and prepared to meet the two dynamos. She listened to their cheery voices for some time before she mustered a morning smile and scuffed in her white socks through the swinging kitchen doors.

"Excuse me hickory docks, birds, I left me eggs and kippers in me lorry."

Her malformed upper lip gave Bridget's speech a muffled, nasal twang the sisters found familiar and endearing and they all laughed at Bridget's cockney rhyme about her socks and absent slippers.

They gathered in a teary-eyed, laughing huddle. The Clemens girls—rusty-haired twins each with a smattering of freckles across her pert nose and the darker, aquiline-featured Bridget—together again. As always, when excited or angry, the adult sisters each fell in and out of the cockney dialect of Nana, their childhood governess.

"We are an odd trio," Belle laughed. "Mummy and Dadda were so strait-laced and proper. And listen to us!"

"Blimey!" Haley agreed. "We all sound like Nana!"

Even Bridget giggled and said, "You've got to admit Mum's and Dad's emotional vocabulary was pale beside Nana's."

The sisters shared thoughtful nods.

Their parents were dead. Nana was gone. Bridget had never married. Belle and Haley were each widowed and wealthy . . . quite wealthy, and more than a little bored.

Years might lapse between good chats, but it never took long for the three to get back to gritty, current reality.

"Geez, if I were with anyone except you two," confessed Haley, "I'd feel too guilty to admit my all too affluent life feels colorless and dull."

"Maybe it's just our age," said Belle, "but when we went back to Kenya last year, I felt like a tourist."

"We *were* tourists," scoffed Haley.

"I've always felt like a tourist," Bridget said.

The twins nodded. They remembered what Bridget was like when she returned to them after The Enclave kidnapping story broke. They and their African friend Karanja had done their best to teach her all the wonders of their new home on that continent and Bridget had tried so hard to fit in. But she was altered—odd—different from the big sister they remembered.

"I have a job in Miami Beach starting up again in June," Bridget said. "I'm not sure I can pull myself together in time."

The twins knew she tended to be depressed and withdrawn. They respected her privacy and figured she would open up to them in her own time. Maybe that time was now.

After a quiet pause Bridget said, "I'd like to try to tell you the real story of The Enclave."

For the next hour they paid rapt attention as Bridget, growing ever more agitated, related the unabridged story of her sexual and religious abuse. For the very first time they heard her story unfiltered through Mum and Dad. They were stunned and sickened by the terror the Rescuers had wreaked upon all the children under their care. Some details had only recently burst full-fledged into Bridget's memory.

"Every woman in my online group of childhood abuse survivors suffers to this day. Depression is a given. Several of us fight insidious, persistent thoughts of suicide. Sexual dysfunction, disassociation and difficulty with intimacy—they're all common."

"That Clovis creep! I'd kill him myself if I ever saw him," Haley hissed.

Belle concurred. "Men like him have no right to exist."

Bridget blinked, swallowed hard and went on, "Two of the women I met in that group were girls I remembered from The Enclave, both younger. One was snatched a year or so after me. It's Reggie. You remember," she coaxed, "the kid who escaped with her brother and blew the lid off the Rescuers and that whole sick, brainwashing, religious cult."

"Sure."

The telling and its aftermath took them until early afternoon. It was a catharsis for Bridget and an awakening for the twins. They felt fury and a deeper empathy than ever before for their dear, sweet Bridey, who had been stolen from them so young and suffered such profound damage.

"I don't know if I can ever recover but the work I'm doing now is so important. We have a plan and it's given such meaning to my life. But emotionally, I'm losing ground."

Bridget told them about the Texas institution where she had lived off and on for most of the last fifteen years. "I need to go back—just for a while—get a firmer grip on my emotions and on my life," she said.

"You go. I can cover your gig in Miami Beach if you like," offered Belle. "I'll have to practice. It will be fun. I'll just pretend to be you. I could use your union card," she said. "I let mine expire."

"I'll come down and observe," Haley enthused. "It'll be an adventure."

Bridget looked at her watch. She swallowed two more of the little blue pills and said, "Well, little sisters." She took a deep breath, "I think that's a great idea. I have a small apartment in South Beach. A friend feeds the pets when I'm gone. Also I know a state-of-the-art makeup artist."

Bridget took her Union Booklet encased in plastic from her purse and handed it to Belle. It was sealed open to her picture. The twins looked at their sister with matching puzzled expressions. "Don't open that yet, okay?"

Bridget excused herself, went out to the truck and brought in a medium-sized cardboard carton with the words POETIC JUSTICE scrawled on one side.

"About that job in Miami Beach . . ." She dropped the carton next to her chair and strode to the liquor cabinet. "The gig is more than just a job." She tossed that comment over her shoulder.

She poured three tall, stiff Tanqueray and tonics, sliced a bit of lime into each and said, "It's after five o'clock in," she looked at her watch, "Zurich. And it's," she handed each a drink, "time to get serious."

She pulled a fat, tattered notebook from the box and handed it over as though she were passing the orb and staff. She picked up a program and smiled. "Have you heard of the off-Broadway show, *The Vagina Monologues*?"

"Yes, yes," they chorused.

"I was there, at this theater," Belle said, indicating the program. "I couldn't even say the word out loud before I saw that show." She thought a moment. "The signs in the subway used to embarrass me," she admitted. "Isn't that silly?"

"I saw a charity production in Hollywood," Haley chimed in, "with movie stars! Vagina! Vagina! Vagina!"

"That barefoot Ensler woman relating those real-life interviews woke me up!" Bridget said. "Until that moment all my meditation was so focused on the black hole of my own navel that all my light and all the light around me was totally self-absorbed. I didn't realize that violence against all girls and all women is epidemic, especially here in America."

Bridget set a laptop computer on the kitchen table and plugged a connector into a phone jack. "I've learned a lot about the Internet. It is a priceless tool for research and information gathering."

The sisters sat around the table as Bridget unfolded her new cause. For each question the twins asked, Bridget had a well-thought-out, logical answer.

The Clemens girls were swapping ideas at a pace they hadn't in years. They were relating like the triplets they had fancied themselves to be when they were kids. And they all became part of The Plan.

A few days later the sisters shared a final solemn hug. Bridget dropped the rental car and trailer at a local affiliate. A case holding her bagpipes and one small travel bag fit on the seat beside her in the taxi that took her to the airport.

Chapter 23

Rave and a Haircut Clip! Clip!

Gillian Waters noted the date on the calendar/clock on her bathroom counter: June 27, 1998. She entered the date in her little ever-present idea notebook. She underlined the 27. In exactly two months, she would turn fifty. "Not bad," she nodded to her steam-diffused image in the mirror. "For an old broad," she added. She liked the dash of gray that streaked her temples and added a distinguished touch to her otherwise mousy-brown hair.

The moderate success of Gillian's writing career kept her living in understated elegance on the sunset side of Sunrise Mountain. Broad expanses of tinted glass opened the whole west side of the adobe pueblo structure to overlook a pool and the sprawling city of Las Vegas. At night the pool appeared to spill over into the star-filled valley of neon. It would be easy to assume her life was perfect.

She smoothed some moisturizer over her face, rubbed the excess into her elbows and thanked her mother for good skin and her daddy for her height.

Gillian's reality was that six years ago Alzheimer's had stolen her best friend and lover of over a decade and transformed Rose into a stranger who wanted only to escape from wherever she imagined she was. Rose's mind had regressed at a grueling, inevitable pace toward darkness till it was absolute. In the nine months since Rose's death, Gillian's anxiety about leaving her private hermitage on the hill had progressed from discomfort to the point of self-incarceration. She didn't even go into that magnificent pool anymore.

Gillian accepted interviews only on her home turf and every material thing she needed was delivered. Reggie, her barber, even made monthly house calls.

Gillian enjoyed Reggie's trips up the hill and the haircutter didn't seem to mind making the drive. She'd delayed her daily four-hour morning writing session for today's visit. She rarely deviated from her writing regimen but her barber's newsy chatter always cheered Gillian and when it came to hair, her precision rivaled that of a plastic surgeon and her touch was firm and assured. It was good being touched. She missed that most of all.

She toweled her hair and combed it straight back. She padded naked to the kitchen and twisted the knob on the fancy-dancy coffeemaker she had set up last night. The automatic grinder whirred and clattered into raucous action. She set two tall mugs, one regular cup and a long iced teaspoon, beside the maker and wriggled the huge Costco-sized vanilla creamer from the fridge.

In her bedroom she slipped into some shorts and a tank top. She dragged a short, backless stool from the laundry room, put it at the kitchen counter and spread a small red dishtowel where Reggie could lay out her tools.

She poured herself the first of the brew that was dripping into the glass pot. She put her nose halfway into the cup like a wine taster and breathed in the steamy aroma. Then, being a hedonist more than a purist, added a slurp of the sweet vanilla creamer. That first cup of coffee was always the best of the day.

• • •

Ten minutes later Gillian was sitting on the stool in her kitchen tugging at the neckband of a blue chair cloth clipped a tad too snugly around her neck. Reggie poured herself a cup of coffee.

She was a smallish woman—on the cute side of pretty. Her hair, a tousled strawberry-blonde, flipped this way and that, just short of her shoulders. She leaned back against the counter and checked Gillian out over the lip of her coffee cup. She reached out and poked her in the upper arm. "Nice." She squeezed her arm. "Firm. And look. Definition!"

Gillian beamed.

"Let's give you a haircut to fit the new you."

"Whoa, Ms. Barber Person! No changes. I love my hair."

"Me, too! That reminds me." She rummaged in her oversized bag and pulled out a magazine rolled open to a picture of Gillian in this very room. She showed her the cover. It was the current copy of *The Mystery Reader's Monthly*. She shoved it into Gillian's hands then pushed her poor client's chin firmly into her chest.

"Check it out," Reggie urged, "page sixty-six." She reached over Gillian's hunched shoulders and pointed with a gray styling comb to a paragraph. "Read it out loud."

"'Waters has a seventh book in the Deadly Sin series due out this year. We visited with her recently at her Nevada home. She is attractive in a sort of "k.d. lang-esque" style. Her salted-brown hair falls over perpetually curious green eyes etched at the corners by time and millions of smiles. Her figure is, as the old song says, less than Greek, but strong and straight . . . if a little thick through the middle.'"

"Damn," Gillian uttered.

"'Waters moves deliberately, yet restlessly as we talk. She rakes long slender fingers through her softly wedged hair. It responds as only good hair and a precision cut allow,'" she concluded.

Reggie did a little Snoopy dance. "Usually they only mention a cut if it's bad."

Gillian asked, "Did you catch that k.d. lang reference?"

"Oh well, Gillian," Reggie said, "I guess it just might pay to advertise. You are, after all, single again after eighteen-plus years."

"Nah, Reg, I'm not ready for that," Gillian protested, cramming a whole boatload of meaning into that simple answer.

They were quiet for a few minutes. Snip, snip, snip.

"Gillian? May I be candid?"

"Okay," Gillian answered with caution.

Reggie pushed Gillian's chin firmly into her chest again and cut her hair against her nape, one tiny parting at a time. "I suffer from clinical depression," she confided.

"Oh?" Gillian said, a little surprised. "I didn't know that."

"I have an incredible therapist. Her name is Darcus Fox."

Reggie scribbled Dark and a phone number in Gillian's ever-present notebook. "She specializes in treating phobias. I just wanted to remind you, people care and . . . I'm sorry if I've overstepped any boundaries . . ." Reggie's voice trailed off.

Another silence.

"I realize you don't know me that well," Reggie began again.

"I know you well enough to like you," Gillian interjected.

"This may not be a good time, but, well, I sort of wanted to ask you a favor." She waited for Gillian to respond.

Gillian grunted.

"I'm interested in meeting with some women—er—a woman in St. Louis that I met on the Internet. It won't be for awhile, but I would like to have someone know where I am, when I do go and that I'm safe."

"Sure, being careful about this sounds like a smart idea. How can I help?" Gillian asked, relieved by the conversation's shift of focus.

"I'll write everything down for you . . . I really appreciate it." Reggie smiled to cover the guilt she felt for being able to tell the half-truth with such total conviction.

Unknowingly, Gillian had been drawn into the plan. It was only the first step. But in was in.

Chapter 24
Gillian Reaches Out
July 14, 1998

Some retro-Joni Mitchell drifted through the house. Gillian slipped Ferron's *Shadows On A Dime* CD into rotation in the six-disc changer. She gazed out the window at the shimmering, late afternoon heat waving over the city. She pushed the switch to lower the shutters. She was surprised to find she was a little nervous.

It had taken almost two weeks of increasing moments of clarity to prompt Gillian to search through her little notebook for Reggie's therapist's number. She phoned and asked if she would make house calls for twice her usual fee. The counselor countered by suggesting a phone session. Now, here she was, awaiting a call from a stranger, whom she was about to allow into the less-than-sordid, nevertheless guarded, details of her private life. She took a hefty, definitely unladylike, draught of her earlier-than-usual glass of wine.

Gads, I hope she doesn't sound beautiful. I'll have to act all Xena-like and defeat my own purpose with machisma bullshit, Gillian mused, only half-laughing at herself.

She sloshed her wine when the phone rang. "Oh, shit, so much for the Xena bit," she groaned and finished off the wine. She walked toward the phone, shaking drops of white wine from her fingertips. When she passed the patio door, the film clip in her head began.

Even walking anywhere near an exit door lately triggered the anxiety and then the film clip. Panic gripped her chest. She didn't know how to stop the sequence once it started. In her mind she opened the door, and as always the faceless person on the other side lifted the two gaping barrels of a sawed-off shotgun toward her chest and pulled the trigger. The roar of the gun slowed the process and the loads of shot spiraled from the twin barrels. She looked down and watched, with genuine surprise, the identical, synchronized masses of metal fragments drilling into her chest, tearing two huge, precise, gaping holes through her body. No matter how many times the clip played, the holes always surprised her.

The phone rang a third time jerking her back to reality.

"Hello," she managed.

Darcus Fox spoke with a faint Bavarian accent that reminded Gillian of her own paternal grandmother. "Ms. Waters?"

"Gillian."

"Gillian. What brings you to seek counseling?"

"I just can't seem to move on," Gillian sighed. "My partner Rose and I were together for eighteen years. We disagreed with fervor at times. What couple doesn't? There were times in the early years when she drove me nuts. Well, when we began to see there was going to be an us," she explained, "she persisted in trying to refine me—knock off my craggy edges. You know, as though I were a fossil to be broken free of my stony matrix." She shrugged self-consciously, aware that she was babbling nervously. "I don't know when she pulled it off, but one day most of my rough mold was chipped away." She chuckled. "Anyway, now, I can't think of a single thing I wouldn't trade to hear ol' Rose crack wise from the other room."

She adjusted the phone to her ear. "I guess you know that each Sinistral and Dexter novel follows the twins through a mystery theme based on one of the seven deadly sins. I've covered pride, lust, greed, anger, covetousness and gluttony. And, as I said earlier, the seventh and final book on sloth, *Inertia* goes to the publisher by the end of this year, Counselor."

"Dark, call me Dark."

She felt calmer now and it occurred to Gillian that she would have no trouble telling Dark about the faceless creep with the shotgun at the door—but the thought of admitting that Sinistral spoke regularly to her made her feel certifiable.

"Rose was soon beyond suffering—at least outwardly. I felt not only helpless and guilty, but also awed by her capacity to endure. I have no desire to meet anyone special or to put my emotions out there again." She sighed. "I've been celibate for so long it's almost a choice." She paused and smiled. "Almost."

"I hear a wistful smile in your voice."

"Yeah."

Ferron's husky voice soothed through a speaker disguised as a book on a nearby shelf:

I hear the city's in a panic
With its first foot of snow

After a heartbeat or two, Gillian went on. "At first she blamed distraction for her absentmindedness. My tool of choice has always been denial," she admitted. "But, the last time we made love—at her insistence—I saw something in her eyes—a lack of something, actually." She grew quiet. "Rose imitated recognition. That moment my role of lover segued into caregiver."

"How did you handle that?" Dark asked, sympathy in her tone.

"I admitted fatigue and hired a nurse. I didn't vent my sexual energy elsewhere," she said. "I ate more, drank a lot more, exercised a whole lot more and wrote compulsively into the single-digit hours of the morning. Rose just faded away. I swam daily in the pool—until the anxiety wouldn't let me out the patio door."

"Well," Dark said with a gentle smile in her voice. "Your condition doesn't seem deeply seated. It's likely been brought on by recent events. Let's get you over the threshold and out into the world again. It's just like getting over a bad habit. It's simple, but not easy. But, Gillian, a neutral setting is crucial to this process. Therapy in your home would just enable and reinforce the agoraphobic behavior."

But if it's snowin' in Brooklyn
You say it's snowin' in Brooklyn

"You seem to be dwelling on step one of a six-step process. It's called precontemplation. You're not sure the effort is worth it. I'll do some testing, if you like, but I'm sure you have what's called an Anticipatory Anxiety Disorder. We could do phone sessions for a while but I think you're ready to have a friend drive you to my office. The professional setting provides a cocoon of safety which is the key to communication and trust between us."

The line was silent for a few moments.

"Okay, Dark." Gillian expelled her pent breath. "Your office. Friday at four."

Ferron's gritty voice quite simply concluded:

Well if it's snowin' in Brooklyn
I'd say snoooow's what you've got.

Chapter 25

Out the Door and Down the Hill

Gillian felt queasy waves of vertigo sweep over her when she stepped from the car and Reggie sped off to find a parking spot. She gaped as the heavily tinted entrance door to Darcus Fox's office receded rapidly and the short concrete sidewalk lengthened into a long tunnel of brilliant yellow and orange flames licking into the passageway. She was contemplating the odds for her running the gauntlet unincinerated when Reggie stepped beside her and hooked her elbow. Gillian ducked her head and they made it in, unscathed.

The windowless waiting area they walked into presented only indistinct forms and shadows after the blinding Las Vegas summer sun and, in Gillian's case, the flaming tunnel to hell. Her eyes adjusted and she saw a dozen comfortable chairs, several burgeoning magazine racks and a woman with tightly permed gray hair sitting, head bowed, behind a curved counter at the far end.

Gillian sat in a straight-backed chair, both feet on the floor and flipped through a *National Geographic*. The clammy sweat on her face and neck felt icy in the air-conditioned waiting room. Reggie sat, legs crossed, next to her, filing a broken fingernail and bobbing her foot in time to the office music.

Dark opened a door. She nodded to Reggie and extended her hand to Gillian. The therapist revealed her Bavarian genes by her choice of footwear and the manner in which she stood in those staunch, practical shoes to take up a little more than her share of horizontal space in the doorway.

Gillian met her intense violet eyes and thought, Oh, my, I don't think those are contacts.

"I am going to guess you are more Dexter than Sinistral," Dark said.

"You're probably right," Gillian acquiesced with a grin. "Sinistral actually intimidates me."

Dark's laugh was rich and unrestrained as she led Gillian down a narrow hallway. There was a whispered purr coming from small devices plugged in beside each office door.

Dark, noting Gillian's curiosity said, "They're white noise machines. They assure that any conversation in the offices cannot be heard in the corridors."

The therapist indicated a choice of seats in a near corner of her rectangular office and walked to her desk at the far end, casually drawing the vertical blinds across the slider in passing.

"You've made a big first step today, Gillian," Dark said. She picked up a translucent, purple clipboard with a silver pen tethered to it by a silver chain. "Was it difficult?"

Gillian told her of the dread, the panic, the faceless person, the shotgun, the twin loads of shot drilling in slow motion into her body, and her surprise.

Dark listened, nodded, making an occasional notation on the clipped form.

"How old are you?"

"I'll be fifty in a month."

"You've got that big one coming up. How do you feel about it?"

"Fifty doesn't seem as old as it used to."

"When did you become a writer?"

"Right out of college I went to work for a newspaper in Montana, one in Phoenix and then *The Journal* here in Las Vegas."

"When did you first realize you were lesbian?"

"Well, before I knew about anatomy or could read, I knew I wasn't born in the right body. My first attractions to girls—I was in the single digits. I didn't have a sexual partner until I was in college."

"Any long-term relationships before Rose?"

"One year with a man. I had to try," she said and shrugged. "And four tumultuous years with a wonderful, oversexed, religious, alcoholic blond barber—bipolar it turns out."

Dark suppressed a smile. "How did that one end?"

"Badly. We went to couples counseling. There was transference. She thought she was in love with the young, male counselor. He was inexperienced, freaked and didn't know how to handle the situation."

"That happens, it's terrible."

"I just sort of walked away and lifeboated from one woman to the next until I met Rose. She was in real estate. She found us the place on Sunrise Mountain. She encouraged me to quit *The Journal* and write books."

"Lifeboated?"

"I never ended one relationship until I had one foot firmly planted in the next. That way I was never alone."

"You told me you were with Rose for eighteen years."

"The last six were basically with her abandoned body. She died long before she laid down for the last time."

"So, essentially you've had almost seven years of mourning. When do you see yourself getting back into life?"

"Oh, Dark. The thought of loving again and hurting like that when it ends—I can't."

"What's your relationship with alcohol?"

That's an interesting way to ask. Out loud Gillian said, "We're well acquainted."

"I imagine you're self medicating," Dark said. "I'm prescribing an antianxiety pill. Take it as directed. You won't need as much booze."

Half an hour later, Gillian stepped outside herself and saw that she was a little less panicked as she maneuvered the escorted dash to the open door of Reggie's car.

Chapter 26

Resurrection of the Panther

Late Tuesday Oct. 5, 1998

Reggie's frenched nail tips clicked a staccato hurry-up song on the keys, not depressing them, just trying to speed up the process from one task to another. "C'mon, C'mon," she admonished in a soft growl. She sat in the dark room. Flight or fight chemicals charged through her system, causing her foot to tap and her teeth to grind. She leaned intently into her work. Drenched curls fringed her face and raindrops still dotted the shoulders of her crumpled raincoat. Her feet were freezing. Her face looked grim in the anemic glow of the monitor until the instant message popped up in the corner.

She had never met the woman halfway around the world who created that message with her voice—at least the adult woman. She barely remembered her as a child. But she admired her as much as anyone she had ever met face to face. They shared the bond of survivorship and were getting to know each other from the inside out.

VenusD: So, it begins?

Lazydaze795: yeah, i'll going to meet them now. i'll take my cell but I may be out of range for a while. v? I'm beginning to remember knowing you and Bridget in The Enclave. My memory is spotty but coming back to me one incident at a time. I was so obsessed with Jazz and me. as i recall, you were older but nice to us. i'm so glad bridget brought us together.

VenusD: Me 2. And because of you we were all rescued.

Lazydaze795: it took what it took to get my butt in gear back then—and bridget's gumption now.

VenusD: Daze, I knew he only had to do nine years. I thought I'd made my peace with that. But now, I can't believe how enraged I am that he will be out there again. I feel so responsible! We can't let him hurt another kid! We can't!

Reggie read the words and could almost hear her snuffle. *She's crying, I want to console her.*

VenusD: Well, we've laid all her groundwork and are steps closer to bringing her plan to life.

Lazydaze795: yes. i'm "snoopying" my computers, as we speak. All your computers will be squeaky clean and free of incriminating data as soon as you receive the coordination message. Belle will send us all new contact info soon.

Reggie slipped the SnoopyDisc into the CD slot. It launched automatically.

"Completely Erase Internet Files!" the screen enticed. "Did you know that your computer tracks everything you do online? These files can be recovered to haunt you forever! Snoopy Disk erases them from your hard disk forever. Forever!" the screen promised redundantly.

The instant message scrolled:

VenusD: You can't know how grateful I am, Daze . . . beyond grateful . . .

Lazydaze795: yeah, i do, v. u did so much of the groundwork in your lab. we all do our part for the good of the whole and hoping for the good of all women. how's the weather in amsterdam?

VenusD: It's October. How else? Cold and dark. I'm using my Seasonal Affective Disorder lights every day.

Lazydaze795: how are they working?

VenusD: Pretty good, I guess. I don't dream of fumbling with loading a gun every night any more. How are you holding up?

Lazydaze795: a little scared. a little excited . . . mostly numb. i'm almost ready to go. the cab's waiting.

VenusD: Daze? Can we meet when this is . . . .

There was a long series of dots before the next letters appeared.

VenusD: . . . over and done? I can only say thank you. Take care, my dear, sweet friend.

Lazydaze795: i know. you're so much more than just a-friend. and yes, we will meet.

Reggie continued with a lot more swagger than she felt:

don't worry about me, kiddo. faking the truth is my forte. hey! i was born into a socialist commune and forged in a theocratic, totalitarian hellhole—where's my 12-step meeting? haha. i knew i would fit into clem's scheme no matter where she put me. i'm no crazier—or saner for that matter—than any of us. i'll be there and hope to let ol' billy boogieman know the gift was from u. goodbye for now.

Reggie signed off the IM with xxxxs & ooooos and set about finishing the job that brought her here, to her house, between redeye flights. Clickety-clickety-click. Reggie typed in the proper sequences and the disk downloaded.

• • •

Halfway around the world, VenusD signed off the IM with a lump in her throat.

Billy boogieman! Indeed!

Reggie jockeyed around the program with the mouse and typed prompted responses in muted bursts. The program swept all e-mail messages from the screen and, she assumed, from the very soul of the computer. She erased her own AOL profile for Lazydaze795 and blocked Willendorph from every means of further contact. It was as if neither of them ever existed here. In essence, she was saying electronically, "Okay, Gillian, you're up . . . set this plan in action. Send the message and get that note to Jazz."

Reggie peered at her watch. Her flight from San Diego had landed fifty-six minutes ago. The cab ride here took twenty-two minutes and in order to board another eastbound flight she needed to be back at McCarran International in forty-two.

She ejected the Snoopy Disc and fumbled between the desk and the file cabinet for her laptop. Her hand slapped around the empty area.

"Oh, no! No, no, no!" she whinged just over her breath. "Damn, I left it at the salon," she remembered. She considered the time. It was too late. "Okay, okay, not to panic," she whispered. "Jazz's cell is charging in the kitchen. I'll just leave a voicemail message for him to stash my laptop in his car trunk."

She initiated the computer's shutdown procedure and expelled her pent breath.

"Farewell, Mistress, it was a pleasure serving you," a seductive cyber-voice cooed.

Just before the monitor went to black, her eye caught the re-flected glint off the silver-plated gun half hidden by papers in the open drawer.

In the utter darkness, she considered what, if any, added courage the heft of the automatic would give her. She brushed the papers aside and touched the cool steel with her fingertips. She slipped her hand around the textured grip and lifted the weapon from its paper nest.

In the darkness the metallic essence of the loaded gun chafed her nostrils and taste buds. She laid the short, cold metal barrel against her cheek and thought a moment of the possibilities.

"Rats!" she uttered.

She forced herself to exhale, dispelling an overload of anxiety, then slipped the weapon back onto the papers. She shut the drawer on that idea. She didn't have time for this. Besides, she knew there was no way to get that piece aboard the plane.

She crossed the dark room, eased the door shut, locked it and returned the key to its hiding place atop the molding above the door.

She brushed her fingers across Jazz's closed door in passing. "I love you, little brother," she whispered.

Her body stiffened. She'd forgotten something—but what? She glanced at her watch as she strode back to her room. She retrieved the key and stood in the open doorway. She ran the beam of a tiny, key ring flashlight around the pristine room. Everything seemed in place.

She chided herself for her silly jitters as she left the house.

The whole Las Vegas Valley was awash in an eerie purple glow. She tightened her collar against the drizzle. Before she slipped into the cab idling steamily at the curb, she lifted a remote control toward the double front doors and pressed a button. A muffled electronic voice ordered, "Armed away. Exit now."

In the house Jazz's eyes sprang open. "Whazzat?" he mumbled into his pillow. He was dimly aware of a voice—then a car driving away. He slid back into a deep sleep and let the incident slip from his memory.

CHAPTER 27

'Cross Town, 'Round Midnight
Tuesday, October 5, 1998

Across town Gillian Waters awoke with a start. She sat up and swung her legs over the side of the bed. She stared out of her bedroom window at the Las Vegas sky and searched for the dream that awoke her. Was it about Reggie, she wondered.

It intrigued Gillian how rainy weather caused the city's lights to infuse the low hanging clouds and midnight air with a mauve twilight almost bright enough to read by.

As she sat on the bed, her chin gradually drooped to her chest. Her dreamer's eye focused on her grandmother's hands plunging with gusto into flour-dusted dough. Her own little-girl eyes could barely peek above the oilcloth-covered pinewood, butcher-block table in the middle of the room. The fragrance of leavening yeast and perking coffee perfumed the heavy air in the sweltering kitchen.

Little Gilly worked the red-and-white checkered oilcloth between the thumb and forefinger of her left hand. Her right index finger hooked over her nose as she held her thumb between her pursed lips. She watched the angular old woman knead the daily dough into submission. Strands of steel-gray hair escaped her tightly twisted bun and clung to the dampness of her face. She pushed the offending hairs away from her eyes with the back of a flour-dredged hand. The old woman straightened and arched her back. Her serious Slavic face softened and her broad smile gleamed when she looked down. Gillian felt that smile come into her own eyes and nestle with a warm glow in the center of her chest.

Gillian's whole body braced as though against a sudden fall. It jerked her awake. She must have dozed again—sitting up. The sweet dream about her grandmother tugged at her memory—but faded by the moment. She was left with an impression of a kitchen . . . a smile and strong, old, mottled hands.

At that very moment her own aging hands yearned for ritual—something rhythmic, repetitive and automatic. Her lips could all but feel the dry, cork-tipped filter and savor the acrid taste of the phantom Viceroy clenched between them. A cupped flame seemed the only requirement to bring the illusion to life.

She uttered the mantra: "I no longer smoke."

There had also been the Rose Dream—she remembered because she dreamed it so frequently. Just moments ago and every night for a week or so she looked into Rose's rejuvenated face, flushed and cresting—a dream-softened focus blurring her features—mouth slightly slack, eyes stoned with passion, lids half-cast.

Gillian felt slightly creepy to be thinking of sex on the heels of such benign thoughts of her grandmother. Damn, she thought, why is the dream-Rose always like this—warm and open—smelling of seawater and honey? She sighed. Well, it's better than . . . she pushed away the inconceivable thought of Rose's present reality.

Echoes of unreleased tension left her feeling edgy and anxious.

She reached to pull her vibrator from the drawer in the bedside table, but decided that the mechanical relief it could afford would feel too hollow, too empty just now.

"Shit!" she griped, and shoved the drawer shut.

Chapter 28
The Ultimate Escape

A restless hour later, the pale yellow rose and black triangle on Gillian's lower leg flashed in and out of the shadows. She'd gotten the tattoo the month after Rose's death. She wanted the numbness to go away. She wanted to feel something—anything—even if it was pain.

Now, moment-by-moment her own labored breathing became the focus of her perfect awareness and all thoughts sloughed away like yesterday's beach debris. A sheen of sweat covered her entire body and the ice block under her heart began to thaw. Sexual frustration and the stark, visceral knowledge of her complete and utter powerlessness in most of life's situations evaporated for the time being. There was only her body now. She could feel the blood in her arms and thighs respond to the pumping rhythm as her rocking movement spurred the flow. Gradually the grinding sensation of the slightly rough terry cloth under her glutes ceased. At every other point of contact between her body and the world, nerves soothed. The device and she became one. The bygone world receded. The past became less momentous. She felt it diminish with each stroke. She was reaching her limit of endurance. She strove for more. She leaned into the feeling with her whole being. She pressed her body into the gathering sensation—then there it was again—vague at first—then beyond all restraint it built into an overwhelming euphoria that exploded and flowed over her. Finally, the ultimate escape was hers.

Exercise. When she worked astride the Healthrider for thirty minutes, pulling on the handles that raised her posterior like a posting jockey leaning into the finish line, the pursuing endorphins consistently overtook her, flooding her sweating body with well-being.

After Dark had helped her deal with the anxiety of leaving her safe harbor, she'd tucked her ever-present mini-notebook with its tethered pen into her pocket and got out and walked in the early morning hours. Then she ran. When the weather was hellishly hot, as it often was in Las Vegas, she worked out at home and in the pool.

This morning her big old black dog Trixter watched with sleepy, up-rolled eyes from her sheepskin pallet as Gillian slowed down and her ragged breathing gradually steadied. Trixter let a huge fang-framed yawn escape around her curled tongue.

The sales slip had declared her lineage as pointer and Labrador mix. Like those breeds, Trixter's attitude was regal, but the white barrel chest on the otherwise slim body of the grown dog suggested some foremother once entertained a visiting pit bull. She was smart though and there was more sleeping to be done. Her soft, brown eyes drifted shut, half-opened for one last peek, then closed for an important nap.

The city lights dimmed as the dawn turned the October sky merely a paler shade of gray. The persistent clouds were an anomaly here in the desert where the sun ordinarily shone every day.

Gillian shuffled across the cold ceramic tile floor of the kitchen and measured out some coffee beans. After she fiddled with filters and water and set the coffee maker grinding she walked naked into her office and booted up the computer.

"Wonder what Reggie is up to?" she mused while allowing the old computer time to get itself together. She didn't mind the pokiness— her primary use for the contraption was writing and storage and, thank the Writer's Goddess, spell-check. She never did understand why she, of the expansive vocabulary, had such a difficult time with spelling.

She unlocked the French doors and stepped over the threshold to the patio. Having recently, thanks to working with Dark, regained the ability, she relished the ease with which she performed this simple act. The cold October air assaulted her naked skin as she crossed herself in mock blessing. At the raised Jacuzzi she scooped handfuls of frigid water and lowered her naked breasts into their icy cups. Her nipples contracted in protest. After doing this several times, adjusting to the frigid temperature, she reenacted her daily liturgy. Her health-nut father had read in some early-day fitness magazine that Katharine Hepburn took daily ice-cold swims. On that evidence alone it became a Waters' family ritual. With four quick strides Gillian reached the deep end of the pristine pool, turned, and, without hesitation, plunged in.

Despite their pre-chilling, she felt the frigid water reduce her breasts a full cup size. It was as though that reaction released enough energy to propel her to the far end of the pool and back. The water approximated the temperature and consistency of a blended margarita, which made the next four and a half laps more arduous.

After a quick, hot shower, she wrapped herself in an oversized chenille robe, and sat at the computer. She sipped her creamed coffee and munched on a stiff piece of cold pizza.

She decided to do some polish work on the fifth chapter of *Inertia* before checking her e-mail. With a second cup of coffee she went to chapter four, cleaned up some dialogue and grappled with a stubborn metaphor. When she got tired, lazy or rushed she had a tendency to *Tell* the story instead of *Showing* it. Readers lost interest if they were always being told, not shown. She scanned the whole manuscript for *Telling*.

Before taking a break to throw sticks to the dog at eight thirty, she logged onto AOL. Her agent wanted an update on her schedule; her pal 'Shell just wanted to touch base; a fellow Ellenhead, her online lesbian group, had sent a joke list; and a cyber-firm pitched ninety-nine secret methods to attract gorgeous women for only $49.99!

She answered her e-mail twice a day. It would pile up if she didn't. She paused a moment to allow herself a wicked grin before deleting the $49.99 offer.

Yesterday Gillian had composed an e-mail to Reggie's cyber-name Lazydaze795 followed by a question mark in the subject box and a short note: "Reggie, Grrrrl, I need a haircut!" It really didn't matter what she typed. The e-mail would either remain unread if all was well—or deleted if there were trouble. She'd given it hardly a thought, before she sent it . . . or after.

Monitoring Reggie's presence on the Internet smacked slightly of soap-opera intrigue or high-dyke drama as lesbian comic and entrepreneur Robin Tyler once called it. Gillian felt it was a little odd, but playing chaperone seemed harmless enough. When she last checked her sent mail list it showed, as usual, that every one of the daily e-mail messages she sent to Lazydaze795 had been left unread. That was yesterday—Monday. This was Tuesday.

Gillian worked until after nine thirty, then microwaved a bowl of turkey soup. She sat in front of the monitor as she sipped the broth. Fragrant steam fogged her glasses and cleared her sinuses. Trixter diligently leaned into Gillian's leg reminding her she was there and would like a taste. After several more sips, Gillian set the bowl on the floor and checked her e-mail. This time she looked at the Mail I've Sent list first.

The list was changed. The bracketed word deleted followed each e-mail addressed to Lazydaze795. "Oh, shit!" Gillian uttered as she fumbled with the mouse and brought up the member directory. Lazydaze795 was no longer there.

She began her calm-the-panic breathing technique, in for six counts, out for six counts—the pervading anxiety slowed a bit. Her hands shook but she fulfilled Reggie's first request in the event she deleted the e-mails. She sent a message to: Belladonis@someobscure-server.com. It said, as per Reggie's instructions:

The lazy one has flown the coop.

"Shee-boy-gun-wis-con-sun!" Gillian muttered through gritted teeth. The link was broken. Reggie was out there, somewhere— maybe in danger.

When I agreed to this monitoring I was housebound. Now, thanks to Reggie, I sought help. She's more than my barber. How can I not try to help her?

But, how? There must be more I can do. Geez, what would Sinistral do?

She fulfilled Reggie's second request by calling Jazz at The U.S. Male Barber Salon for an appointment. She mentioned that Reggie was her regular barber.

"Stylist," Sinistral prompted her to add out of deference to his creative ego.

She would hand the sealed envelope to Jazz in person. Reggie had emphasized that she must wait six hours after sending the e-mail message to Belladonis.

"Be gentle with him," she had stressed, "and prepare him a bit before giving him the letter."

Jazz checked his crowded schedule and said he would see her at four thirty as his last client of the day.

Chapter 29

Jazz

Gillian arrived twenty-five minutes early for her appointment with Jazz. She was writing some random thoughts in her little book when the receptionist gave her a blinding white smile and a plastic glass of chilled white wine. She took a sip. *Mmmm, nice touch,* she thought.

Her first clue might have been the way the man held his shoulders as he made his way across the salon—he kept them perfectly level, like a dancer's. Or perhaps it was the slightly bitchy edge to his voice as he walked through his domain greeting patrons that triggered a ding, ding on Gillian's gaydar. Or, she supposed, the blue eye shadow and rainbow-sequined half-shirt might have been the tip-off.

Reggie always spoke fondly of Jazz, so Gillian assumed he was a good guy. She was feeling guilty for not taking Reggie's request more seriously and figured that if she were going to launch a search for her missing barber she had to start somewhere and probably the sooner, the better. Perhaps Jazz would remember an event or a name that would be helpful.

"*Since they worked together, there's a good chance they formed a sort of gay alliance*," Sinistral suggested, assuming, as Gillian did, that Reggie was on the team, as it were.

Gillian was not sure when Sinistral had begun speaking to her. The fictional detective had probably uttered her first suggestions halfway through the third Deadly Sin novel *Appetite for Pretense* when she devised her own escape from an impossible predicament. She had suggested that Gillian change her wristwatch to a large face type so she could smash the lens and use a shard to cut her bonds.

At first Gillian was afraid she had stepped off the deep end. She was certain it was just a matter of time before she was declared certifiable. *Wouldn't communication with my own figment be a sure sign of schizophrenia or some other mental malady?*

But, in time she got used to Sinistral's intermittent presence and gradually came to regard the teenage sleuth as a muse—a snotty, know-it-all muse.

Jazz's voice broke into her reverie. "Ah, Ms. Gillian."

Jazz was compact, buff yet supple, fair and almost hairless. "Reggie does such a fine job with your hair!"

He sat her in a chair and asked, "What can I do for you today?"

Then he spun her around leaving no pause for an answer, stopped the chair facing the mirror, crouched down, his eyes looking directly into the mirrored reflection of hers and said, "Perhaps I could just shorten this up the tiniest bit." His voice was a purr . . . or a soft growl.

His chin brushed her shoulder and she noticed his subtle cologne. If an aroma were tangible, this one would feel like an expensive cashmere sweater.

"I don't want to change what Reggie's done with your hair," he said. "It's perfection!"

Jazz's face was soft and free of angles—almost childlike. His wavy blond hair was cropped short on the top. The rest was clipped close in the current neo-Marine recruit style that male offspring of longhaired '60s parents seemed to prefer. Their hippie-era folks had fought the powers-that-were to grow their locks as long as their genetics would allow. Long, flowing, Rasta twisting, or huge, puffball Afros—hair had been the badge, the freak-flag, their symbol of revolt. Little wonder the next generation rebelled in the opposite direction.

Gillian studied Jazz's face as he assessed her hair. A parade of tiny studs marched in rainbow-colored order along the outer rim of his right ear. When he raised his arms to lift her hair straight up, he bared a sculptured midriff. A small, purple stone glittered from a gold ring that pierced the knot of his navel.

"Have you heard from Reggie?" Gillian asked, as he brushed her hair in deep, smooth strokes and hefted its weight in his fine-boned fingers. "I'm not sure when she's supposed to get back and I needed to be well-coifed for . . . uh . . . an appointment. Friday," she lied. "Or else I would have waited. I hope she won't feel . . . I've been unfaithful," she trailed off.

"Oh, that was convincing," Sinistral jeered into Gillian's inner ear.

"She's been away for a few days. I got a message on my cell phone this morning," he said as he reclined the chair and began to shampoo her hair. He stroked his fingers through her hair and worked the shampoo into a fragrant lather and rinsed it.

After restoring Gillian to her upright position, he worked the conditioner to the ends of her hair and massaged her scalp.

His hands are stronger than they look.

"Probably a new amour . . ." His hands flitted slightly. His eyes did not.

"What's this?" Sinistral noticed his humorless eyes as he lowered Gillian to the sink for a final rinse.

Gillian did not want to seem too eager—just a little nosy. Jazz snapped the chair upright and briskly toweled her hair.

"Wonder if that's so?" Gillian said in a muffled tremor.

"Oh, you know our Reggie—wild, older men . . . or women— expensive scotch and party, party, party!" he said.

"No," Gillian admitted, "I don't know her that way. She was kind to me when my Rose died. We talked about emotions and loss."

"Ah, I remember," he recollected in a more serene manner, "she talked about you." His voice had dropped a few decibels. "You're the writer."

She nodded.

"She likes you—says you're torqued," he added. He concentrated on parting the under edge of her hair horizontally. He held the rest up and out of the way with large clips.

"If torqued is positive, I'm flattered," she said.

"That's where I've seen you. She has the magazine article about you pinned up in her booth." He pointed at the framed page in the booth across the aisle.

"I don't suppose you know where she is?" Gillian asked.

He pushed her head forward until her chin was pressed firmly into her chest. This move effectively stopped all verbal communication on her part. If she attempted to move even slightly he muttered, "Nah!"

He combed the hair smoothly against the nape of her neck and meticulously cut a tiny amount equal to the length of an eyelash. He lifted each section of hair ever so slightly, incorporated it with the next parting, which he then cut with one precise snip. Gillian could feel him perform the same step over and over. He kept tension on each section. Gillian knew she was in good hands and would not have to pay for the meager information she was receiving with a bad haircut.

"I forwarded her passport to her this morning," Jazz interjected into his gossipy monologue to which Gillian had only been half-listening.

She stiffened.

"Aargh! Don't move, sugar," he responded.

"Passport! She had a passport?" Sinistral anguished as Gillian stared at the vicinity of her own navel. *"She didn't say a word about going out of the country. This could get complicated."* Thoughts churned. Sinistral started to panic.

Gillian hissed through clenched teeth, "Shhhhhh!"

"I'm sorry, sugar, was I yammering?"

"Oh, no, not you. I mean," she stammered, "I just remembered something I forgot to do."

"Ah," he nodded.

Gillian tried to quell her reaction to the passport revelation. *How odd.* She took a moment for detached observation. *I didn't think I felt this involved. Oh, dear, it's Sinistral! She's taking over. I never should have made her a Sagittarius.*

When she mentioned the passport again she tried to sound casual.

"Hmm? Oh yeah," he said, "the passport. It arrived in the mail yesterday. She sent me a stamped, addressed envelope last week and asked me to forward the passport as soon as I got it. Oddly, there was a large No. 1 clipped to it."

From a leather holster mounted on his back bar, Jazz withdrew a hair dryer shaped like a silver pistol with a large barrel. Gillian stared in fascination as the gun shot air into her damp hair and built volume and shape into the precision cut. The noisy dryer gave her time to form her next question.

"So," Gillian went on when her hair was dry. "Is all her mail delivered here, to the shop?"

Jazz stopped and looked directly into her eyes reflected in the mirror. His brows flexed inquisitively. "I thought you knew," he said. His eyes narrowed.

She felt her own green eyes betray a little too much curiosity.

"Reggie is my best friend and my roommate," he said. Something in the reaction he saw in Gillian's eyes made Jazz want to elaborate.

"We were raised in the same foster home," he said. "We protected each other like—sisters." He stood there, behind Gillian, suddenly like a tall little boy wearing mommy's shoes. He was quiet. His face clouded. "I feel as though there is intrigue here—Reggie might be in danger," he confided in a whisper before he could stop himself. "I don't know what to do." His voice faded even more as tears gathered on his lower lids. He daubed them with care so as not to muss his eye makeup. Gillian greatly admired his technique—never having mastered it herself.

He held up a hand mirror.

"Nice cut," she said.

He brushed the hairs from her face and neck, shook the haircloth and led her to the cash register.

Intrigue here. Interesting. I chose the same word. Aloud she asked, "So, you forwarded her passport to St. Louis?"

"St. Louis?" Jazz regained his poise. "No, the prepaid envelope postmarked New York was addressed in big block letters to a Hector Jimenez at a post office box in Miami Beach."

"Miami Beach?"

"The last call I got from her came from San Diego. What is she doing in San Diego, New York or Miami Beach or . . . or friggin' St. Louis? And who the hell is this Hector Jimenez?" he pleaded.

Gillian checked the clock by the desk as she paid him. She never wore a watch. Something in her physical makeup caused watches to stop. Still, now that she was out in the world again, she would have to start arriving places on time. The evening had barely begun. They could beat the crowds.

"Grab your coat, Jazz," she said, "You need some food and we've got a lot more to talk about. Very nice cut," she repeated, when she caught another glimpse of herself in the mirror beside the exit door.

Chapter 30

Sifting the Digs for Clues

Until the last decade of the twentieth century, the western foothills area of the Las Vegas Valley was all sand, sagebrush and sidewinders. Now the oversized, tightly packed, earthen-tone stucco homes with the magnificent Mexican red tile roofs had become like the crackerboxes of the fifties, except no longer made of ticky-tacky, and gone, to varying degrees, upscale. They were as alike as magnificent emperor penguins and like those flightless birds defied identification except by their own—in which case sobriety would definitely be a factor.

The interior of Jazz and Reggie's home reflected a Southwest art-deco flavor, a lot of pale neon and pickled oak. Jazz took a key from the upper frame of Reggie's bedroom door. The room was spare and neat—showing not much in the way of popculture or, for that matter, any type of decor. An old Gateway 2000 Vivitron 15 stood on the computer desk. A tangle of wires disappeared neatly into a hole behind the monitor, lending the illusion of organization. The system was shut down and no clutter marred the pristine surface of the desk.

Gillian pulled out her little notebook and pen and began to list and diagram objects in the room. A dartboard mounted on a large cork square on one wall. A Mitsubishi television on the opposite wall with a VCR. A couple of old Hitchcock movie tapes on the bedside table. She picked up one.

"Gads, what ever happened to Farley Granger?" she mused as she made a note of the tapes' location. She entered each fact into the notepad.

"Who?" Jazz asked.

"Oh, just an old movie star from the fifties," Gillian answered. "Does Reggie have a laptop?"

He looked in the space between the computer desk and file cabinet then remembered, "Oh, it's in my trunk."

Gillian gave him a quizzical look.

"That's what her message on my cell phone this morning asked me to do."

"Oh."

"How odd," Jazz murmured a minute later.

"What?" Gillian asked.

"Oh, it's just our old Barber School textbook. It's on the floor next to the bed. Alopecia is bookmarked and highlighted."

Gillian shrugged. "Baldness?"

"Yeah," he responded. "Probably old notes, from school."

"Hmmmm . . ." chimed in Sinistral.

Jazz used a cable guide to decipher the VCR programming. It was set to record an "Ellen DeGeneres HBO Special" and two segments on public television, one about the new Televangelical movement in the South and the other a debate about the registration of convicted sex offenders.

Jazz looked slightly relieved. "It seems Reggie is planning to return—or else she left unexpectedly."

As the computer booted up Gillian slid the desk drawers open one at a time. In the second drawer, silhouetted against the papers and stationery items, a silver .32 automatic lay in stark relief.

Gillian picked it up gingerly, using a tissue. She sniffed the metal. No odor of gunpowder. She held the grip firmly as she released the clip onto the papers and pulled the sheath of the barrel back. An unspent bullet skittered to Jazz's feet. The distinct sound of the sheath being thrown and the shell's landing drew a sharp gasp from Jazz.

"Oops!" she said and shrugged her apology. She placed her thumb into the gap at the base of the gun barrel. She peered down the spiraled bore. Light reflecting into the barrel from her thumbnail revealed more than a little dust on the rifling. "This gun hasn't been fired or cleaned in a long time," she uttered and made a note.

The Windows95 desktop held only the usual icons and a search of the aol30A file showed several humorous sound waves, some game components and what appeared to be a dozen other innocent files. Gillian opened a new carton of floppies and downloaded some interesting looking files. She wondered if Lazydaze795's online account was invalid, or if Reggie had just blocked her. Unless she could figure out Reggie's password it would be impossible to explore her activities on the Internet. Gillian's own password fed in automatically on her home computer . . . it isn't as secure but a lot less hassle than typing it in each time. She crossed her fingers. She clicked the AOL icon twice. In a moment it came up Regster1. She pressed the little triangle next to the name—if there were additional users, a menu of alternative names would drop down. There were none. She tried to sign on with Regster1. No such luck. A message box asked for a password.

She tried Reggie's zodiac sign, Libra . . . no. Jazz recited Reggie's social security and barber license numbers. Gillian looked at him quizzically. He grinned. "I have a thing about numbers." She tried several combinations of those numbers. No. He suggested several significant dates. Nothing.

"*Try LazyDaze,*" Sinistral prompted.

"Hello, Mistress," a seductive female voice greeted them.

"We're in!" Gillian said.

"*Way to go. Grrrls Rule!*" Sinistral affirmed their success.

Gillian grinned, and glanced back at Jazz for approval. He was engrossed in a picture taped on the inside of the bedroom door. The left vertical edge of the picture was torn.

The extreme close-up photo showed a boyish man from the back with his face looking over his shoulder. The larger-than-life profile showed a smooth hairless head, one soft innocent eye and a beatific smile. The photographer had caught his subject in front of a beveled glass window in The Rainbow Refectory that diffused sunlight into a halo framing his head. But the focus of Jazz's rapt attention filled Gillian's chest with a vague apprehension. A needle-sharp dart was stabbed into the neck.

"This is probably important," Sinistral whispered in Gillian's ear.

"Duh!" Gillian replied under her breath as she moved closer. "I wonder if we should call the police?" she thought out loud.

"Oh, that would be great," jeered Sinistral. *"Officer,"* she mimicked. *"I have this friend on the Internet who doesn't talk to me anymore. She deleted my e-mails and told me to take action if she did that . . . and, oh yeah, she has stabbed a picture!"*

"Do you think they would be interested at this point, Gillian? And, if they were, this," he indicated the dart, "might not present Reggie in the best light."

Gillian shrugged and carefully pulled out the dart. She peeled the tape from the door and removed the picture. The dart had been plunged so violently into the target that the hollow core door was dimpled under the blow and several splits in the wood radiated out from the point of impact. Gillian and Jazz looked at each other.

Gillian spread the creased target flat on the computer desk and looked closely at the entire picture. The page was larger than most magazines, more like one from a coffee table book or the size the old *Life* magazine used to be. The dart puncture was in the man's neck just above the collar. Gillian smoothed the wrinkled impact area and a closer examination revealed four tiny moles surrounding the ragged dart puncture.

"Oh, my God!" they exclaimed in unison.

Jazz knew the horror Reggie must have felt when she discovered the familiar pattern of moles on the neck of this famous televangelist.

Gillian could only imagine.

On the back of the punctured picture was the continuation of a story about the new televangelical movement of the nineties. The article, called "Reclaiming the Rainbow," illuminated the ups and downs, saints and sinners, and the enormous amount of capital flowing to the self-proclaimed shepherds from the absolute poorest segment of America's working flock. Jazz read aloud: *The evangelists seem to be divided into two groups, although neither is defined by its poverty. The groups are thought of as the Billy Grahams and the Elmer Gantrys.*

With a twinge of guilt Gillian began to download Regster1's old files as she listened to Jazz's narration.

"It's not snooping, Gillian. She pulled us into this," Sinistral rationalized.

The story probed the depth of the pop-ministry's power, and the deep-seated need in its followers for slick and easy answers to life's countless quandaries.

As Jazz read on, she downloaded as many of Reggie's files as she could fit onto disks—letters sent and received, favorite places and Web sites. There was a lot. She hurried and didn't linger to read much. She felt a little sleazy and intrusive. She would have preferred to respect the private thoughts of her friend.

The Graham list is shorter than the Gantry list and seems to have more credence and sincerity, while the Gantrys are often perceived as slick hustlers—the pro-wrestlers of religion.

"Now here," Jazz observed, "the writer deftly covers his derriere."

But, it is all in the perception of the beholder. What is blatantly apparent to one viewer might be absolutely shrouded to another.

There were no saved e-mail letters from Belladonis. The only information in the Belladonis online profile said:

Belle is a female, lives on Long Island, NY. She plays the bagpipes. Twigging new sites on the 'net gives her a thrill. Her favorite colour is plaid. She loves to surf on the water as well as online.

"Oh, yeah! That Long Island surf is gnarly!" Jazz sneered. "And, what the hell is twigging?"

Gillian noticed the American Heritage Dictionary was on Reggie's computer. She looked up twigging and answered his question. "It's British slang for discovering, observing, noticing."

"The man in the picture is most likely Clovis Ransom," Jazz said. "Except now he calls himself Marcus Hollister."

Gillian shuddered. Jazz's face shifted to a more intense concern.

South Beach is nicknamed the American Riviera. The Versace mansion where the designer was slain is within two miles of The Rainbow Refectory as is the club where the movie Birdcage *was filmed. The gay presence in the area makes San Francisco's Castro Street look like a Southern Baptist picnic ground. It seems an unlikely setting for a religious-right conservative organization to put down roots. But, as polls tell us, twenty percent of any population is always disgruntled, and in the affluent South Beach area, that twenty percent is bound to represent quite a large chunk of change.*

Gillian signed off Reggie's Internet connection and shut down the computer.

"Farewell, Mistress. It was a pleasure serving you," the fickle cyber-wench murmured.

"My calendar is free for a few days, Jazz. I lied about the Friday meeting."

Jazz grinned and hugged her. He dialed the airport, made reservations and wrote down the information for Gillian.

Gillian flipped open her cell phone and scrolled to her niece's home number.

Two years ago Gillian's niece Cora had fallen in love on the Internet with a Venezuelan poet/under-the-table construction worker in Miami Beach. The whole family had adored the husband she divorced. They'd kept him close until he died of a malignant brain tumor and a broken heart. Most of them profoundly, unforgivingly disapproved of the poet. Gillian had never believed a woman should live her life to make others happy. She'd understood when Cora joined her poet in Florida.

Gillian speed-dialed Cora. Nowadays, she was front office manager at the Casbah del Mar Hotel, a beachfront resort in Middle Beach.

She and her husband lived in South Beach, only four miles down the coast. After several rings it switched to an answering machine.

"I remember! Cora and that poet guy publish The Lincoln Road Informant." Sinistral reminded Gillian.

Gillian dialed again. This time Cora answered. "Hi, honey," Gillian greeted the sleepy voice answering the phone, "I know it's late. I need some information . . . and a small suite at the Casbah." She continued in earnest. "We're on our way to the airport now."

She gave Cora the Reader's Digest condensed version, just enough to make getting back to sleep a problem for Cora. The red-eye left at 10:20 p.m. and arrived in Miami at 9:57 a.m. with a transfer in Atlanta. "We should be to the hotel by eleven a.m. When does your next paper come out?"

"Day after tomorrow," Cora said.

"Cool!" she responded. "Save me a quarter page ad space, will you, darling, and nose around to see if you can flush out an honest private detective, preferably female?"

"Will do."

Gillian signed off with her half of their traditional signature phrase: "Remember, the early bird gets the worm."

Cora recited her part. "But the second mouse gets the cheese. See you tomorrow morning, Aunt Gilly."

Sinistral and Gillian smiled.

Chapter 31
Up! Up! Into the Fray

Back at The U.S. Male, Jazz pulled some cash from the strongbox in his office, slipped his passport into his pocket and left some money and scribbled some instructions for his assistant manager.

On his way out, he grabbed a spare charger for his cell phone and then locked up. He slid into Gillian's car.

"Wait," he said and jumped out. He pulled Reggie's laptop from the trunk of his car.

Up on Sunrise Mountain they stopped beside the mailbox at the top of the driveway.

"Nice digs," Jazz said looking down at the home and the panoramic view.

"Thanks," she said as she reached out her window to collect a fistful of mail.

She left Jazz to fend for himself in the main room. "Get yourself a drink from the bar if you like."

Gillian tossed some underwear and toiletries into the bag. "Here, Trixter," she called and chucked her under the chin when she ran to her. She slipped her a cookie and locked her in her safe room with a doggie door.

The number she had dialed picked up. "Shell, will you be able to check in on Trixter while I'm out of town?" she asked. "I really don't know . . . several days?" With her free hand she stripped and pulled on her leather traveling pants and a light turtleneck. She hopped into her office pulling on a loafer. "Thanks. Thanks, Shell."

She grabbed a box of blank floppies to use in Reggie's laptop and, at Sinistral's insistence, pulled the fireproof strongbox from the closet shelf, retrieved her passport, her zip drive and the zip disc copies of her latest manuscript.

"Thank you, thank you, thank you, my friend. Smooches to Bev," she said, and zipped the suitcase shut and headed for the door.

Gillian's working class background had never allowed her to justify the exorbitant premium on first-class airfare but Jazz was without compunction. He upgraded and said, "You're with me and we need our rest." That was fine but what a shame to waste all that comfort sleeping.

At some level of her psyche, comprehension was dawning full-blown that this was not a game but something as serious as a Category Five hurricane. Certainly the mutilated picture of Reggie's abuser implied ominous possibilities. That fact, combined with what Gillian and Jazz perceived as an Internet conspiracy, added up to a potentially volatile state of affairs.

She dozed and awoke with a start. The plane was dark. She pulled the laptop from under the seat in front of her and lowered the tray. The glow from the screen highlighted Jazz's cheek and jawline as he slept.

Did Reggie have retaliation in mind? Would she sacrifice her own freedom—or even her own life—to punish Clovis? Who of us really knew what primordial acts lurked in our own arsenal—much less another's?

Gillian tried to imagine Reggie's reaction when she spotted her abuser's picture in the magazine. Had she been in the salon? Had she seen the moles over some patron's shoulder? Or, had the magazine been left open to the page in a friend's home or in a dentist's reception room? Had the sight stripped away all the civility gained by therapy? Did Jazz's feral sister yearn to slash flesh and gnaw bone? In whatever manner Reggie had come upon the article, Gillian's heart ached for her.

Gillian pulled reading glasses from her carry-on. She rummaged around and found her green tin of uppers—Altoids. The mints burst on her tongue and sent a cool sensation through her sinuses and lungs. The mint rush cleared her head.

She flipped open Reggie's laptop. She checked the icons and stored files and did not find much. Then, "Oh, my," she exclaimed just under her breath. "What's this?" There was a floppy in the laptop.

It contained stored e-mail letters. The first was from someone called Keepntabs. Had Reggie left this deliberately? Or, was this the first chink in her plan?

To: Regster1

Keepntabs: Geez! I guess it constitutes Good Behavior when you don't attack a little girl or boy while in custody. Duh! Could the scarcity of little children here at the Fortress be a factor? He leaves protective probation in Oct. Relocating to the southern California coast. Hope he doesn't meet any youngsters on the train! I'll let you know time frame. Nighters.

The second file was from Clemensuk. Odd name. Online names often meant something. Gillian always tried to decipher them. She read the letter sent in March, well before the Rainbow Refectory article.

Dear Regster1, I feel as though no coincidence occurred when I was in the 'survivors' chat the night you came in and told your story . . . our story, really. The fact that you feel, as I do, that your life is on hold until some closure can be reached, is a bond I can almost touch. Let's talk in real time. Okay? Do you like Hitchcock? Tell me your snailmail address I'd like to send you a tape. I've found two more survivors who appear interested in helping in any capacity. All the others seem to have come to grips and are getting on with their lives. I wish we could feel that way— you and I. They seem to have found the secret to taking back their power from their boogieman. We sure tried. Wish we could have!

Oranges and Lemons, Kid.

Oranges and Lemons . . . Oranges and Lemons. The phrase niggled at Gillian's past until her mental filing system delivered a quick flash from her childhood.

Eight-year-old Gillian turns one end of a jump rope. The other end is tied to a slim boxwood tree that casts dappled shadows on the cracked sidewalk in front of her house. The intermittent whir of a push mower chatters in the background and the smell of freshly mown grass perfumes the summer air. The rhythmic slap of the rope and the skipping feet of the little red-haired English girl from up the street keeps time as she chants, "Oranges and Lemons, say the bells of St. Clemens . . ."

The figment faded.

"Aha!" Gillian whispered melodramatically. "Clemens—the church in the rhyme and UK—United Kingdom, they add up to 'Clemensuk'. Maybe our letter writer comes from London near St. Clemens or at least England."

"*Hmmm. Or maybe she just thinks Mark Twain was a lousy writer,*" Sinistral interjected.

The only other fragment Gillian could recall was: ". . . and here comes a chopper to chop off your head!" *When they tell kids' tales, those Brits are a laugh riot.*

Gillian's eyes drifted shut, the laptop timed out.

Chapter 32
. . . To Share a Slice of Time
Tuesday 10/6/1998 10:50 p.m. PST
Haley Baxter

Haley Baxter sat in a dingy motel room leaning against three limp motel pillows propped against a wall-mounted Formica headboard. The stuffy room was redolent with the saline scent of old sex and fabric never quite dried. Her pale legs, crossed at the ankles, were covered with a sparse, velvety blond fuzz and her thirty-four years were belied by a dash of freckles across her nose and a tousle of short auburn curls framing an angelic face.

She fingered a slim cylinder with reverence. Every few seconds she slid a tiny fletched dart into the tube and lifted the mouthpiece to her lips. She gathered her quiet anger and with a crisp *Pffft!* exploded her breath into the tube, propelling the tiny projectile into a target on the wall some four meters away. The very center of the bull's-eye bristled with tiny slivers. She rarely, if ever, missed anymore—not at any distance. She wiped the moisture from the corners of her mouth with the back of her hand, inadvertently brushing the off-center hairline indentation that divided her upper lip and made piping more difficult.

Pffft!

"I need a little more sedative. Me nose isn't numb yet," she informed the empty room as she pulled a tall, brown bottle with a white collar from the minibar.

She pried the cap from the frosty Guinness and eased the thick creamy head to the top of a tall, plastic San Diego Chargers cup.

"Cheers, Luv," she toasted the silent images on the television, and took a deep draught. She licked the velvety foam from her lip and let the dark ale's icy edge cut through the viscous film of her thirst.

Pffft!

Karanja would be proud, she thought.

Karanja and Kenya were twenty years in her past but often in her thoughts lately. The boy's lessons had been well-learned.

"I heard you play the pipes." Karanja's singsong voice caressed her ears from years and miles afar. "I know you have the power." She remembered how he had placed the knuckle sides of his curved fingers over her heart and indicated, "Here." Then he added, "I can teach you to find your eye."

He had.

Pffft!

She drained the Charger cup, leaned back to cradle her head in the nest of her laced fingers and closed her eyes to better savor the glow that was spreading over her skin and finally numbing the tip of her nose.

"That's more like it," she cooed in a sigh of gratitude. Her lips tingled.

She began to hum Kenya's Anthem in the soft, sweet style Karanja's mother had taught her. The Swahili words came back to her, as did the melody extracted from an ancient African lullaby:

"Ee Mungu nguvu yetu Ilete baraka kwetu Haki iwe ngao na mlinzi

Natukae na udugu Amani na uhuru Raha tupate na ustawi . . . " she sang.

O God of all creation,
Bless this our land and nation.
Justice be our shield and defender,
May we dwell in unity,
Peace and liberty.
Plenty be found within our borders.

The old stories of Africa were so vivid they often inhabited her dreams. Now, in her ale-induced doze, random thoughts and memories streamed like beer bubbles to the surface—unfiltered.

Her father's people had been white colonizers, and Karanja's ancestors had descended from the original warriors and chiefs of the land. Ignoring the racial code of the day, Karanja's father, Jomoto, and her father, Andrew, became fast friends. She watched them dance on the inside of her eyelids, frisking and stalking through the high grass waves of the savanna. All that had changed when the life they lived was washed away by the tsunami-force wave of history called the Mau Mau uprising in the early 1950s.

Andrew and his family were among the white colonists who had been driven from the continent by fear of racial reprisals. He'd finished his education in England, married and fathered his first daughter, Bridget. After he took a position with the British Diplomatic Corps in Washington, D.C. the twins, Belle and Haley, were born.

When Bridget was snatched from them early in 1972 her family exhausted every means of finding her. Televised pleas from Mummy and Dadda had turned up nothing. After eighteen months they had reached an agonizing decision to return to Kenya where they had hoped to lessen their inconsolable grief while aiding that country in its struggle for progress.

She flashed on the move back to Kenya, Africa, the land of their father's childhood. She recalled Dadda falling to his knees upon learning his friend Jomoto was dead—killed in the fight for independence. The tears he shed then were compounded by the ones left unshed for Bridget.

Jomoto's son Karanja was then fourteen. Jomoto's wizened father, Kyoto, and Karanja befriended the family anew. But this time the Brits were guests in Kyoto's country. Karanja took it upon himself to teach the girls wilderness survival. They taught him to play the bagpipes, but he was steadfast in his refusal to wear the plaid kilts even when he played for Dadda's funeral.

When Bridget was rescued and returned to her family, the twins and Karanja had done their best to teach her all the wonders of their new home. She'd tried but even Mummy found her oddly different from the happy girl they remembered—utterly altered.

The urge to pee forced Haley to open her eyes to the reality of the dingy motel room. She flushed the toilet and rinsed her hands. She yawned as she pulled a dark wig over her rusty hair and crammed a San Diego Padres baseball cap on backward. She looked at the kitten calendar on the bathroom wall. Saturday night would be dark and moonless. The new moon was a sign that the plan was in sync with providence, she assured herself.

Walking to the spot farthest from the bathroom she spun on her heel and, *Pfffft*—she puffed a dart into the furry space between the kitten's eyes. Dead center.

She put down the dart gun, picked up her chanter and played a soft riff. The burnished wood of the slender instrument felt warm and familiar. It fingered the same as her pipes and had a similar resonance, only much quieter.

She locked the door, turned up her collar against the dampness and trotted in the soft sand toward the lapping surf. She would be alone there. She knew she played like an angel, but was sharply aware of the fact that most people preferred listening to bagpipe music from a distance—a great distance.

Tuesday 10/6/1998 11:50 p.m. MST
Gillian

Gillian's head nestled into the soft wing of her first-class seat. She missed her tiny airline issued-pillow pressed against the tourist-class-window—haha, not a whit!

Her sleepy focus slipped past the porthole into the open sky. The green wingtip light of a westbound plane winked in the inky distance. *Ships that pass in the night.* She drifted to sleep. The little red-haired girl kissed Gillian's dream-cheek and walked out on the silver wing to play her pint-sized bagpipes.

"Okay, Sinistral, I get the Clemensuk-bagpipe connection," Gillian muttered, "Go to sleep!"

Tuesday 10/6/1998 11:50 p.m. MST
Reggie

Reggie shifted her body toward the tiny window. She had no idea what had awakened her. The cabin lights were dimmed. She raised the little plastic window shade. Far in the distance she spotted the starboard light of another plane flying east.

Life goes on, she thought. And tomorrow the same, and a week from next Tuesday. She fought a slight queasiness in her stomach. The quick turnaround had been stressful. I'll be back in San Diego in time for breakfast, she thought. Haley is probably there already.

The rendezvous in Key West had gone well. She missed Bridget but felt recommitted. Belle was so intense. Her passion was probably what kept them all motivated.

Reggie had learned that as soon as Belle received the e-mail from Gillian, she'd flown to Key West. That e-mail had been automatically forwarded to the entire survivors' network and the wheels had all been set in motion.

I would feel so much better if the passports were already there at the house in Hillcrest or at the very least they would arrive tomorrow. I hope I can carry out my part of the plan. When it's done we'll all bask on the beach for at least a week—in Venezuela. After that, there'll be plenty of time to figure out what to do with the rest of my life.

It was invigorating to overcome helplessness and finally take action. It would be particularly good if that action could exact retribution for Jazz's stolen childhood, her own, and of course, VenusD's. Simple survival is good, she mused, but not good enough.

There was fear. She was not sure if it was of failure or success.

When she was a child she had stalked the night and when the time was right, she had been a warrior. And felt alive. She so wanted to feel that way again.

Reggie's eyelids sagged and she drifted back into a shallow, fitful sleep. Anxious shadows populated her dreams, stalking her—wielding guns and knives and fear.

Wednesday 10/7/1998 1:50 a.m. EST
Belle McCreedy

It was pleasant on the balcony in the early morning hours. A slight offshore breeze ruffled Belle's auburn hair. The ebb tide swishing out on the long smooth beach sounded like deep rhythmic breathing. The humidity was becoming familiar to her—Key West had been even sultrier.

Before Belle ever met Reggie face-to-face she was a heroine to her. She was the reason her family got their Bridget back. They'd gotten to know each other online, and seeing her *face-to-face* was just an additional lovely identifier, not *the* identifier. Getting in touch with each other's commitment was a source of positive energy for all of them.

Reggie and Haley seemed to get on nicely, Belle reflected with a smile. They'll perform well together.

She mulled over Bridget's intricate plan, devised to weave her—and dozens of other abuse-surviving women—into one cohesive force. Her attention to detail was worthy of any field general's planning, against all odds, to win a crucial and righteous battle. Her plan harnessed the raw energy and expertise of each woman to wake the world and drive home a powerful statement. A statement that would be heard.

Belle remembered the statement verbatim:

Patriarchy of the World, you cannot go on abusing your women and children without regret or a backward glance and expect to escape punishment. Vengeance may be the Lord's but justice will be served in this life. You may wheedle and twist the system to escape severe punishment but we are everywhere. Seventy thousand women are raped every year in the

U.S.A. and the leading cause of death of pregnant women is murder.

We know the effects of sexual abuse can include chronic anxiety, low self-esteem, problems with intimacy and sexuality, severe depression, suicide or persistent thoughts of it as a final refuge from the pain. Alcohol or drug abuse, eating disorders or multiple personality disorder can ensue.

We survived in spite of you but you stole pieces of our lives. We are among you in all walks of life—and we will see that you pay the price for the devastating havoc you wreaked upon our innocent, young lives.

Belle closed her eyes and pictured the herpetologist in Amsterdam plying her chosen profession with precision—using electronically maneuvered, mechanical hands—her own having been rendered useless by a pedophilic religious fanatic when she was eleven. The thug had spread his poison around the world for twelve more years. Then fate delivered him to her and she orchestrated his arrest and saw him sentenced to ten years. But now he was free and she knew he would destroy more children's lives.

Another genius, determined not only to survive, but also to live well. But for her, too, the depression ebbed and flowed—Belle opened her eyes and gazed seaward, "—like the tide and my dear, sweet Bridey," she whispered into the wee hours of the Miami morning.

Chapter 33
Clammy in Miami

Jazz held the heavy door open and Gillian rolled her luggage from the air-conditioned comfort of the Miami airport into the dense, humid reality of Miami.

"Argh," she gasped.

The soggy air clung to her whole body like steamy tendrils of warm saltwater taffy. After years in the desert she'd forgotten how the mugginess dragged at her and weighed her down. Her hair drooped, her energy plummeted—but, on the positive side, her skin really perked up.

"Well," Gillian sighed to Jazz with wistful optimism, "at least the cab will be air-conditioned."

It wasn't.

After the tollbooth, the traffic moved briskly across the Julia Tuttle Causeway to the beach and the Casbah del Mar Hotel.

The Moroccan marquee sheltering the hotel entrance was held aloft on the well-muscled shoulders of a quartet of twelve-foot jinni emerging from their lamps. Porters hustled their bags into the cavernous air-conditioned lobby. The dry, cooled air snatched the leaden feeling from their shoulders and delivered freshened air to their grateful lungs. Their footsteps echoed as perky taps on the vast marble floor of the foyer and the pastel decor soothed their weary eyes.

Gillian checked her image in the mirrors that framed the elevators. She looked more rested than she felt. Jazz's eyes danced about taking it all in. Hard to believe a Vegas boy could be so impressed by decor.

"I adore it!" he exclaimed. "It's only slightly influenced by art deco, but it's wonderful!"

They stepped from the elevator on the ninth floor and sank into plush carpet the color of a rich merlot. Their bay view suite overlooked the Intracoastal Waterway and the city of Miami. A lovely bottle of her favorite Siegerrebe chilled in an ice bucket on the counter. Several bottles of Pouille Fuisse and some cold, grilled chicken waited in the refrigerator.

Appraising the fully equipped and well-stocked kitchen prompted Gillian to note, in her best Bogie accent, "Ah, definitely a classy jernt."

There was a knock at the door. Jazz opened it and Cora burst in. A tall woman, her features were attractive and even, her shoulder-length hair curly and generous. The whole effect of Cora was one of gorgeous, flamboyant efficiency.

"Isn't the weather glorious?" she enthused. "It was so humid up until last week."

Gillian's desert heart conceded that everything was relative.

Cora acknowledged Jazz with a smile as she gave her Aunt Gillian a long hug and then quickly produced a short list of investigators—all female. In exchange, Gillian pressed a folded paper into her hands and made the introductions. Cora opened the note. "You want this in tomorrow's paper, right?" Cora asked.

"Yes," Gillian answered, "and can you be sure some papers are left at the Rainbow Refectory?"

"Sure, I would anyway. They run a schedule of their services in the paper." She started to leave then leaned back through the doorway. "Anything you need, ring the desk! Tell them you're mine!"

Gillian checked the time. A little early for wine but some cold chicken would be great with a bottle of tonic water.

Jazz picked up his cellular, a chicken leg and, as an afterthought, a tiny MP3 player holding Rita Mae Brown's latest mystery. He was off to pick up the rental car and stake out the post office. Gillian settled in to call investigators.

The first woman on the list was out of town. The second call garnered a flip young secretary and an investigator who sounded bored with life and uninterested in the Internet aspect of this case. The third answered her own phone on the second ring, "Rachel Bracken here." The voice was small—very small. To match her body, Gillian guessed. She sounded as though she were playing at a faster speed than she was recorded.

"Good morning, Ms. Bracken," Gillian began, "your name was given to me by my niece, Cora . . ."

Bracken's answers were quick and forthright. She seemed bright and interested in the case.

As a result of an earlier investigation, she possessed some knowledge of, access to, and contacts in the Rainbow Refectory. Plus, she spoke fluent Spanish and computer-ese.

She agreed to meet Gillian and would come by the hotel at two p.m.

After a swim in the seaside pool, Gillian showered, pulled on a pair of Bermuda shorts, a khaki tank top and a pair of Birkenstocks. She was drying her hair when the phone rang announcing Rachel Bracken.

Gillian deliberately set her gaze at about the level of the doorknob so as not to register surprise at the detective's presumably short stature. When she pulled the door open she found herself looking directly at the hem of the woman's elegant silk suit jacket.

Gillian raised her gaze to one absolutely level with her own. That would make Rachel Bracken five foot ten or so. Her summer-weight suit was a shade lighter than a mid-July sky and hung from her squared shoulders and modest breasts in understated grace. Her short, blondish hair was combed straight back, tucked behind her ears and flipped slightly at the nape of her neck. A swoosh of sky-blue streaked the hair above her right ear. That and the tiny diamond twinkling in the cleft where her left nostril flared placed her firmly in a generation more recent than Gillian's.

My, oh, my! Gillian smiled her appreciation and gestured her into the suite.

"You old horndog!" Sinistral scoffed when she felt Gillian's relief that using free weights had toned her droopy triceps.

"Ms. Waters," the thirty-something woman said, proffering a business card and a confident handshake.

"I'm familiar with your work," she said smiling into Gillian's eyes.

"You're kidding!" Gillian answered with genuine surprise. "A bona fide detective reading my stuff . . . my dear, politically incorrect mother would have called that a busman's holiday."

"I like Sinistral's cocky humor, too," Rachel said, still chuckling. "The series is an entertaining read."

An entertaining read. That was what Dark called it. A nice way of saying, It ain't Faulkner. That's fine. Immortality has never been my goal.

Gillian glanced down at the detective's card, "You're also," she raised a quizzical eyebrow, "an attorney?"

"Yep. I am a member of the Florida bar," Rachel said, "but I like this work much better."

"Why's that—may I call you Rachel?"

"Certainly. Well, I was with a firm in St. Petersburg for seven years and as Ferron so aptly put it, played with the big boys."

Ferron? She quotes Ferron? Hmmmmm.

"I worked outrageous hours, made contacts all over the Southeast, earned a ton of money and an ulcer that laid me low. I had time then to think and admit to myself that I hated the breakneck grind of it all. I love it here on South Beach and I set my own pace."

Gillian noticed that Bracken's voice was just fine in person.

Gillian located the ingredients to brew a pot of coffee as she told the tale of Reggie, Jazz and herself as succinctly as she could. Rachel listened, and made brief notations in a small leather-bound notebook. Gillian switched on the coffeepot.

"I was able to get a young runaway out of the Rainbow Refectory last year when her father and mother traced her here to the Beach," Rachel said. "I've felt creepy, cult-like vibes from that place since the beginning. This Marcus Hollister guy isn't just another religious wacko though," she stressed. "He's mesmerizing and plays on people's fear and anxiety. He's extremely disarming. I'm surprised he isn't in politics."

Gillian and Sinistral agreed that Bracken seemed to be a perfect fit for the job.

"He doesn't deny his attachment to The Enclave, you know?" Rachel added.

Gillian's internal attention switch snapped to alert as Rachel continued, "He claims to be one of the rescued children."

"Oh, dear," Gillian admitted her shock. "That wasn't mentioned in the article." She shuffled through some papers and handed Rachel the folded magazine page.

Rachel's expression was guarded as she smoothed it on the coffee table and touched the dart hole. She turned the page over and skimmed the text.

"I remember seeing this picture and reading the story. It was in *Rolling Stone* last April or May. There was more about Marcus Hollister on another page," she added. "As I recall, his family, strict Seventh-day Adventists, moved to Arkansas after their reunion and planned to deprogram him. The parents were killed and Marcus was injured when their small, residential hotel burned down. Marcus was sixteen. One of his hands was severely burned, but he escaped."

Great recall.

"Since Reggie had the magazine picture, more than likely she's aware of the whole story," Rachel added.

"One thing bothers me," Gillian mused. "Reggie said that Clovis was almost grown when she was ten. He must be at least nine or ten years older than her and she is thirty-one. That would make Clovis forty or so. This," she gestured toward the magazine picture, "does not look like the face of a forty-year-old man."

"I know," Rachel agreed, "he's like a boy . . . smooth face, high voice, slender build. I noticed he had some barely visible scars on his face, maybe from a facelift? Or, perhaps Reggie was mistaken. Maybe she saw the moles on another, younger boy and mixed them up in her mind."

The phone rang.

"Aunt Gillian," Cora said, a slight urgency in her voice, "turn on Channel Seven on the cable box! It's that Marcus Hollister guy!"

Rachel pulled a blank videotape from her briefcase, slipped it into the VCR and pressed Record.

Gillian analyzed the man on the screen. He seemed to glow with an inner light. It was eerie. He probably had his own lighting crew, luminous makeup, soft focus, a slightly upward camera angle . . . all in all, a great camera artist. The words he was saying sounded hopeful and positive and were spoken in the guileless voice of a prepubescent boy. The message of damned-them vs. saved-us was subtle. The whole effect was one of authenticity and divine inspiration. *I want to see this dude up close and unaided by technology.*

The camera panned the congregation. The cathedral was packed. Marcus chose people at random from the vast assemblage in the sanctuary, asked their names and a little something about why they were drawn to the Rainbow Refectory.

Gillian recognized the routine. "Watch," she said. "In a half hour or so he'll go back and say something else to them recalling their names and their personal stories."

"How could he memorize all that? Photographic memory?" Rachel asked.

"He probably uses an earpiece receiver. I've been told entertainers like Debbie Reynolds do that in their act," Gillian suggested.

"I love Debbie Reynolds," Rachel offered.

"Me, too," Gillian exclaimed. "I had the opportunity to shake her hand once and look into her hazel-green eyes and tell her I had such a crush on her when I was fourteen."

"How brave of you," Rachel said.

"I did it for all my sisters who would never get the chance. I'm afraid I made her uncomfortable," she recollected. "I didn't mean to. Anyway, someone keeps notes on the information during the first part of the show," Gillian said, picking up the thread, "and feeds it back into the headliner's ear during the latter. Not a thing wrong with that endearing trick in show biz."

"Sure, I can see how that could ingratiate the entertainer to the audience. Not particularly ethical in religion, though," said Rachel.

"Or money-gathering for salvation!" Gillian added.

Two heartbeats later Rachel and Gillian shot a glance at each other.

"Great minds . . ." they both said.

"You thought of it, too, didn't you?" Rachel asked.

Gillian nodded and said, "Wonder how we could get access to the source of the whispered message?"

"Better yet," Rachel upped the verbal ante, "be the messenger." She scribbled something in her book. "I'll work on it."

Sinistral was pacing between Gillian's ears. All three of their minds started focusing on the possibilities.

They watched the glossy television production a while longer.

"This guy looks so androgynous . . . even neuter. It's hard to see the child molester in him," she said, and then rolled her eyes. "As though the monster's appearance would reveal his nature," she censured herself. "Reggie talked about a dark, scraggly beard. This guy doesn't look like he could grow one."

"Yeah. He makes me think of someone else—an actor or someone interviewed on television . . . or . . ." Rachel dangled the thought out loud.

"That bald head—there's not a shadow of dark hair roots," Gillian noted.

"And there is something about his eyes," Rachel added scribbling furiously in her little leather notebook. "I see what it is," she said tapping the face on the screen. "Innocence? Mystery? Nope! Like the Mona Lisa . . . no eyebrows! He's shaved off his eyebrows."

"Ah, good observation." Gillian nodded her respect. She switched off the sound. The silence felt a little abrupt and even a little awkward.

"Well," Rachel said as she got up and smoothed the wrinkles from the front of her slacks. "I have some understanding of the case and think I can be of help. Shall we work together?"

Gillian grinned, nodded and reached to shake her hand.

Zzzsszssss! It wasn't audible but felt like time-warped, static electricity—but on the pleasure end of the scale. Gillian released her hand.

"I'll have to run it past Jazz," she said, "I'll pay you for today either way." With a nervous grin, she reached for her beach bag.

Rachel held up her hand with a smile and a little shake of her head.

"Oh. Okay. So, tomorrow?"

Rachel agreed.

This is going to be interesting. Rachel waited for the elevator. *I wonder what this Reggie and the girls are up to. My first guess would be—no good.* She dialed her cell. "Hello, Esther Beck? This is Rachel Bracken." She pictured the older, pink-clad cleaning lady who didn't just do it for the money. "I'm going to need some help in the Rainbow again . . . There might be two of us . . . say in a day or two. Thank you, Esther. You're a treasure."

Gillian did some editing, sifted through the manuscript searching for passages that could benefit from some added sensory descriptions. She lost track of the time as she always did when in writer mode. Jazz came home. No passport action at the post office.

• • •

Jazz was back at the post office when it opened Thursday morning. Gillian worked on *Inertia* for a couple of hours. Today she was what she thought of as 'thinking funny' and looking for opportunities to shoehorn in a little more humor. Writing was the only way she knew of to keep her mind out of the here-and-now, and into the there-and-then. It kept her from speculating about Reggie and her exploits.

About ten a.m. the phone rang. Jazz sounded as though he'd just sprinted out of an aerobic class. "Reggie isn't here!" he blurted.

"What?"

"She's not here in South Beach. Some Hispanic guy, maybe Hector, picked up her passport and some others," he panted, sounding winded and anxious.

"Take it easy, Jazz. Breathe, dear boy," Gillian urged.

"The guy took the passports and put two of them in each of two envelopes that were already addressed. I stood right next to him. He had to match a number 'one' or 'two' attached to each passport to a large numeral on each addressed envelope. Maybe he doesn't read . . . or maybe he's a little slow."

"Why do you sound so glum?"

"The envelope with Reggie's passport is addressed to San Diego."

Both of them were silent.

"Our theory is toast," Jazz gulped.

There was a knock on the door. Gillian answered it still talking on the cell. Rachel came in. They swapped smiles. Rachel kicked off her shoes and draped her jacket over the back of a chair. She walked right into the bathroom off the master suite like an old buddy.

Gillian had to admit she was puzzled by Reggie's presence on the other coast. "I'm sorry, Jazz," Gillian said softly. "But we still have a little time. Did you see where that guy sent the envelopes? Did you get the used ones?"

"I did better than that, Gillian," he said, "I distracted him with a twenty-dollar bill I dropped on the floor. He didn't see it at first. I pointed it out to him. When he bent over, I snatched the envelopes off the counter and shoved them up my shirt. I handed him the used ones. He dropped them in the mail slot without even looking. I circled back a little later and saw him eating an ice cream cone. But I'm afraid there might have been surveillance cameras."

"Gads, our Jazz is a federal fugitive!" Gillian laughed.

"What?" Rachel called from the other room.

"Jazz," Gillian cajoled, "you may be a postal thief but you are a genius! This is fabulous news. She's far away from Clovis. Were the new envelopes stamped?" she asked as an afterthought.

"Yeah . . ." he answered.

"Oh . . . well . . . hey, technically the guy hadn't mailed them yet—no federal crime!" she said with aplomb. She didn't know if that was true or not, but she felt reassured. "Just bring them home, dear boy."

Gillian was pondering the situation. *I like the way Rachel gives the impression she's just hanging out. Well, that was a totally unrelated thought.* She felt a twinge of something stir in her stomach. *Was that anxiety?*

"I remember!" Rachel called from the bathroom. "I just remembered who the guy was, you know, the guy who Marcus Hollister reminds me of." The water ran briefly. She emerged from the master suite drying her hands on a small, mauve towel. "He was called Do, like doe, a deer, remember?"

Gillian looked blank.

"You know, Heaven's Gate—the Hale Bop comet people? I think his name was Marshall . . . Yes! Marshall Applewhite. Marcus looks a lot like him, only on lower doses of amphetamines!"

Gillian saw what she meant. It wasn't the looks, but the look. It was the pale pate and childlike features—something in the eyes, the irises surrounded by white. Marcus had just shaved his head and ratcheted it down a few notches.

They gleaned as much information as they could from Reggie's online stuff. They were picking at the chicken and sipping bottled water when Jazz returned with the envelopes.

Rachel took the large post office envelopes, studied them and went into the kitchen area. She put them in the freezer. "Makes them easier to open," she answered the unasked question. "You know—with less destruction."

Jazz popped the top on a cola drink and they sat around the small table to look at the compiled intelligence. All the pages and scribbled scraps were there, along with Reggie's laptop set up with an online connection. Rachel added her leather notebook and Gillian her idea book to the resource table.

"How do you suppose this one ties in?" Jazz wondered aloud as he picked a page from the pile. It was a copy of an e-mail that Cora had printed for them. Rachel read it aloud. It was from someone with the screen name Keepntabs.

"Geez! I guess good behavior in California consists of not molesting and maiming another little child while in custody. Duh! Could the scarcity of young girls here at 'The Fortress' be a factor? Protective probation ends Oct. Relocating southern coast. Hope he doesn't meet a little child on the train! I'll let you know the time frame. Nighters!"

Gillian remembered reading it on the plane.

"Sounds like Keepntabs might work at The Fortress," Jazz noted. "See, they say here, not there."

"Hmmmm," Rachel murmured, glanced at Jazz's watch and flipped open her cell phone. Kinsey's in the Santa Barbara area—too far south, she thought. Then she said, "I know . . ." She searched the menu then entered a number. A distant phone rang twice.

A sleepy female voice answered, "Mahoney."

"Hey, girl! Did I wake you?" Rachel asked.

"Yeah, up all night. I'm definitely getting too old for this job," the voice replied.

"How are things on your ocean?" Rachel asked.

"My ocean is great. Any late hurricanes stirring up yours?"

"None of the weather variety at the moment, but I do have a whirlwind of information I am trying to sort out. Do you know of any sex predators targeting children who are being released about now in your neck of the woods? Or what facility is nicknamed," she referred to the slip of paper, "the Fortress?"

"The only sick perp I can think of offhand due to be turned loose on the public anytime soon is that Billy Ray Ripley guy. You know, the a-hole who victimized a girl in a religious commune in Kentucky. He caused her arms to be snake bit and they had to be amputated."

"Snake bit?" Rachel asked.

Jazz sat up. His eyes widened and his face blanched.

Rachel noticed Jazz's expression and said, "I'm putting this on speaker."

"The cult was what they call, *Signs Following*. Comes from the Bible, Matthew I think. It was pretty big in that area of the country. Besides handling snakes, some congregations drank poison and handled fire, too. Lot of groups hid out when it was made against the law. Billy-boy was on the loose for twelve years before he was caught. He was serving time for his abuse of the girl and child porn. Jerkoff only did nine years and served his probation on the prison grounds of Northern California Correctional—otherwise known," the voice on the phone paused for dramatic effect, "as the Fortress."

"Could that religious commune have been The Enclave?"

"Maybe so, I'll check."

"When does he get out?" Rachel asked.

"It was hush-hush, but I think he might be out now."

"Thanks, K.C. I owe you. Just call."

"I will, Rachel. And I'll check on The Enclave shit and for any other perps and let you know. 'Bye."

"That was a PI I know in Northern California," Rachel told them what was said before they could hear the conversation.

She asked Jazz, "Do you remember snakes?"

"I didn't until I heard you ask. Snake bit?"

"So, you do remember snakes?"

"Yeah." The horror flooded back. "I saw it. And later I remember her leathery, twisted arms." His trembling soto voce was barely audible. A moment later, and louder, he added, "And I remember her before with regular arms. I liked that girl. She was nice to me."

"Are you okay?" Gillian asked.

Jazz shrugged.

"Maybe you should call your counselor."

Jazz gave a thoughtful nod.

As soon as Rachel thought it appropriate she steered the conversation back to the business at hand.

"Both of the envelopes in the freezer are the standard post office two-day delivery type. Each has large block letters spelling out a name and address: Reggie Cowels, on Arbor Drive, in San Diego and Bridget Clemens on James Avenue in Miami Beach."

Jazz nibbled on a chicken leg and drained the can of cola. "Her name was Josepha."

The women looked at him.

"I just remembered. A big oaf named Billy Ray was sweet on her."

They nodded and Rachel made note of the most recent name to crop up.

"The New York return address that Jazz memorized is probably bogus," she said. "I'll check that out." She scribbled a few words in her leather notebook then placed it back on the table. She donned plastic gloves and handed them each a pair. "Well," she suggested, walking to the freezer, "let's see what these girls look like."

She lifted the chilled flap on the first envelope, then the second, disturbing the seals as little as possible. The numerals in black ink were on the backs. She slid two blue passport booklets from the envelope marked one. Each had a scrap of paper with the numeral 'one' clipped to it.

The first passport was Reggie's. Gillian opened it to the headshot. Jazz touched Reggie's picture tenderly. His left eye twitched as he looked into the serious face staring into the camera that captured a momentary glint of defiance in her eyes.

The second passport belonged to a Haley Baxter. She had a girlish face with a dash of freckles across her nose, a halo of auburn hair and a quizzical smile.

The second envelope also contained a passport belonging to a Belle McCreedy bearing the same birthdate and the same youthful face as Haley's, but sporting a wild mane of a similar auburn hue.

They must be twins, Gillian thought.

"Duh!" mocked Sinistral. *"Or the same person."*

The second item wasn't a passport but a union booklet vacuum-sealed in a plastic envelope. The booklet itself was held open to the photo of a somber young woman with the same clear hazel-green eyes as the twins. Bridget Clemens, thirty-seven, born in London, England, had dark shoulder-length hair with severe bangs. She wore outdated, oversized, heavy-framed glasses. A thin scar ran through her upper lip to the base of her nose.

"You don't see that so much anymore," Gillian thought aloud. "Probably improved surgical techniques." The booklet appeared to be used and tattered.

"Oh!" Jazz said quietly. "I just remembered a big girl at The Enclave with that sort of scar. An older boy told me they called a scar like that a harelip. I thought it was caused by a real hair and couldn't figure out why they didn't just snip it. She talked funny. She was nice to me, too. She whittled whistles from twigs and little animals from peach pits. She even taught Reggie to play tic-tac-toe and that African game about planting the seeds."

"I think I know her too," considered Rachel as she double-checked the address on the envelope. "I'm sure I've seen her . . . right here in Miami Beach." She tapped her fingertips together. "At the Rainbow? That's it! She played a bagpipe solo at the Rainbow Refectory—ahhhh, late last year."

Gillian and Jazz both looked at Rachel with incredulous admiration. "In my business a person remembers that sort of stuff," she explained. "When she played, there was a spotlight on her and the house was dark. She wouldn't recognize me," Rachel added.

Jazz wandered a few feet away, distracted by the mute image of Marcus Hollister on the television. He released the mute with the remote and listened to the choirboy voice. He shook his head. "I don't know—I think I would have remembered that voice."

Rachel mentioned how he reminded her of Marshall Applewhite.

"He—Applewhite, he was castrated, wasn't he?" Jazz asked.

Rachel and Gillian simultaneously snapped a look at him.

"In my line, a fellow remembers that sort of stuff." His eyes added a coy trace to his otherwise straight face.

"That might account for the feminine softness and the high voice," Gillian suggested, "mightn't it—like a eunuch?"

Rachel shrugged ignorance and asked, "But how would that happen?"

Jazz was typing on the laptop. "Maybe he seduced the wrong little kid and someone other than the law caught him," he said without missing a stroke.

"*Hmmmmmmm*," Sinistral and Gillian uttered in unison.

"Wait! Listen to this," he exclaimed. "In Clemensuk's profile she says:

I play soulful pipes in the key of life the colour of which is, at best, a grayish-brown.

"How morose," Rachel said.

"But, the most interesting part is," Jazz crowed, "she and Belladonis both spell colour with a 'u'!"

Sinistral said, "*Bingo!*"

"Do you think they are both British or do you think they are the same person—or twins?" Rachel asked. She scrutinized the passport photos again.

"Their online profiles seem so different—almost diametrically opposed." Jazz reflected. "Dual personalities?"

"Do you remember any British kids at The Enclave, Jazz?" Rachel asked.

He shook his head. ". . . I don't think so. Well, maybe that little girl with the cleft palate. I guess her talking funny may have been part an English accent, part the deformed lip."

Rachel reached around Jazz's shoulders with both hands. Her manicured fingertips skipped over the laptop keys. She Googled Bridget Clemens.

Recent entries alluded to her musical career. Her bio mentioned little of her personal life except a paragraph about her life in Africa after years of being held at . . . "Voilà!" she uttered. "The Enclave."

They stared at the screen, each processing the new information. Bridget Clemens—an Enclave survivor, too.

"I'm checking Belle McCreedy and Haley Baxter. Nope. Maybe with the last name Clemens." *Click, click, click.* "Nadda."

"What are these girls up to?" Sinistral wondered.

Gillian picked up Belle McCreedy's passport. The birth date showed she was thirty-four. The face in the little blue passport was freckled and the hair was decidedly red and unruly. Her pleasant face looked generic and familiar.

"Wait," Gillian said. "This passport says she is in Hong Kong and her arrival back in Tampa is stamped—" Gillian counted on her fingers, "next Monday morning!"

"Oh, shit!" Jazz riffled through the pages of Reggie's passport and chimed in, "Reggie's says she landed in Frankfurt, Germany Wednesday and returned—next Monday from Belgium!"

"Haley's is the same as Belle's. They both indicate that they've been in Southeast Asia for five months," said Rachel. "The documents sure look authentic."

"Reggie's passport looks exactly as I remember. Except, of course, the trip to Germany. That can't be real," Jazz said. "See? Here are the stamps from our trip to Scotland."

"A damn good forgery, if you ask me," Gillian said peering closely at the various entries.

"Probably only the recent stamps are forged," said Rachel.

"I think the most important question here and now is . . ." Rachel paused. She fixed Gillian and Jazz with a sober look. "What is the plan here? Is there anything more I should know? I find it's best to be up front. What is it you want to do?" They were silent. "I mean, do you want to stop Reggie and talk to her to keep her from making a mistake? Or do you want to unmask Hollister? Or both? Or," she suggested, "is there another agenda?"

She reached over and held Jazz's wrist, to check the time. "I never can keep a watch going. They always die on me," she explained.

"Me, neither," Gillian declared with a quizzical glance. "I mean, me, too . . . not. I can't . . . either."

"That's because you two are witches," Jazz said matter-of-factly. "You play with time." They both looked at him. He just smiled. "I read it somewhere. Witch Energy Wreaks Havoc with Wristwatches."

Rachel regarded him for a moment, then said, "I'll phone an associate in Paducah and check the names of the rest of the survivors of The Enclave, but in the meantime, if one of these girls kills Clovis, this might be a murder-conspiracy case."

"Do we think that's what they have in mind?" Gillian asked growing even more sober. "I figured my mystery writer's mindset was just pole vaulting from motivation to . . . And, frankly, I wonder if it's such a bad idea. I guess I have a vindictive valve in my scribbler's heart. But what alternative form of closure can we offer Reggie? I know vigilante action can get out of hand but in this case Hollister is too big for the law to look at much less touch—without more conclusive evidence. I mean, even with that evidence . . ."

"She's right." Jazz chimed in. "Look how the O. J. Simpson fiasco has haunted our collective memory. Famous athlete, butchered wife, a truckload of DNA—not guilty?"

They pondered that for a beat or two.

"There are a couple of obscure e-mail messages that could support the killing theory," Rachel responded, shuffling through the collection of printed e-mails. She picked one. "This one is from Clemensuk."

I'm working on a fury for the whole genre. I find that when I direct my hatred toward just one person who has harmed me, the job is so much easier.

"Likely, most of their online communications," Rachel added, "were in private chat rooms. There would be no record of those conversations, unless someone saved and printed them . . . like this one."

"Gillian." Jazz stood in front of the television. The tape of the Hollister segment ran mutely. He paused the action. He studied the full screen headshot of Marcus Hollister closely. "I think he has alopecia totalis. I don't see any eyebrows or . . . eyelashes. I've only seen the disease twice before," he said. "Reggie used to talk about his hair falling out in clumps. I think if this dude has a scar on his butt and no dick, he is Clovis. On second thought, even if his dick is intact. And, yes, I believe Reggie could be capable of killing Clovis," he said quietly. "I remember her saying that if she thought he or any other man were hurting little children, she could kill." He added, "I wonder what became of the real Marcus Hollister?"

Gillian had transferred each separate clue from Reggie's room to its own sticky note. Rachel was going through the evidence collected on the table. She looked at Jazz and scribbled in her notebook. She picked up a yellow sticky note written in Gillian's hand, and said, "Gillian, which Farley Granger film?"

Gillian reacted with a blank look.

"He made two . . . with Hitchcock right?" Rachel elaborated. "*Rope* and *Strangers on a Train.*"

Oh my, another interesting aspect to this fascinating woman. She knows old movies. Gillian conferred silently with Sinistral who agreed.

After a moment Gillian realized that Rachel was referring to the videotape in Reggie's bedroom back in Vegas. "*Strangers on a Train,*" she answered as their eyes met. Gillian felt a long dormant flush in her chest and on her cheeks and a weakness in the muscles of her inner thighs. She responded to the rush with eloquent silence.

Rachel's focus shifted away from then back to Gillian. Their eyes locked for a heartbeat.

She averted her eyes, took a sip of water and looked at the sticky note in her hand. "Do you remember Bruno?" she asked. "And what was the name of the character Farley Granger played?"

"Guy Haines," Gillian replied, her flush slowly subsiding.

"Oh, yes, Guy." Rachel acknowledged the reply and noticed Jazz looking confused. "It was a movie, Jazz, an early nineteen fifties Alfred Hitchcock film. Guy and Bruno are two strangers who meet on a commuter train. They make small talk about their lives. Each of them has a person in his life that he feels keeps him from independent wealth or happiness. As a plan to solve each man's problem

Bruno suggests they commit each other's murders. This would leave no motive to trace back to the actual killer."

"So, Gillian," Rachel asked, "what do you think? You figure perhaps our girls are strangers on a cyber-train?" she mused more than asked, looking out the window at a yacht gliding up the inland waterway.

After a moment Rachel started, blinked hard as she gathered up her notes and headed for the door. "I have a few things I want to pursue. I'll be in touch later." She let herself out.

Chapter 34

An Occasional Man

Rachel stopped for a newspaper in the lobby. She shook her head at a headline below the fold: GAY U. OF WYOMING STUDENT CRUCIFIED ON A DESOLATE RURAL FENCE.

She stepped out of the dehydrated, super-chilled air of the Casbah del Mar and greeted the welcome humidity with a sober thought: Homophobia—alive and well in America.

Her Isuzu was sweltering but she didn't turn on the air conditioning right away.

Interesting team, Gillian and Jazz, Rachel thought as she headed north.

It's strange to feel that old rush of attraction to a woman after so long. It's okay to savor the echoing electricity, but that's all.

"Shit!" she uttered. "I know what I need. It's just been far too long," she said to the rearview mirror, "since I've indulged in my

'occasional man.' It's been weeks since I've even visited Ms. Turbator, "
she thought, alluding to the electrically operated lover who lived under her mattress.

At the next stoplight she activated her cell phone and switched on
the air. She scrolled to a contact and connected.

"City desk," announced a man's voice.

"Vincent Todaro, please," she said.

A pause and then a sorghum-smooth voice drawled, "Todaro."

"Vincent, Rachel Bracken here."

"Ah, Rachel, my love. How are things at the Beach?"

"Same old same old, Vincent, hope you're well. I need you to squir-
rel around and see what information you can dig up on that Enclave
case in your neck of the woods some twenty-plus years ago."

"Sure, I remember it. Anything in particular?" he asked.

"Yeah. All of it and I need some follow-up on the old man's boy,
one of the ones that got away . . . Clovis. Also, one of The Enclave's
victims, a Marcus Hollister. Just fax it to me, por favor and muchas
gracias. I'm going home and unplugging my phone."

"Just a moment, Rachel," he said and put her on hold. "Back.
Cassidy says some E.J. Dumase . . . Derfelt . . . anyway last name
began with a 'D', was searching for the same information—a couple
of months ago—July or August."

Hmmm, Rachel thought. That was well after the *Rolling Stone*
article. "Male or female?" she asked.

"Cassidy never saw the person. Handled the whole exchange by
e-mail. The guy—er, or gal dropped all the right names for Cassidy
to go out of his way and take the time. He's faxing the whole enchi-
lada to you right now."

"How did he know the last name began with a 'D' and what was
the e-mail address?"

"The person sent a thank you check. He cashed it. Didn't keep a
record. Didn't keep the e-mail addy either."

"You're aces, Vincent. Thanks and thank Cassidy."

Rachel manipulated the buttons again, "I need the area code for
Arkansas."

"What city?"

"Arkadelphia," she replied.

When she finally located Jim Sanders she found his eighty-eight year-old mind as sharp as ever. "On the off chance I can't dig up an answer I know exactly who to call to get it—my big brother Chet," he told her.

Jazz yawned. "I think I'll try to grab a few winks." He went into his room.

"Well, well, well," Gillian said after a minute. She clapped her hands and snapped her fingers to get out of her head and on with the day. "An invigorating swim. That's what I need," she announced to the empty room.

Gillian preferred swimming naked, but in deference to hotel protocol she eased into a tasteful, sage green swimsuit that exactly matched her eyes. She threw the hotel's complimentary—and sinfully plush—white terry cloth robe around her shoulders, donned sunglasses, dropped a half-used tube of greasy sunblock into the pocket of the robe, and strode to the elevator.

After ten vigorous laps in the tepid, seaside pool, the last vestiges of her energy drained from her body as smoothly as the chlorinated water slid from her well-oiled skin. She collapsed onto a faded pink, upholstered lounge chair. The salty sea air and hypnotic rhythm of the nearby surf lulled her into a deep doze. Moments later she found herself in a phone booth—underwater. Rose was with her. The folding door was rusted shut. They were trying to tip the booth over so they could escape.

Gillian was bone-and-gristle tired. "Gotta get us out," she sobbed. "Gotta save Rose!" She threw herself against a side of the booth again and again. "I'll get it next time," she vowed and prepared to throw herself into the glass one more time. The oxygen in the booth was almost exhausted. With the tenderest of touches, Rose slid her arm around Gillian's shoulder and nuzzled the spot where her neck and shoulder met. Gillian felt a thrill prickle her scalp and turned to look into Rose's eyes.

"Dear, sweet, Gilly," Rose said, "can't you see?" She made Gillian look down, "I am already dead?"

Rose's lifeless body lay on the floor of the booth.

Gillian sobbed, "No! noooo . . ."

"You have to save yourself now, my love." Rose faded. The phone booth faded and Gillian, gasping for breath, opened her eyes to the blinding Florida sun.

At eight forty-five p.m. Rachel heard her fax machine, and then the printer fired up. She flipped open her phone and dialed. "Sanders, you frosty old night owl. How the hell have you been? I'm sorry I was so abrupt this afternoon."

"I'm great and don't you give that another thought," he said. "I just sent you some information."

"Great. But, I thought we could talk. What did you dig up about young Marcus Hollister?"

"Well, I remembered his surviving a hotel fire that killed his parents. The hospital records have been purged, but my guy spoke to a night shift nurse at the hospital in Gurdon, Arkansas. She said she recalled the incident vividly. She was right out of nursing school and it was her first life-threatening burn case. She remembered Marcus and said she talked to an E.J. Dilley or some last name that started with a 'D' last spring about him."

Hmmmm, E.J.D. again. Rachel felt the twitch of a quizzical eyebrow.

"As a result of the depth of his third-degree burns, gangrene set in and Hollister's left hand was amputated. The nurse verified that."

"Ah. So that would explain the glove."

"Yep. You know how I've made it sort of a hobby to keep track of the unidentified John and Jane Does found in the state over the years? Well, there were a lot more of them when the mob ran Hot Springs and again during the Civil Rights movement. But anyway, a number of years after the fire in Gurdon, some human bones were found in the woods near another wide spot in the road called Malvern. There were animal teeth marks on the bones. A shard of a left ulna suggested that the hand might have been surgically removed. No positive identification was possible, but I always thought it was Hollister—until Hollister started preaching and being noticed."

"Hmmmm. So, what started the fire?"

"Hollister's father—smoking in bed."

Rachel felt a twinge. *What am I missing?* She signed off and realized she wasn't a bit tired.

She poured herself a glass of wine and went outside. She sat on a tilted chair, her feet propped on the balcony railing of her thirteenth-floor condo overlooking the beach. Her fingers flitted over the keys of her laptop as she used a special news bureau search engine to investigate Reggie, Jazz and Marcus Hollister. Most of the older information about them was limited to The Enclave incident. She read one of Hollister's more recent entries.

His dramatic eruption from the swamps of the Mississippi Delta to evangelical fame had come on the heels of a decade of heavy drinking in the juke joints of backwater Arkansas—a self-imposed exile from civilization. He reemerged to testify at revivals and tent shows along the riverbanks, elevating his ten-year-long debauchery to his "wilderness" experience. He soon amassed a following, his own ministry and a tidy bankroll.

Boy, there's nothing like a reformed debaucher. Rachel stared out at the black, silver-fringed surf and riffled through her mental phone list. "Who else might have a bit of pertinent information?" she asked the wind.

Well, I do remember an E.J.'s Bistro in Hollywood Beach. That would be way too easy. She got the number from information.

At the busy eatery up the coast a few miles, cultural artifacts from the Sixties and Seventies covered the walls and lent an informal atmosphere to the noisy place. She remembered that on the wall beside the register was a small, sun-bleached plank of driftwood burned with the phrase: The House That Pot Built.

E.J. was out of town. Rachel left her name and number.

Chapter 35
Rachel: Out & In

Gillian and Jazz plotted their immediate strategy over hot mugs of creamy early morning coffee. At least it was early morning by Vegas standards. Here in Miami it was after nine.

"Okay," sighed Jazz, still groggy after a fitful five-hour doze, "I'll take the passports to San Diego and keep track of Reggie." He rubbed his hand over the blond fuzz of his sparse morning beard.

"Cora got you on a charter flight to San Diego," Gillian said, checking her notes. "It's for some World War II fighter pilots' convention and they'll be picking up some folks in Atlanta and Dallas. She also booked you into a motel in Hillcrest for tonight and you'll pick up the rental car at the airport."

"Cool," said Jazz, planning aloud. "Then I'll find that house in Hillcrest this evening and put the passports in the mailbox once I figure out what's going on."

Reggie was his primary concern. He knew she would never do anything to harm him. He and Gillian would be within easy reach of each other with their cell phones.

"We'll deliver the other envelope to Belle," Gillian said, "and find out what we can about Marcus Hollister."

"I wonder . . ." Jazz hesitated, searching for the words. "I wonder if maybe Rachel should NOT be involved in this."

Gillian's expression couched a silent protest.

"I was just thinking, there's the matter of conflicting ethics if things happen." He hesitated. "Or if the law gets bent . . . or broken," he added solemnly. "No matter what, I don't want Reggie endangered—from either side of the legal system."

Gillian reluctantly agreed.

Jazz answered a knock at the door and Cora strode in brandishing a copy of *The Lincoln Road Informant* and lugging a huge pump pot of more hot coffee.

"This ought to start the good brother squirming!" Rachel said as she walked in behind Cora, reading her own copy of the small local paper.

Cora put the thermos on the bar and flourished *The Informant* like a matador's red cape. "Look what I have for you, Aunt Gillian!" said Cora, referring to the banner headline that asked: WHATEVER HAPPENED TO CLOVIS RANSOM?

"Wow, Cora!" Gillian took the paper and held it at arm's length. "This is perfect!"

"Well, you'll write the article for next month's issue," said Cora. "Write about how your research for mystery novels ties into the Clovis search. I'll bet our readership goes way up."

Gillian nodded with a smile. Cora poured herself half a cup of coffee and continued, "*The Informant* is only an ad-driven rag, you know. Its job is to entice customers to the Lincoln Road Mall. It's not really a newspaper, per se." She took a gulp of the piping hot brew.

That niece of mine always did have an asbestos throat.

"It's more of a newsy paper. So, the headline is sort of arbitrary. It's good to be boss." She finished off the coffee. "Oh, and by the way, four dozen copies were delivered to the cathedral this morning."

Gillian grinned. "Thanks!"

Cora kissed her on the cheek and smiled to Rachel and Jazz as she let herself out.

Rachel dropped her briefcase on the floor by the bar and poured herself a cup of coffee. She added a double glug of cream, hitched herself up on a barstool and picked up the conversation as though she had never left. "I spoke to Paducah." Gillian and Jazz turned matching quizzical faces toward her. "You know, Kentucky," she answered the looks. "Old news stories confirm the Google search. Bridget Clemens *was* a survivor of The Enclave."

She referred to her notes and went on, "Her family is British. They were working with the consulate in Washington, D.C. when she was snatched. The family searched for months, hired detectives and offered reward, you know, the usual. They finally gave up and went back to the father's boyhood home in Kenya, with some sort of loose attachment to the Peace Corps."

She skimmed the notes and continued. "There were three daughters . . . conflicting information as to where the first daughter was born, London or Kent. The twins were born in D.C. Dad taught them all to play the bagpipes, speak Swahili and some other African dialects. Bridget was born with a deviated septum or cleft palate—a harelip. Her younger twin sisters were named Haley and Belle. No congenital defects."

She looked up. "I checked the 'Net and the deformity occurs only about once in four hundred births."

She continued reading. "When Bridget was freed from The Enclave, the mother came back stateside, retrieved her daughter and returned to Kenya. A dozen years ago, both parents were killed in a boating accident. Bridget left Africa and moved back to America. She was a professional musician. One of her twin sisters, Haley Baxter, resides in Myrtle Beach, South Carolina, but is on an extended visit to Southeast Asia with her twin sister Belle McCreedy. I phoned Belle's home in New York," Rachel said. "I schmoozed up the resident housekeeper and she told me that all Belle's mail is being forwarded to Bridget's place in Miami Beach."

"Was?" asked Gillian a little slow on the uptake. "You said Bridget was a survivor and was a musician."

Rachel's demeanor sobered. "Oh, her body was found this spring—hanging from a rafter right in front of the pulpit in a—" She referred to her notes, "—Baptist church in Houston."

Jazz gasped.

"Oh, my," Gillian whispered.

After a moment Rachel continued, "Yeah, Bridget is dead." She paused. "And I have no idea who the woman is that's playing bagpipes at Hollister's cathedral," she added, "but it is not Bridget Clemens."

This bit of news hung in the air like a bad odor as they each contemplated the implications.

Jazz looked at his watch. The time was only seven forty am in Las Vegas. He broke the heavy silence, "Geez! You've been busy!"

"Most of my contacts are night people," she said and continued. "Marcus Hollister survived a hotel fire that killed his parents. Old hospital records have been purged, but my guy spoke to a night nurse at the hospital. She remembered the incident vividly. She remembered Marcus and said she talked to an E.J. Dilley or some 'D' name last spring—about him." Rachel looked up from her notebook, "It was after the *Rolling Stone* article."

"Maybe E.J. is a female. It could have been Reggie and company," Gillian interjected.

"Hmmmmmm." Rachel considered the possibility and scribbled something in the notebook. Then she went on. "Here's an interesting bit of information." Her voice took on a conspiratorial tone. "Because of complications, Hollister's left hand was amputated."

Gillian and Jazz were startled, once again, by a verbal bomb.

Rachel held one palm outward to stave off questions until she finished. "Last night I chatted with a buddy who is an old, I mean old, reporter in Arkadelphia, Arkansas. He said that ten or twelve years after the fire in Gurdon, some gnawed-on human bones were found in the woods. The end of a left ulna looked as though the hand had been surgically removed. No positive identification was possible, but my buddy always thought it was Hollister—until Hollister started preaching in nineteen eighty-nine."

"Wow," Gillian said softly.

"If Hollister's left hand isn't a prosthetic device," Jazz chimed in, "that would be evidence that the man is an impostor, right?"

"I used to think the white glove he wore was an affectation like the teenage Michael Jackson," Rachel said. "The old guy is searching the records in central and southern Arkansas for me, trying to find any mention of Clovis—legal, medical or evangelical. *The Informant*," she read from the paper, "says there is a Saturday twilight service and Dark of the Moon Show at the Rainbow Refectory and two services on Sunday. What do you say we drive Jazz to the airport now and go hang out at the cathedral? You could sort of get an idea of how the place operates, see if that headline caused any stir, maybe do a little sleuthing," she added. "I'll let you talk this over." She excused herself and walked into the master suite.

She dialed her cell. "Hi, Esther. We will see you at the Rainbow today. Thanks."

"What do you think?" Gillian asked Jazz.

"Well it seems we have to reevaluate Rachel's role—again. Her professional connections and talents are certainly invaluable," Jazz admitted.

"I think we would be foolish to let her go," Gillian offered.

"Yeah." Jazz sighed, "I agree."

"I'll talk to her about your concerns for Reggie's safety," Gillian assured him. "And I'll broach the subject of any legal ramifications."

She and Jazz programmed their cell phones to speed dial one another with the single numeral nine. Stealth took some forethought.

"*Gillian*," Sinistral nudged verbally, "*I've got an idea for a story!*"

Gillian hoped Sinistral didn't notice that she rolled her eyes.

Traffic was brisk across the causeway after they dropped Jazz at the air terminal. In the air-conditioning of Rachel's Rodeo, Gillian relaxed and covertly checked out Rachel's profile. *That slash of color in her hair is really quite cool,* she thought, *sort of a fashion statement. I rather like it.* As they made their way back to the beach Gillian said, "Rachel?"

"Hmm?" Rachel replied.

"What is your . . ." She searched for the words, ". . . legal policy if a client breaks the law? Or in the course of investigating—a law is breached?"

Rachel's slight smile lifted one corner of her mouth. "Well, Gillian, I play that by ear. If I feel uncomfortable with a case, I just withdraw. I won't jeopardize my client, my case or my own code. I'll let you know how things feel. Okay?"

Gillian nodded. "Nice car," she added.

"Ah, this ride," Rachel replied. "Lots of room, good visibility and there are so many of them, I fade into the traffic when I'm tailing someone."

Gillian broke the brief silence that usually follows when women discuss cars. "I just had an idea. I'm going to do a new book about The Enclave and the aftermath."

"A bit serious for Sinistral, isn't it?" Rachel asked.

"Oh, well, we all grow up," Gillian answered, "But, do you think that would land me an interview with Marcus Hollister?"

Rachel chuckled, admiring the ingenuity. Then she smiled and nodded. "That would also explain my involvement. I'm a research assistant gathering information for you."

Rachel's gleeful smile, turned full on Gillian, flowed like honey down into her chest. *I freaking love that diamond.* Her eyes lingered on the base of Rachel's perfect nose where the stone sparkled like a tiny dewdrop on a pale pink rose. *Oh, dear, I'm still such a push-over.* She grinned, relishing the feeling. She stared down at the posh houseboats moored along the glassy channel, and asked, "How do you feel about big dogs?"

Sinistral beamed!

Chapter 36
Dead Woman Flying

The dark-haired woman with the hooked nose and harelip spoke in a loud, irritating voice. Her words were a bit distorted by a slightly deformed upper lip and a British accent. Her bangs slashed a severe line above her dated, oversized glasses. She was making a fuss about the flight to San Diego. She bought the ticket, but let it be known to all around her that she was unhappy about the price.

"It's so much more than I saw advertised," she groused. The woman behind the counter explained once again that the lower price was for booking a flight ahead of time, not the day of the flight.

The irate woman turned and spoke to the man behind her. "I'm buying this ticket for a flight later today—what possible difference could it make when I book it? It's corporate thievery!" She twisted down and around and made sure he looked into her face.

The man was bored with the delay—but he clearly did notice her face. It was flushed with anger.

She huffed her way to the nearest restroom. In a stall she lowered the lid and sat down on the oval seat. She pulled down the little metal shelf and set up a mirror.

She pulled off the device that depressed the skin running through her upper lip to her nostril. She wrapped the contraption in toilet paper and placed it in her purse. She pulled the false bridge from her nose and rubbed the lip area, massaging cream into the crease until it softened. The oversized glasses and long, brown wig went into the bag also. With a large hair pick she shaped her unruly locks into a barely restrained shoulder-length mane of mahogany red curls. She placed the ticket she'd purchased into a brown envelope.

Belle, now looking her vivacious self, stepped from the restroom and strode back to the ticketing area holding a brown envelope. She spotted a woman wearing exactly the same get-up she had just removed. She walked up beside her and slipped the brown envelope with the airline ticket into her hands. The woman turned and walked away. From that moment on, whenever anyone spoke to that Bridget impersonator, she would hold her hand to her throat and mutter her only word of English, "Laryngitis." In San Diego she would lose the disguise and board her flight home to Guyana.

"Good morning, Belle! Welcome back!" Belle smiled to her own reflection as she strode out the terminal door.

The traffic was unusually light along the causeway this Friday morning. She pulled the disguise on before she got into her own neighborhood. There was an envelope propped in her screen door. The envelope contained her passport. *Good.* She studied the last few stamps in the little blue book, and nodded. She did not notice the gray Rodeo parked across the street.

Belle opened the door and was greeted by a familiar fluorescent bulb-like buzz. The glass vivarium was densely planted. She cooed to her charges as she checked the misting system and tapped some special food into their habitat. The formulated blend mimicked their native nourishment and kept their poison production deadly. Without that special formula the tiny frogs were just colorful pets.

The wee buzzing frogs were classified as Dendrobates Azureus. They sported brilliant blue undersides and legs. They differed from one another only in the pattern of the shiny black spots on their turquoise backs. On the front top of the tank hung a small wooden sign that said: dendro-*Bate's Motel.*

A few minutes later Belle returned to the tank and cooed, "Well, my little pretties, it's time to earn your keep." She set a small silver case on the table near the tank. She raised the hammered-silver lid, revealing several pairs of stud earrings wedged into velvet slots. She pried up the floor of the box. On the right side of this layer were four tiny pretreated darts inserted sharp-end-first into holes designed specifically for this purpose. Each hole lay directly beneath an earring slot.

The first step was almost as familiar as writing her name. She had prepared darts many, many times while living in Africa, although not using this particular poison source.

Four untreated, fletched slivers, each not much bigger than a thorn, filled the slots on the left. She considered treating them. "Nah," she uttered. "If four darts don't get this job done I'm not sticking around for a war." She left the untreated slivers in the left half of the receptacle.

For the next, less familiar step she would need to make some preparations and take some precautions.

She blew air into a pair of rubber gloves to check for leaks, slipped them on her hands and rolled up the extra-long cuffs to cover her forearms. She opened the deep tank and selected a tiny blue frog. She held the creature in a gentle, yet firm grip. The beating of its heart against her rubber-clad fingertips felt like a tiny, vibrating cell phone. She held the colorful creature near the warmth of a lightbulb until a bead of moisture formed on its back. Deftly she withdrew a pretreated sliver from the right side of the silver case and dipped the tip of the dart into the drop of venom on the frog's brilliant back. After a moment, she returned the sliver to its slot. She repeated this procedure with the second, third and fourth slivers, placing each in the slot provided. She returned the frog to its tank and secured the lid. She tugged the gloves inside out and put them in a small cardboard container. She replaced the earring-studded layer and snapped the little silver box shut. She placed the cardboard box containing the contaminated gloves in a toxic waste disposal container.

The darts had been purchased in Amsterdam last month. The customs guy had barely looked at the contents of the little silver box—the earrings were simple, obviously inexpensive. The hidden darts were pretreated with toxin from the Phyllobates Terribilis, the most venomous of the jewel-like frogs. The second treatment from Bridget's blue buzzers would boost each dart's potency and speed its effect.

Belle always took precautions. She blew into a slender tube and peered down its interior to be sure it was unobstructed. Actually, the whole tropical frog business was her sister Bridget's thing. Belle grew pensive remembering that she had fallen heir to the hobby and all its accrued apparatus—as well as a new mission in life—just last spring.

She slipped the hollow tube into the special pocket set into the inseam of the left knee-high boot of the pair she would wear tomorrow night.

Chapter 37
Casing Rainbows

Rachel and Gillian parked a block from the Rainbow Refectory complex and locked all their unnecessary belongings in the little safe between the front seats of the Rodeo. Rachel pulled a sleeve-like sock up her leg. It fit snugly just above her ankle. She slipped a few dollars into a pocket in the sock. She added her PI license and the safe key. She pulled a compact .38 automatic from the locked glove box and double-checked to see if the cartridge clip was full and one was in the chamber. She tucked the car key into the hideout sock and slid the gun into a holster nestled in the small of her back. It did not break the line of the classic lightweight pantsuit she wore. She considered slipping an extra clip into her sock. Nah, she thought and admonished herself for even considering it.

Gillian kept some money, her driver's license and a little red Swiss Army knife.

The Refectory's foyer was spacious and uncluttered, white marble, beveled-glass and light everywhere. Gillian picked up a flyer about tomorrow night's service and read the name of their treasured resident soloist—bagpiper Bridget Clemens.

"I thought she was supposed to be in Houston," Gillian whispered.

"Not to mention . . . dead," Rachel added.

A dozen or so visitors milled in the circular vestibule and took photos of the grandeur. Blue velvet ropes and two large, steel-haired men in identical gray suits blocked admittance to the long hall off the lobby.

"Tweedle Dee and Tweedle Duh," Sinistral sneered.

On the same counter as the flyer was a stack of Cora's *Informants*. The headline blared the question about Clovis. Gillian picked up several, as did Rachel, intending to leave them here and there, improving the chance they'd be seen and read. A moment later a small, rat-like man in a white linen suit surged from the crowd behind Gillian and swept up all the remaining *Informants*.

"Oh," he said to a woman who was just reaching for one. "These are last week's issue." He hugged the papers to his chest and turned away. "I'll bring back the current ones, momentarily," he added and scurried up the hall.

One guard unhooked and held the rope aside for him. Gillian gave the woman one of hers and set the rest back on the table. Rachel did the same except for one she rolled up and carried with her.

"This is the current issue," the woman told her companion. "I wonder why he thought it wasn't."

Rachel followed her instincts—and a cleaning lady dressed all in pink—to a small side door that gave access to the complex's sanctum sanctorum. A gaggle of women wearing similar pink dust caps, pale pink hospital scrubs and oversized sheepskin slippers drifted soundlessly throughout the vast amphitheater. Their sheepskin-shod feet polished the white marble floors as they systematically moved about dusting and burnishing the pews and every surface in the vast beveled glass cavern. Every pink-clad woman wore a matching mask covering the lower part of her face. They looked like a cheerful group of industrious medical students gleefully gathering to witness their first autopsy.

The pews were a blinding white. All the metal surfaces were chrome. Huge rolls of carpet were chocked at the top of each aisle. Gillian half expected a fog machine to float a layer of mist on the white marble floors and complete the dreamlike, rock concert effect.

"The stage is gigantic," Gillian whispered.

"His sermons are extravaganzas," Rachel whispered back. "There's always fire and lightning and sometimes floods."

They stepped out from under a dropped ceiling at the back of the hall. Directly above them, where the cathedral walls began to curve to form the dome, a bank of mirrors slanted inward.

"Behind those mirrors are the security and control booths," Rachel said.

The one-way glass was barely perceptible because it reflected the alabaster whiteness and light of the interior.

Stepping back under the overhang, Rachel pointed out the various stations of interest in the spacious vaulted room. In the center front stood a dazzling white pulpit. Behind that, a deep stage sprawled practically from wall to wall.

"The pulpit raises and lowers to below floor level. Leaves a clear view of the show," Rachel said.

To the left of the stage stood a magnificent white organ embellished with silver vines and flowers that matched the chromium graduated pipes, the tallest reaching almost to the dome. On the right a small balcony jutted out some twenty-feet above the floor. It provided a spot for the soloist. The Bridget impersonator would have to play a bagpipe solo there tomorrow night. The choir loft was at the same level on the opposite wall. Along both sides were the required exit signs over large double doors.

Rachel's whispering lips brushed Gillian's ear sending tiny shock waves cascading along neuronal paths lighting up all her erogenous zones and curling up her toes. Her eyes shot wide.

"Up there, on the left," Rachel whispered. "Look past the dais.

See that small door? That one accesses Hollister's private quarters."

Neither that door nor another on the back wall had an exit sign, only a tiny red light above each.

Replacing traditional stained glass windows depicting saints and the Stations of the Cross were monumental leaded, beveled glass windows stretching skyward and curving to form a dome where a huge multifaceted crystal orb rotated refracting rainbows everywhere. Inadvertently Hollister had introduced the definitive symbol of gayness in the latter twentieth century to surround a congregation that reviled the lifestyle. The women grinned at the irony of a disco ball at the apex.

"The architect must have been on my home team," Gillian whispered.

"Or perhaps just influenced by *Priscilla, Queen of the Desert*," Rachel added. "But Hollister, ever capable of turning lemons into lemonade, recouped by renaming his cathedral the Rainbow Refectory and his mission, Reclaiming the Rainbow."

Gillian watched with curiosity as Rachel dialed a number on her cell phone. "That—" she gestured upward with her eyes and her head, "is more than likely where the 'messenger' roosts, too. I read," Rachel whispered, "that the cathedral's systems manager was in charge of an Atlantic City showroom before he came to work for Brother Marcus. It was in an article about the Rainbow Refectory's vast array of lighting and sound effects."

Two heartbeats later a wiry and mature black cleaning lady stood upright and casually checked her vibrating beeper. She began gliding up the aisle toward them. She came to a stop at a supply cart parked in the aisle ten feet away. She lifted a limp bundle from a lower shelf of the cart, set it on the floor and straightened up. While she busied her gnarled hands spraying a clean rag with some aerosol antistatic solution, she nudged the bundle under the pew. With a sharp punt, she scooted it back to the last pew right in front of them. Then she sprayed her woolly slippers, tucked a few damp strands of silver hair into her cap and pushed the cart toward the front.

Rachel stepped up and grasped the back of the pew with both

hands, leaned on her straightened arms and casually surveyed the arena. Covertly, with her right foot, she hooked the bundle and slid it back to Gillian who picked it up and tucked it under her arm.

Sinistral gave Gillian a mental high five.

In a restroom they ripped open the bundle and found two clipboards with attached pens, two sets of booties, face masks and dust caps in the same pale pink as that of the cleaning crew and a box of surgical gloves. But, instead of tops and pants there were two full-length exam coats that fit easily over their street clothes.

"Esther comes through again," Rachel enthused. "She's a fine woman. Lost a daughter to Jonestown. I made arrangements with her this morning." She gestured to the badges clipped to the collars of the coats. "The folks these belong to are on vacation." Rachel's attached badge bore a mug shot of an older woman with long gray hair. Gillian's belonged to a tall, young black man with good bone structure . . . oh, well. She flipped the badge to the reverse side and trusted people's inattention to detail.

Rachel's clipboard held a hand-drawn layout of the complex. Adjusting their surgical masks they reentered the sanctuary. Rachel crammed the wrapping from the bundle deep into the large trash pocket on a cleaning cart that she and her fellow inspector scooted past. Gillian filched a can of polish and a cloth.

As the inspectors edged their way to the service door, they heard a sharp, "*Pssst!*"

They turned in time to see ten cleaning women each nod three times in unison, then strike the chocks holding the five tightly coiled carpet cylinders, allowing them to unfurl down the converging aisles. The runners whirred as they shot downward like blurred, tumbling silver daggers aimed at the pulpit. Gillian and Rachel stared at the spectacle in silence, glanced at each other then returned to their task at hand.

Rachel said under her breath, "Always move with confidence, the cameras are on and often monitored."

The diagram showed the first door labeled equipment room. That was where a cleaning person would normally go. "The second door is marked Stairs," Rachel said. "Now, we chat about our clipboards, push through this door, turn right down the hall and turn directly into the second door on the left." She paused. "Ready? Now!"

While Gillian expected a little more originality from Rachel, she conceded that professional maintenance people did tend to achieve a certain invisibility. Not only that, they were needed regularly and usually had access to everywhere and anywhere in a complex. Plus, the diagram Rachel's contact had drawn was quite detailed. The service stairways didn't seem to be under surveillance except at the main floor entrance. Gillian wondered what the odds were that they would remain unnoticed when they walked through that second door.

Gillian pushed the bar and shouldered the door open. She held it open and Rachel brushed past her. The door closed behind them with a barely audible *whoosh* and a click. They feigned interest in Rachel's clipboard and, chatting idly, strode past the first door on the left and through the second. Once they were off camera they pulled down their face masks and breathed sighs of relief.

On the first landing Rachel pushed a door open. It was a small dressing room. Straight through the room was an opening covered by a heavy, black curtain. She pushed it aside and stepped onto the soloist balcony.

Gillian's phone vibrated. "Aunt Gillian!" Cora's voice came over the phone a little too loud.

Rachel grimaced and Gillian let the curtain fall back over the opening and whispered, "A little softer, honey. We're snooping in the Rainbow now."

"Oh, okay. Guess who just called me?" She posed the question in a stage whisper.

Rachel stepped back into the room.

"I can't imagine," Gillian answered smiling to herself.

"Marcus Hollister, himself!" Cora dropped the name like a bag of buckshot.

"Oh, my, why?" Her eyes met Rachel's.

"He wanted to know about the Clovis story and invited me to do an interview with him . . . hehehe," Cora ended with a snicker.

"Wow!" Gillian whispered. "We suspected something was afoot when they swept in and removed the stack of *Informants* from the lobby. I'll be in touch, thanks so much!" She disconnected before Cora could tell her to be careful. "Did you hear that?" she asked Rachel. Rachel nodded.

They continued up the stairs. The door at the top opened onto a narrow corridor. After a hundred and fifty feet or so the hallway turned right and widened to about twenty feet across. Cantilevered smoky glass windows all along the right-hand wall provided Gillian an unobstructed view of the sanctuary and a touch of vertigo when she looked down. The sanctuary viewed through the backside of the mirrored glass was dim and foreboding.

Almost the entire left side of the wide hallway held items stored in an orderly fashion. The first racks held vestments, choir robes and several suits that would have caused Elvis to turn and stare—all stored in transparent, zippered bags. Under the racks stood multiple pairs of shoes in boxes or plastic-wrapped in perfect ranks. Beyond the clothes racks were stacks and stacks of chairs and long, folded banquet tables. There appeared to be thousands of each.

Up ahead, another hundred feet or so, two box-like structures jutted into the hall. The word SECURITY was stenciled in no-non-sense letters on the window of the first door. Directly across the hall, between the stacks of chairs, was a large utility elevator and next to it a door marked RESTROOM. Rachel listened for a moment at the security door then peeked in. No one was at the controls. A dozen monitors displayed ongoing scenes from many vantage points on the vast property. Some of the cameras covered the pews where two thousand followers would sit during the service. Cameras focused on the door to the left of the dais where Marcus would enter the sanctuary, as well as the outer lobby, the halls leading up to the main areas and the entrances. The parking lot was also under observation.

"Pretty heavy security for a house of worship," Rachel pointed out.

Running water followed the sound of a toilet flush. Gillian and Rachel pulled back into the shadows among the stacks of chairs. The restroom door opened. A security guard emerged. His thinning hair looked damp, as did the opened collar of his uniform shirt. The tails of his loosened tie were shoved between the third and fourth button on the front of his shirt. He paused, an expression of pain twisting his face, and then he turned and dashed back into the facility.

Rachel grinned and took advantage of the guard's obvious gastric distress to slip into the surveillance room and do a quick equipment check. It was fairly basic. Flickering monitors were labeled by location. She picked up one of the several walkie-talkies charging on the counter and slipped it into a pink pocket. She noticed a couple of weak spots in the camera system that she knew she could sabotage pretty easily. To begin with, she maneuvered the knob that directed the remote controlled camera in the service hall, aiming it a little higher. That way a person could turn toward the equipment room, duck down and enter under the utility stairs undetected. Once she accomplished this, she removed the knob. She pulled a pen from several standing in a coffee cup on the desk, inserted it in the stem of the knob and spread it until half of the stem broke off. She reinserted the useless knob into the hole and put the broken piece in her pocket.

The toilet flushed. She replaced the pen and got back to the stacks just as the guard emerged from the restroom. They both held their breath as they watched him return to his booth. They moved on.

Just beyond the security room the hall opened up for a dozen feet. Then there was a second cubicle equipped with a desk, chair, microphone, pads, pencils, computer, a high-intensity lamp and a few reference books. Rachel thought it was probably the post of the voice that whispered in Marcus's ear. The room was dimmer than the hall. Rachel gave the area a thorough scan. She stooped and fished out a crumpled piece of paper from the shadows behind the wastebasket. She flattened it and they both bent over to read the writing in the dim light. The cryptic scrawl said *Luv Parks wants to know if Simon will ever stop gambling. (right side-front)*

"Bingo!" Rachel gloated. She smiled at Gillian and touched her arm lightly. Gillian felt a distinct twang in her chest that had nothing to do with Luv Parks or her compulsive Simon.

Wow, my magic twanger still works! She smiled back. There it was again—the eye lock. Rachel in a pink dust cap and pink scrubs was, without a doubt, the single most desirable woman with whom Gillian had ever prowled a church.

"Exciting, isn't it?" Rachel queried with what might be construed as a double entendre or perhaps even mind reading.

Gillian grinned more broadly yet.

I love the zipper of smile lines that run up her cheeks when she grins. They're like multiple parentheses framing her glee. Rachel blinked at the intensity of her own thought. She shrugged. "I've got an idea." She chuckled to cover her perplexing feelings, unfurled her copy of *The Informant* and circled the name Clovis in the headline and scribbled: *Ask about this! Alice B. Tokemore (left of center)* She laid the paper on the desk.

They looked out for the guard then circled the structure. The entrance to the sound and light booth was accessed from the opposite direction. While the booths shared a common wall, that wall did not have a door. The sound and light booth had two chairs, a long desk, a large soundboard, earphones, a computer, a panel to control the banks of lights and a hand-operated device to aim a spotlight mounted outside the one-way glass. The choir loft was to the left and down twenty feet or so. The small balcony for the guest soloist was at the same level on the right. Gillian was having fun. After all, this was a church! What could happen if they were caught sneaking around? She was just researching a story. Right?

Rachel walked back to the monitor's desk. "We could distract this guy," she suggested. "Somehow get him out of here and talk to Hollister ourselves." Her cell vibrated. She flipped it open. It was Mahoney in northern California. "Hey, K.C." Rachel whispered and listened. "Thanks."

After a moment Rachel, in hushed tones, said, "My contact in California says that escaped Enclave pervert Billy Ray Ripley is on the move and heading for Cardiff-by-the-Sea or Encinitas. Let's go." She glanced at the clock on the wall. "The cleaning crew will be getting ready to leave about now."

Gillian was calling to warn Jazz about the pedophile's approach and striding toward the stairs right behind Rachel. Too late for them to get out of sight, the security guard emerged from his surveillance booth. Gillian's stomach clenched. Rachel was quick on her feet. With one continuous move she turned to her right, lifted her face mask into place and grabbed a chair off the top of a stack. She signaled for Gillian to do the same. Holding the chair so that it covered most of her badge, she walked directly toward the guard.

"Smile!" she hissed.

Gillian did.

He had seen a movement, but was startled to see the two pink creatures emerging from the shadows.

"Hi," Rachel said with muffled enthusiasm. "We were just getting a couple of chairs to put in the changing room . . . you know, so we can sit down when we change our shoes . . . and stuff."

The guard started to turn and gesture to the stacks and stacks closer to the stairs. Rachel stopped him halfway. She looked down at the chair she carried. "Green . . . you know, to match the . . . green room!" Gillian held up her chair to cover her ebony badge picture. Her smile weakened and she hoped he would not notice her chair was purple.

"Ah," the guard acknowledged their sense of decor, and led them all the way to the stair doorway. He held the door open as they passed him. He gave them a thin smile and hurried back toward the restroom before the door whooshed shut.

Rachel and Gillian power-walked out of the Rainbow high on adrenaline after their close encounter of the scary kind. Rachel said, "Let's take a swim break. There's a very cool beach a mile or so north of your hotel. I always keep a suit in my trunk."

"Sure . . ." Gillian had not a clue why she sounded so hesitant. Sinistral poked her. Hard. "Actually, that sounds great," Gillian said.

They loped to the Rodeo laughing like hyperactive teenagers.

Chapter 38
On The Beach

Haulover Beach was almost deserted for a late Friday afternoon. Rachel sized up the area, and whipped off her bikini top. The crashing surf muffled the sound of Gillian's sharp intake.

Twirling the strip of cloth Rachel said with a grin, "Did I mention that it's a suit optional beach?"

"No," Gillian laughed. "I'm sure I would've remembered that." The air was salty and the blossoming trees at the edge of the sand were abuzz with pollinating bees. Their foray for nectar stirred up the flowers and added a heavy hint of honey to the sea breeze.

The lingering adrenaline, the nostalgic bouquet and the slightly risqué situation made Gillian feel suddenly . . . frisky. She trotted to catch up to the semi-clad woman striding boldly along the beach. They walked to the water's edge and skimmed flat stones and shards of seashells through the frothy curls that rushed to swirl around their feet.

Offshore a pod of surfers waited for the next big wave. Now and then the wind grabbed their gleeful whoops and cheers and wafted them in with the surf.

"Were you surprised that I brought you to a nude beach?" asked Rachel, breaking the silence but not taking her eyes off the horizon.

"Pleasantly," Gillian answered and skimmed another shell.

"I knew if I waited for you to do something," Rachel went on, "we would be at the airport sending you back to Vegas before you spoke up." She paused. "And I didn't want . . . not to know . . . what you would be like."

Gillian's face and neck felt suddenly bloodless and her ears roared. She squelched an inner protest and reached to weave Rachel's slender manicured fingers with her own. Their feet left twin trails of prints in the narrow wet band of darker sand that greeted the incoming tide. Simple words like . . . nice and fun slipped into her thoughts. Their shoulders were dead even and their hands swung at the same level. Gillian glanced at Rachel's profile and slid her eyes down over the graceful elegance of her small breasts. A wry smile crept around the corners of Rachel's mouth as she felt Gillian's eyes caress her.

Gillian stopped and disengaged her hand. She shrugged out of her suit top. Her own breasts were on the B-side of small and retained their firmness, albeit, at a slightly lower elevation. She dangled her top by a crooked finger and hung it over one shoulder. She took Rachel's hand again and they strolled on.

"I'm for a swim," Rachel said and stepped out of the rest of her suit. It lay on the sand like so much flotsam washed ashore.

Gillian uttered a low moan that was half growl and reached for Rachel's waist pulling her breasts to her own, feeling the contact between thousands of mutual nerve endings. Her head felt light when she pressed her lips to Rachel's.

Rachel dropped to the sand and pulled Gillian down. They faced each other feeling the grit under their knees. She took Gillian's face in her hands, slid her hands deep into her salted brown hair and pressed her own kisses on Gillian's waiting mouth.

Gillian enfolded Rachel's slim body. There was no hurry. She felt her passion reciprocated. She melted into this astounding woman . . . this thrilling woman . . . this magnificent woman. The smell of her and the salty sea air swirling with the scent of honey filled Gillian with the sense of possibilities.

She was back in life. Kneeling in the gritty sand at this precise spot on the planet was exactly where life intended her to be. She was feeling long untapped passions with the perfect person with whom she was destined to share this little slice of time.

A small voice speaking Spanish sweetly insinuated its way into her consciousness. At first she thought it was Rachel's voice in her ear but she felt her startle, also.

By increments Gillian realized where she was—felt the daylight—became aware of the public situation, the unknown laws and a small, naked child standing beside them. Only then, with Venusian effort, was she able to withdraw her embrace and hold Rachel at arm's length. They both looked down and grinned.

A little brown cherub of a girl punctuated her singsong phrases with a tiny salute that shaded one squinting, jet-black eye from the afternoon sun. She turned, did a little jump and scampered up the beach with jubilant delight.

A wide-eyed Gillian looked at Rachel for an interpretation.

"Tender kisses are like angel smiles," she translated.

Gillian grinned. They agreed there had been nothing angelic about those kisses. They reluctantly surrendered to the idea of deferred pleasure.

"Now, I could really use a swim," Rachel said. "How about you?" She turned and trotted into the breaking surf. Gillian watched with profound appreciation. She stripped off the rest of her bathing suit, then, ever the Virgo, gathered it up with Rachel's and tossed them both up the beach away from the rising tide. She sprinted in gleeful, naked pursuit and sliced a breaking wave with her outstretched fingertips.

Chapter 39
Cars, Planes and Commuter Trains

Jazz's flight landed at four o'clock San Diego time. Arriving planes usually made a sharp westward descent, skimming over the hills that sloped abruptly to the bustling city on the harbor, but today's final glide took them eastward from offshore.

When he picked up the peppy, low-key Japanese car awaiting him at the airport, he admired Cora's taste. He bought a *Thomas Street Guide to San Diego and Vicinity*, a thermos bottle, several candy bars, a Padres baseball cap and, as an afterthought, a pair of oversized, mirrored aviator sunglasses from a rack.

Jazz parked and went into a gourmet coffee shop on Harbor Drive. On the passenger seat of the little rental car his cell phone vibrated several times in his absence.

He climbed back in the car, toting the full thermos and savoring a steaming, paper-collared cup of sweetened espresso. He headed east toward the little urban community of Hillcrest mere minutes from the airport.

Variegated flags fluttered boldly along the business district streets. Many automobiles sported rear windows that shimmered with oily, multicolored tints and the preponderance of rainbow-themed yard ornaments bore witness to the gay community's foothold in the area. Jazz followed the narrow streets as they skirted the canyons and wound behind Mercy Hospital.

A low chain-link fence surrounded the front yard of the little pink house on Arbor Drive. There was no car in the driveway, nor any parked in front. A frayed rope swing swayed from a gnarled branch of a pepper tree that drooped over the tiny yard. A mailbox attached to the gate of the three-foot fence was too small for the blue-and-white cardboard envelope containing the passports.

The louvered shutters were cracked for ventilation, revealing the flashing blue signal of a television playing. He parked and watched.

The sun set around half past six and the cool evening fog rolled in. Jazz pulled his Windbreaker on and rolled up the windows. He crossed his arms and, slouching down in the seat, tucked his fingers in his armpits for warmth. He watched. And watched.

Eventually, a light went on in the television room, another illuminated the other front window briefly, and then went out. He watched. He downed the last of the tepid coffee directly from the thermos.

At about ten he heard the theme music of *Law and Order*, Reggie's favorite television show. An hour later, the closing theme cut off and the light went out. He could hear someone closing the windows and the shutters. A light went on in another window. In ten minutes the house went dark.

He waited an hour, then drew a deep breath and stepped from the car. He strolled past the house to the corner and back. There was no activity on the sleepy block. He lifted the latch with the silent stealth of a cat burglar, and pushed the gate open. *Screeeech!*

The bottom edge of the sagging gate dragging over the uneven sidewalk resounded like two-dozen grimy fingernails scraping across a blackboard. It echoed in the foggy street, magnified by the background hush. Jazz blanched and stood stock still. Nothing. He reminded himself to take a breath, lifted slightly on the gate and opened it up all the way. He went up the short, cracked concrete walkway and climbed the three faded and peeling barn-red steps. He propped the oversized envelope against the screen door and made his way back to his car before he exhaled.

He checked the mirror and pulled smoothly away from the curb. He zigzagged up a few streets and wended down a few others. He couldn't drive around the block because of the canyons but after a few dead-ends, wound up across the street from the house again. He could see the envelope.

"Sweet dreams, Reggie," he whispered and went to the motel to grab some sleep.

Parked in front of his motel room, his spiffy rental car clicked as the engine cooled. His cell phone vibrated a few times. Then all was silent.

Chapter 40
No Turning Back

At seven thirty the next morning the envelope was still propped against the screen door on Arbor Drive. Vestiges of an evening fog bank lingered. The tinted windows of Jazz's little white rental car shrouded his presence even in the daylight. So he settled in. He unwrapped his Breakfast Jack and munched away. When he finished the last french fry he put all the trash into the little white bag. He finished the piping hot coffee, added the covered cup to the trash bag, twisted the top and tossed it in the backseat. Time passed.

He felt his eyelids drooping so he reached for the thermos of fresh black coffee. He poured a cup and noted the time—nine fifty-five. He unwrapped a candy bar, chewed it slowly and melted the chocolate from his teeth with the hot coffee. The damp morning mist was burning away and the sun was peeking through. The air grew balmy and the closed car got a little stuffy. He opened the passenger side windows halfway and lowered the left rear window an inch or two. The soft flow of air made it easier to breathe.

Jazz concentrated on the house and tried to pick up Reggie's vibes. More hours passed. He nearly dozed off. He poured more coffee. The envelope was still there. The sun passed its zenith and headed for the ocean. He drove to a nearby gas station to use the restroom. He wasn't gone fifteen minutes. The envelope was still there. He dozed.

The car got hotter. He rolled the passenger side windows all the way down. For a few minutes he watched in distracted fascination the blur of a gray-and-white mockingbird darting and thrusting at a very fat, very annoyed red cat. The bird kept up the harassment until the intruding feline scurried down the street and away from the bird's nest. *Scrappy little shit, just like my Reggie.* He looked back at the pink house and sighed.

"Whatcha doin', Mister?" The tiny voice wrenched his attention and he whipped his head around and for a moment thought maybe he'd dozed off and imagined the voice. He lowered his startled, wide-eyed gaze directly into a small dirt-smudged boy's clear blue eyes staring from the bottom edge of the window.

Jazz's whole body jerked again and his heart flew into high gear. Fortunately the plastic thermos cup he'd fumbled was almost empty and not enough time had elapsed to allow the coffee to reach his bladder. As he attempted to reinstate his composure, he briskly fanned his face with the *Thomas Guide*. The voice from the little mouth hidden by the car door said, "You got a pretty ear."

Jazz reached up to touch the row of earrings and said, "Thank you."

Then he pulled his tinted glasses down, peered over the rims and growled, "Didn't your mommy ever tell you not to talk to strangers?"

The little boy jumped back to the sidewalk and his eyes flew open. "You're a stranger?" He ran off screaming, arms flailing, into a maze of bungalows to the south.

"Oh, no," Jazz analyzed. "This could be trouble!"

He started the car and darted from the curb without a look or a signal. An ear-grating skid was accompanied by the impotent protest of a tinny, falsetto horn and a decidedly female British voice yelling, "Bugger!" A pale blue Fiat stood just short of his left front fender.

"Odd," mumbled Jazz, "Brits are usually such polite drivers!" He watched in the rearview mirror as he proceeded to the corner. The Fiat backed into the driveway at 419. By the time he turned around and cruised past the house, the woman who drove the Fiat was inside and the envelope was gone.

Jazz pulled around the corner and negotiated a U-turn, not an easy task on such a narrow street. He parked between two other white cars on the street that abutted Arbor Drive to the west. From this vantage point he could see the front of the Fiat and both escape routes. He was sipping coffee directly from the thermos when he saw Reggie open the hood of the little car.

Oh, God, she looks great. She was wearing blue jeans and a white T-shirt. Tears filled his eyes. She and a dark-haired woman lifted off the car top and put it in the trunk. He had forgotten that the engine was in the rear in this model.

He cracked his window a tad. Minutes later he heard a car door slam. Reggie came into view and tossed a soft travel bag and a small black case into the backseat. She was wearing all black. She walked out of his view.

He heard another slam and a throaty rumble. The little car bolted out of the driveway, turned right and drove directly toward him. It turned left. For a single heartbeat the law of time was revoked and the woman in the passenger seat of the Fiat stared straight into Jazz's startled eyes. He knew that the tinted window reflected the blue sky and fluffy clouds and stopped her gaze short of reaching his. Nevertheless, his heart tripped over its next beat.

The dark shoulder-length hair, the glasses and the scar that ran through her lip—it was Bridget Clemens!

The adrenaline surging through his muscles caused him to overshoot the correct gear and the little Japanese car stuttered in pursuit.

Reggie ducked in and out of traffic like a gypsy cab driver in the

Manhattan theater crunch. Jazz's little white rental car was agile and quick and he managed to stay on her trail. She pulled into what looked like a driveway. The sign said Bachman Place. They threaded their way down the narrow, steep winding road that snaked into Mission Valley. They were the only drivers on this path and Jazz struggled to lag back so as not to be seen. Bachman emerged onto Hotel Circle. Reggie turned east then nipped left under the freeway and merged into westbound Highway Eight traffic. Jazz was back within two car lengths when they went up a fly-over ramp that lifted them over a few southbound lanes then swooped down and funneled them north on Interstate Five.

The weekend traffic was heavy but steady. Fortunately, the Fiat had a whip antenna with a purple wispy thing at the end. Jazz was able to see the violet tassel even when the little car was hidden by traffic. After they merged to the left several times they both cruised in the center lane. After several minutes Jazz activated his cell phone and pressed speed dial and nine.

"Gillian," she answered her newly familiar voice accompanied by East Coast traffic sounds.

"Gillian," he echoed.

"Jazz! I've been calling you. Did you get my messages?"

"Geez, no. I always forget to check."

"Well, the Ripley guy is on his way to Cardiff-by-the-Sea or Encinitas."

"I'm tailing Reggie north on Interstate Five now . . . and guess who's with her? Bridget Clemens," he answered his own question.

"Interesting! Things, as Alice said, are becoming curious-er and curious-er! We saw the late yet very active Bridget Clemens yesterday. She came home and took the passports in."

"I looked right into her face from not three feet away!" Jazz insisted.

"We were across the street, but it sure looked like her here, too." Gillian said.

"Wow," he exclaimed. "Are you all right?"

"Rachel had to make an emergency trip to Tampa last afternoon.

I took a sleeping pill and slept in really late. No, no, I'm fine. She just got back. We're on our way to the Rainbow now."

"Uh-oh, it looks like they're getting ready to exit at Solana Beach," Jazz said while negotiating across two traffic lanes and accessing the exit ramp, two cars behind the little Fiat.

"Solana Beach? Not Encinitas? We figured they were going to intercept the creep at a train station in Encinitas. You be careful. I think they're going to that train stop to maybe kill the guy!" Adrenaline raised her voice a pitch.

"Wa-tha-fu!?" Jazz gasped audibly. "How did we come to this conclusion?"

The little Fiat exited to the right up a ramp, which curved counterclockwise back over the freeway. They were headed toward the beach. The area east of the freeway had looked hilly and residential but just across the broad white strip of I-5 the road sloped westward to the silver-blue Pacific Ocean. A thick roll of gray fog devoured the horizon keeping its resolute promise to come ashore every evening.

The Fiat turned sharply to the right. By the time Jazz found a parking place the two women were already in the Solana Beach train station. He trotted into the station. The clock tower showed three fifty-five. He joined the dozen or so people milling about and managed to stay out of the sight of Reggie and the other woman who were peering up the track to the north.

Several minutes past four an Amtrak train pulled into the station. Two men and seven women disembarked. Reggie and her pal scrutinized the two men. Only one of them carried luggage—a drab cardboard-colored suitcase. Reggie's gaze settled on him. The brawny man lumbered across the tracks to where the northbound train would board. Maybe, Jazz thought, he intended to double back on another train.

Jazz consulted a timetable and noted that although the Amtrak and the Coaster followed the same route, the southbound Amtrak had not stopped in Encinitas. The man could catch the next northbound Coaster. It would indeed stop there.

The women held a brief discussion, then Reggie's Bridget-look-alike cohort left in a brisk trot to follow the man with the suitcase to the Coaster stop. Reggie jogged back toward the parked Fiat. Meanwhile, the other woman seemed to be engaging the big man in small talk.

Jazz was already running for his rental car while keeping an eye out for the Fiat. He heard the little Italian car grumble to life, saw gravel tossed into the air, and watched as the pale blue sports car shot out of the lot and fishtailed toward northbound 101. The fog bank was rolling in fast, turning the late afternoon a misty gray.

Traffic on 101 was a bitch. Jazz could see Reggie holding a cell phone between her shoulder and her ear as she snaked her way through the bumper-to-bumper cars creeping north. Jazz assumed she was in contact with her cohort and he stayed as close behind her as he dared.

He watched the northbound Coaster clatter past.

As they pulled into Encinitas, the lowering fog caused the lights to halo and colors to fade. Up ahead a figure stood by the roadside hugging its arms around its body while alternately springing up and down on its toes and running in place. It was either a signal or a method of generating warmth. Probably both. Reggie pulled up to the figure. The hazy apparition solidified into her cohort and climbed into the little car.

They traveled up the road a few blocks, pulled a U-turn and nosed into the curb in front of a bar. Jazz idled nearby as the women opened the trunk and reinstalled the car's roof. Since there was room now, they moved a large case from the backseat into the trunk. Bridget removed a wooden cylinder from the case before she slammed the bonnet shut. Then the two women settled down to watch the entrance to the bar.

Jazz figured if he had to follow them in the fog and the dark, chances were he would lose them. He needed to decide on a plan of action now. He turned off his lights and pulled into the curb halfway up the next block. He flipped open his phone, pressed speed dial and then nine.

"Gillian," a whispered voice answered.

"Gillian, they're watching the door of a bar. The guy must be in there. It's so foggy, I've got to do something or it may be too late. Should I go warn him?"

Gillian thought for a moment. "Can you do that and not be seen by Reggie?"

"Maybe there's a back entrance," he pondered. "I'll check." He slid the dome light switch off, eased out of the car and clicked the door shut. He skulked north alongside the building, staying in the shadows. The collar of his Windbreaker was turned up to the chill and his baseball cap pulled low on his brow. He trotted away from the bar and turned left at the corner. Just behind the row of shops on the main drag there was a dirt easement.

"Gillian, I'm heading into sort of a dirt alley now," he informed her.

He entered the dark path and jogged southward as quickly as the patchy fog and uneven terrain would allow. When he came to the cross street he peeked from the darkness. He could just make out the women's silhouettes in the Fiat. He jammed his fists into his pockets and lowered his head as he crossed the side street. Reggie would be hard-pressed to recognize him even if she did notice his shadowy figure.

There was a dented, green Dumpster on the side of a concrete slab lit dimly by a single yellow bulb next to the rear door to the bar. The door was unlocked. He could see his breath. Gillian could only hear a brushing sound and strained breathing.

"Gillian, I'm going in the back door now," Jazz whispered. "Oh, shit! Oh, shit! Oh, shit!" he muttered as adrenaline flooded his bloodstream. He made sure the cell was set to vibrate and flipped it shut.

The fetid air in the dingy hall made his eyes water. He clutched a clean folded handkerchief over his nose and mouth and peered through a bamboo-bead curtain. The burly man he had seen get off the Solana Beach train earlier sat at the bar.

Gillian heard the phone disengage. "Jazz! Jazz," she begged. There was no answer. "Damn," she uttered as she frantically hung up and pushed speed dial and nine—four rings and then his voice mail. "What have we gotten ourselves into?" she asked herself as she shut her phone. Her gut churned with dread.

Déjà vu swept over Jazz like nausea when he parted the beaded curtain and went into the bar.

Chapter 41
Dark of the Moon

Rachel and Gillian planned to settle in before the technicians and security guards took their positions for the Saturday evening service. As they passed the array of outfits on racks, Gillian saw what she was looking for—the stack of plastic shoeboxes. She peeled the plastic lid from the top box and removed one shiny, pointy-toed, patent leather shoe and replaced the lid.

They cleared a three-foot aisle behind the chairs from the booths area to the elevator. This would allow a quick, hidden retreat to the elevator in an emergency. They waited on chairs in a nest they formed among the stacks. From that vantage point they could see two of the flickering screens in the security booth. Those screens were supposed to be focused on the two stairways coming up to this area. One did, the other did not. The latter out-of-kilter camera showed a railing and a wall.

Gillian took the pilfered walkie-talkie and stepped into the open elevator when they saw men coming up the opposite stairwell. She propped the elevator door open slightly with the pointy-toed shoe and turned off the interior light.

The technicians arrived.

Gillian sat on the floor of the elevator and waited. She tried a few times to ring up Jazz. "Sheboygan," she groused each time his voice-mail message engaged. She soon found herself writing dialogue in her head. A new book was playing itself out in her imagination. She wondered if it would be possible to track the life of the noted evangelist back to The Enclave—to fill in the blanks and the motivations. Maybe stir up the demons that drove him. This creative thinking filled time as smoothly as sand in an hourglass.

The tech turned up the sound when Hollister took the stage. The crowd hushed in anticipation as the houselights dimmed. Gillian could hear Hollister speaking. Gradually his voice intensified to ranting and emoting. The congregation began moaning. The machine-driven wind whipped through the audience as lightning flashed and the theatrical storm built to a crescendo.

Rachel crawled over and tapped on the elevator door.

Gillian took the cue. She pulled the shoe free and allowed the elevator doors to shut. In the guise of Hollister's new assistant from New York, she said in her best Bronx twang, "Attention all personnel, a mandatory meeting will be held in Reverend Hollister's wing during the music and fireworks. Set all controls to automatic. Be prompt." A walkie-talkie tried to ring in. "No exceptions!" She turned the device off.

Two more bolts of lightning, a dramatic pause and the houselights came up. The crowd burst into raucous applause and cheering. Hollister stood on his marble pedestal as it rose to its fullest height. The audience hushed. "My faithful followers, it gives me great pleasure to share with you my heavenly piper, Bridget Clemens!" As the pulpit receded from the limelight, Hollister stepped to the stage and sat. The houselights dimmed and a tiny spotlight fixed upon the piper's balcony. The pipes emitted the full, rich tones of "Amazing

Grace."

The technicians grumbled at their summons and put things on automatic. Their complaints were silenced by the stairwell door whooshing shut behind them.

Rachel tapped on the elevator door again then trotted down the hall to slip a couple of chairs into the push bar to prevent or at least delay access from that stairwell.

Gillian rigged the elevator door open again. Rachel sat down at the monitor's desk and slipped on a pair of earphones.

Damn! Jazz went into that bar over an hour ago and he's still not answering his cell. Things aren't tense enough here; I have to worry about him. She fiddled with the thin silver cylinder that emitted a ruby-red laser beam. She would use it to warn Rachel of someone's approach. She sighted along the barrel and danced the red dot right in front of Rachel. Cool. Rachel snapped her head around and saw Gillian was just practicing. She smiled. Gillian soon grew tired of the toy and tucked it in her pocket.

Rachel turned on the speaker in the control room. The keening pipes were tearing into the melodious heart of "Grace." Gliding just under the melody a slightly discordant bagpipe shriek of agony sent shivers up the spine of anyone within earshot. After a few minutes the tune segued into, "Oh Happy Day!" Then another vaguely familiar song wove its way into the forefront. Gillian hummed it under her breath trying to remember the words . . . dah-dah-dah-de-dah-dah-dah . . . then it was gone and "Grace" was back. The choir began its lengthy medley with "Grace" as the pipes faded like a dying asthmatic.

In the darkness of the soloist's balcony Belle was seized by the need to verify the fact that Hollister truly wasn't who he claimed to be. *Damn. We should have done this before.* By the light of a tiny flashlight she replaced the lethal dart with an untreated one. If there were no reaction she would abort her plan.

The spotlight was on the choir loft. Their set ran precisely thirty-two minutes and was punctuated by Saturday night's *New Moon* pre-programmed light show and pyrotechnics. Hollister sat motionless as the choir sang. Only his left hand in its white glove resting on his knee was slightly illuminated by the dimmed houselights.

Rachel also studied him with absolute concentration. "You are a consummate showman," she mused just over her breath, "but why couldn't you also be who you say you are?"

As if in answer, Belle chose that moment to puff the untreated sliver into the back of Hollister's gloved hand.

His body tensed and his arm jerked up slightly.

Startled, Rachel lost her grip on the microphone but caught it as it fell toward the floor. Her fingers clutched the switch. She did not notice the red light that indicated the mike was live.

Hollister brushed at the twinge on the back of his left hand and looked down to pull a sliver from the white glove. He twirled it between his thumb and forefinger. This was no insect stinger. It was symmetrical and had tiny flares. He slipped it into his vestment pocket and noticed a small red stain beginning to bloom on the white glove covering his left hand. Dawning realization propelled his right hand to cover the stain . . . but not before Belle, Rachel and Gillian all saw it.

"You bloody, buggering, murdering bastard!" Belle snarled pulling the small opera glasses from her eyes.

"Geez, man!" Rachel gasped. "Is your glove bleeding?"

Hollister shot bewildered eyes skyward then pressed his fingers to the earpiece in his right ear and darted his eyes to the mirrored windows near the ceiling. Gillian jumped back as though she could be seen. Rachel felt his eyes penetrate the one-way glass and bore into her own.

Hollister pulled his left hand to his chest and edged his chair back farther into the gloom, furtively scanning the entire sanctuary.

When Gillian saw him pull back into the shadows, she retreated behind the chairs near the elevator. "Let's get out of here," she uttered in a stage whisper.

Rachel held up two fingers signaling to wait a couple of

minutes.

"Prosthesis, me blooming arse!" Belle growled. She reached for the treated dart and knocked the silver case to the floor. Just short of panic she pulled the penlight from her pocket and swept it across the floor, retrieved the tiny, deadly missile and hastily slid it into the blowgun.

Hollister's eyes panned past the shadowy depth of the little soloist balcony but a momentary speck of light caught in his periphery. He snapped his eyes directly at it and watched it go out. "Ms. Clemens, are you a naughty girl?" his whisper was covered by the music.

Belle peered into the shadows onstage. He was gone!

Hollister crossed the familiar stage. Tiny lights outlined the steps and pathway toward the utility doors and the upper level. The doors sighed shut behind him and he took the service stairs two at a time. The soft Italian slippers he wore with his vestments muffled his footfalls.

"Oh, my God . . . where did he go?" Belle gasped. A flood of adrenaline and assorted alarm juices surged through her body. Belle slipped the loaded blowgun back into the false seam in her right boot. *I'd better flee this scene.* She shoved her things into the case and pushed her way through the thick velvet curtains.

Something heavy and metallic smashed into her left temple. Spider webs of somnolence gathered in her head as she felt herself twisted by a powerful arm clamped across her neck and under her chin.

The concentrated pressure of the sleeper hold diminished her breath and restricted the blood flow to her brain. Someone was behind her. Her knees buckled and in the subdued light of the little anteroom, she could see a trickle of blood on the back of that person's left hand. The other hand held a stubby automatic to her right temple. The glove was gone and the lightweight brace that usually held the fingers rigid hung from his wrist by ribbons of gauze. She lost her hold on the bagpipe case and it slipped to the floor.

His voiced growled in her ear, "Let's go see your little friend in the booth." His words swam in the thick fog swirling in her brain. He dragged her into the hall.

"I have a little friend?" Belle wondered. The force of the hold on her chin had dislodged the device that simulated the harelip. The wire cut deeply into her lip and gums and blood began to drip on the left sleeve of the man's white robe.

"Damn!" He uttered and pushed her away with a threatening gesture that signaled, "Quiet." He grabbed the device from her mouth. He looked at her disheveled wig and said, "What have you done with my bagpiper? Take those off!"

Belle wavered as the room kept tilting. She removed the wig and glasses, stooped to set them down but lost her equilibrium and let them slip to the floor. Hollister dropped the wire device on the pile. A dribble of blood soaked into the white net lining of the wig.

He grabbed the phony piper by the upper arm in a pinching grip and prodded her with the gun to climb the stairs. When they reached the turn in the hallway he peered around to see if it was clear. He put the nose of the gun up under her chin and dragged her toward the security booth.

Gillian became aware of them when she first heard the door at the top of the stairwell whoosh close. She fumbled with the laser pen and tried to dance the tiny light all around Rachel. "Oh, no!" she panicked. Then she remembered her technique and sighted along the barrel of the pen. She depressed the button. The tiny red light swept across her own eyes, filling her vision with brilliant red pain. She managed to replace a scream with a sharp intake of air. "Oh, shit, oh, shit, oh, shit!" she screamed in her head. "I'm holding it the wrong way!" She fumbled the pen and narrowly caught it before it clattered to the polished floor. It was too late. When her vision began to clear, the sight of the gun Hollister held against the woman's face snatched Gillian's voice right out of her throat.

Hollister with the woman in tow was in front of the security booth. Two more steps and he was able to see Rachel, half-standing, dressed all in pink, gripping the microphone and wearing earphones.

She was peering intently into the dark sanctuary.

Gillian melted into the chairs and became as invisible as she could. The two figures loomed between her and Rachel. She watched, held her breath and wondered who it was. There was so little light. *Oh, It's Belle!* Gillian scuttled behind the chairs and kept apace with their progress up the hall. Her sheepskin slippers rendered her footfalls soundless.

Hollister palmed the snub-nosed gun, drew back his hand and struck a sharp blow to the side of Belle's head again. She sagged. He let her slip to the floor where she sprawled unconscious.

Gillian froze.

Hollister strode toward Rachel. She couldn't stop him. He had a gun. Should she yell to warn Rachel? Could she?

"No! Wait!" Sinistral entreated.

Hollister entered the booth on silent feet and grabbed Rachel out of the chair, brandishing the gun in her face. The earphones and mike clattered to the floor causing a screech in his right ear. He yanked out the earplug and dropped it on the floor.

The chokehold on Rachel's throat compressed the air and blood flow and a gossamer veil could be seen slipping across her eyes. She pulled on his arm with both hands. He scooped up the microphone, turned off its switch as well as the one on the control board that, like a keen knife slitting a throat, severed the music.

Through the glass, backlighting Hollister and Rachel, huge multicolored fireworks burst in the sky of the cathedral. None of them reacted to the cascade. The sound of the explosion barely penetrated the glass. The Saturday evening *Dark of the Moon* light show was under way.

Hollister dragged Rachel around to the sound booth. He grabbed a handful of purple plastic cable ties from a chipped coffee mug with a Dolphins logo. "What makes you sniveling, whining women think you can come in here and try to destroy all of this?" He swept the air with the fistful of cable ties. "Did you really think I would just roll over?" His shouting escalated.

Rachel, visibly fighting the urge to surrender to oblivion, released her right hand's grip on his forearm and reached to the small of her back.

Hollister dropped the ties and grabbed her hand. He released the chokehold and with his left hand felt the bulk of the compact gun in the small of Rachel's back. "What's this?" he asked and reached under her jacket to yank the small automatic from its hideout holster. He lifted his vestment and slipped her weapon into his back pocket. "Are you cops?" he snarled.

As she regained consciousness, Belle's face reflected her effort to encompass the strange woman Hollister had in tow.

Gillian tapped her nails on the floor by Belle's face. Belle peered into the shadows and saw another pink woman! She blinked and tried harder to clear her head. She reached in her boot for the blowgun and had managed to pull it out partway when Hollister, with the first pink lady in tow, delivered a shove with his foot to her shoulder blades.

Belle pitched forward, moaned and thrust her leg under the chair in front of Gillian, hiding the half exposed tube from Hollister. Gillian saw the protruding tube and held onto the boot as the battered piper struggled out of it and to her knees.

A look of resigned panic crossed Belle's face as her foot slipped free of the boot and she realized her weapon was gone.

"Over here!" Hollister ordered and pointed to a spot in the middle of the hall. He picked up a few of the cable ties and ratcheted one around each of Rachel's wrists, threaded another through the first, yanked her arms behind her back slid the connector through the other wristband cinching it snug. She was manacled as securely as any arrested felon—and there was no key. He shoved Belle down with her back to Rachel's and trussed Belle's wrists together in front of her.

Hollister began to pace and scream a tirade. He gestured and threatened with the gun. Belle started to protest and without hesitation he swatted her once again with the palmed automatic. She slumped sideways.

"Jesus! Jesus! Jesus!" he spat. He pulled the stained vestment off and tore off the brace that still dangled from his left wrist. "Jee-sus! Now I have to kill you!" He threw his hands into the air.

"Stupid! Stupid!" he spat in their faces. "Don't you know how powerful I am? I advise world leaders. You saw all the people here. They depend on me." He lectured his predators like children. "This is like a small city. I save people. I am a channel and they are healed. I am wealthy beyond your dreams and you expect me to give it all up because of something that happened all those years ago? I had to do away with him! He was a useless slug of a man! A drunkard, a self-pitying cripple."

Gillian thought he was probably referring to the real Hollister. She shoved the penlight laser in her pocket and pulled the blowgun out of the boot. Silently she uttered, "Geez! Why couldn't it be a gun like Rachel's? It's a goddamn peashooter." She looked in the boot. There was nothing more. She could see the fletched end of the tiny dart just beyond the mouthpiece.

Maybe it's a tranquilizer dart. Maybe I just have to hit him anywhere. Okay, I can do this. I blew a pretty mean peashooter in my day—

But this was real. She knelt down and was grateful for the dim lighting and the adrenaline that shrouded the pain of her knees grinding on the polished floor. She scooted behind the chairs to the opening. It was just about where he was pacing. The bound women were to his left.

"Do you know how many years I've worked and prepared?" He raised his hands, and the gun, threw back his head and shouted, "Gaaaaaaahd! Why now? Why ever? Arghhhhhh!"

She had one shot. She had to get closer and right now. Gillian sized up her options. Maybe I can rush out and knock him off his feet . . . and then what? A plan began to form in her head.

She pulled off the fluffy polishing slippers. She lay flat on her back near the wall. She slipped one of the oversized lamb's wool footies under her behind and the other under her shoulder blades. With her knees bent, she put her feet against the wall and scooted her behind as close to the wall as she could. She watched him downside-up from her prone position. The next time he halted his pacing and delivered a protest skyward, she held the blowgun to her mouth and straightened her legs sharply. Her body, mostly on the sheepskin, shot noiselessly from between the chairs and came to rest a dozen feet into the hall—out of the shelter of the chairs . . . in plain sight!

Rachel's mouth formed a shocked O.

Gillian took a deep breath, refined her aim almost straight up, closed her eyes and exploded her breath mightily into the mouthpiece.

After a heartbeat, she opened her eyes. He stood there, looming above her. In gradual increments, he lowered his gaze to hers.

Oh, my God! I missed!

Panicky thoughts screamed in Gillian's head, which was filling with fluffy white cotton balls effectively blocking all audio input. She blew again and again into the empty tube. It made a series of impotent hissing sounds. She fumbled for the laser light in her pocket.

Hollister peered toward the floor and brought his gun to bear on her blanched face. She could see the rifling in the barrel. It looked as though the bore could launch a bowling ball. She watched in frozen horror as the knuckle on his trigger finger whitened with increased pressure.

"Reggie and Jazz say Hi!" she braved.

Hollister's eyes widened in what might have been comprehension. He gave a little cough from the back of his throat and after one more eternal moment, from a great height, he pitched forward into a heap across her legs. She lifted her head and his lifeless eyes looked directly into hers. The laser pen rolled out of her gloved fingers with a tinny *clink*. She saw the makeup covering hairline scars under his cheekbones and at his jawline. She shuddered and a slight whimper escaped her lips. "Aaghhh . . ."

The other women first looked toward the sound of Gillian's frantic puffs on the empty blowgun then up at Hollister as he coughed and fell. They all slumped in silence for a full minute.

"Rachel," Gillian finally whispered, "are you okay?"

"Fine," Rachel responded.

"Belle?"

Belle was puzzled about more than just the fact that they knew her name, but first she had to see where he was hit. "I'm cool," she said as she crawled over to Marcus. With her bound hands she rolled Marcus off the second pink lady's legs and onto his back.

Gillian shoved her hand into her pocket and pulled out her little Swiss Army knife. She pried open the biggest blade and sawed through Belle's plastic handcuffs.

Belle was pleased to see that both the women wore surgical gloves, too. She fished the penlight from her pocket and ran it all over the front of the Marcus's body.

Gillian scuttled to Rachel's side. Rachel leaned her head into Gillian's shoulder. After a moment Gillian slipped the blade between the plastic restraint and her wrist and began sawing.

Belle looked puzzled for a moment, then stood up and studied Gillian's abandoned woolly slippers. She calculated the dart's trajectory. Then stooped to put her hand under the man's neck and lifted. His head fell back and his mouth gaped. She played the light on the roof of his mouth and smiled. With two surgical-gloved fingers she reached back toward his palate and pulled out the tiny dart. She flourished it before her mystery cohort. "Nice shot," she said to Gillian.

"*Nngh*," Gillian replied. She still clutched the blowgun.

Belle pulled Rachel's gun from Hollister's trousers and slid it to her. Rachel nodded her thanks.

Delicately holding the dart between her thumb and forefinger and wearing only one boot, Belle clumped down the hall to the restroom.

Gillian wrapped her arms around Rachel. She nestled her face into Gillian's neck and said, "Intense!"

A toilet flushed and Belle emerged from the restroom. She reached under the chairs, retrieved her boot and pulled it on. She crossed to Gillian, pried the blowgun from her clenched grip and slipped it back into its hiding place.

Gillian wanted to kiss Rachel's hands but she just cooed and massaged the red indentations on her wrists. After a poignant moment she felt a blush bloom from her chest and her pulse rushing in her ears. She stood and said, "I want to see his butt before he wakes up."

Belle looked at her quizzically but undid the slender leather belt and pulled the pinstriped slacks to his knees. When she rolled him over they saw Reggie's heroic handiwork from all those years ago. It looked like the laced closure on a football.

Reggie will be pleased, Gillian thought, to hear how many stitches it must have taken just to close the surface wound.

"Cool!" Rachel said.

"Let's get out of here!" Gillian said. "We need to talk! And we'll leave him—" she gestured to the half-clothed body on the floor, "—with a lot of explaining to do."

Belle reached down and picked up Hollister's discarded vestment, the laser pen and the scraps of plastic ties. She saw the blood from her lip on the sleeve. She bundled everything together.

"I'll be two minutes," Belle said and dashed to the anteroom by her balcony. Gillian and Rachel checked the hall area and got on the elevator.

As an afterthought, Rachel walked across the hall to the control room, pulled some cables free to disable all the cameras.

Belle picked up her bagpipes case, the disguise glasses, wig and wire harelip device from the hallway floor. She pulled a union card sealed in a plastic bag out of the instrument bag. Her hands were shaking. The card showed Bridget looking seriously into the camera. Belle kissed the picture lightly, tore open the baggie and dropped the untouched card to the floor along with a small scrap of a fortune cookie message that read, POETIC JUSTICE. She shoved the vestment and disguise into the case and dashed up the stairs, down the hall and slapped the mission statement beginning *Patriarchy of the World* on the body and leaped into the service elevator. Rachel released the door. A rattling of the wedged hallway door and the sound of pounding fists faded as they descended.

They walked in brisk lockstep toward the entrance, past the velvet rope, out of the complex and off the grounds. The choir was winding up its post-fireworks medley. The last strains of "Amazing Grace" floated after them. They broke into a synchronized trot.

"Do you have a vehicle, Belle?" Rachel panted.

Belle's face registered surprise again but she shrugged and said, "I rented the car with Bridget's ATM card and license weeks ago. I had it wiped clean before tonight's service. It's back there in her parking space."

They loaded Belle's bagpipes in the back of Rachel's Rodeo.

"About Hollister having explaining to do . . ." Belle began.

They didn't dispose of all their surgical gloves, disguises or vestments until they were miles away—and then only one piece at a time. The harelip device was just a balled up wire by the time Belle removed the cap from the hollow post of a chain-link fence surrounding a parking lot and dropped the twisted wire in and replaced the cap. The insert holding the darts was dropped to dissolve in the inland waterway.

Chapter 42
Poetic Justice

Inside the beachfront bar in Encinitas, the burly trainman got up, looked at Jazz and shrugged toward the back entrance. Everything in Jazz's being screamed for him to stay out of that dirty alley and away from the brute, but his options seemed to lean heavily toward—none. He wasn't willing to give this randy guy what he seemed to be expecting but at least getting him out the back door was a good start.

Maybe I can convince him to leave the area and avoid Reggie all together. Oh, God, I hope so. He caught the closing door and started down the five steps to the dimly lit alley. Scary *déjà vu* vibes caromed around in his head again like scattering billiard balls.

The last traces of daylight were fading fast. A murky layer of slate-gray fog lowered the sky and muffled the surf. The air was chilled and heavy with the fetid smell of rotting seaweed.

An abrupt scraping sound spooked Jazz and he turned to bolt back to the bar.

The huge man was fast. He grabbed a handful of Jazz's jacket and yanked him around into a jackhammer punch to the left side of his face and fireworks burst behind his eyes. He bounced off the metal railing and landed face down on the littered concrete.

"Pervert!" the man spat. "Fuckin' boys upstate don't mean a fuckin' thing don't give you fuckin' punk pansies the okey dokey to come on to me on the outside," he snarled, "so maybe I'll just teach you not to jump to fuckin' conclusions."

Any memory of the attack slipped before it could grab hold. The pain of his rib cracking from the behemoth's sharp kick awakened him as he rolled across the pavement and curled up like an injured armadillo. He felt his cell phone in his Windbreaker pocket. Half in reflex and half by intention, he punched two buttons.

Sitting in the Fiat in front of the bar, Reggie pressed the phone to her left ear, listened, and whispered, "Jazz?" There was only a scuffling sound and then a foghorn. She raised her head from the phone and caught the fading foghorn sound in her right ear. She looked at Haley and covered the mouthpiece. "Did you just hear a foghorn?"

"Yeah," Haley looked puzzled. "There's an ocean and it's foggy."

Reggie strained to listen again and flinched when Jazz's anguished voice rasped in her ear, "Oh, God! Reg, the alley!"

Then, again, when a prissy falsetto voice mimicked, "Oh, God, Reg, the alley."

Jazz began to croon in a whisper, "Itsy bitsy spider . . ."

Reggie didn't process how Jazz got there, only that he was there—in the alley. She sprang into action, shoved Haley out of the car, and headed for the nearest corner. Haley scrambled for her backpack and raced after her in a dead run.

The behemoth delivered two pile driver punches to Jazz's chest, then picked him up like a duffel of dirty laundry and threw him on his belly halfway up the steps to the bar.

The hefty trainman held Jazz in place with his left hand as he unzipped his own pants and worked them down. He pulled a foil packet from his shirt pocket, hummed to himself as he tore off the top with his teeth and rolled the enclosed sheath down his turgid member.

A voice from the dark alley entrance grunted, "Bugger!" in a raucous, guttural Cockney growl.

The trainman snapped his head toward the voice and the dart struck him between his startled, gray eyes. He fell to his knees and toppled over before he lost his erection.

The two women stepped into the circle of light. Reggie shoved her cell phone into her pocket as she dropped to the dirty concrete steps to cradle Jazz's swollen and bleeding head. She reached down and gently pulled up his trousers. She wept softly and chanted, "How, how, how did you get here?"

The other woman's eyes were dry. She tossed Reggie a pair of surgical gloves. Still confused by Jazz's presence, Reggie managed to tug the gloves on without letting him go.

The woman shoved the blowgun into her bulging backpack and pulled out the small video camera with the attached light and ordered, "Reg! Chill!" She held the camera toward Reggie. "This dart will only last twenty minutes!"

Reggie took off her Windbreaker and fashioned a pillow for Jazz's battered head. She prepared the camera as the other woman pulled a large hypodermic syringe and a vial from a plastic bag. She filled the hypo, then slipped the vial and bag into her pocket. She nodded to Reggie.

Reggie turned on the power and the camera lights flooded the alley. The other woman glanced around and spotted Jazz's cell phone. She picked it up, turned it off and put it in her pocket.

Reggie began taping.

Jazz, in the slow process of regaining consciousness, watched groggily as the women went to work. The second woman sure looked like Bridget.

She swabbed the trainman's skin and plunged the needle deep into each of the muscle groups in the trainman's right forearm. Then she refilled the hypodermic and did the same to the left.

The dark-haired woman with the hooked nose and harelip turned and looked directly into the camera. She spoke in a loud, irritating voice, her words a bit distorted by the deformed upper lip and an accent. Her bangs slashed a severe line above her dated, oversized glasses.

With the timbre of London's East End, she began. "That was a drug containing Thiopentone. Injected into the muscle this drug causes severe necrosis. We call it poetic justice." She paused. "Now he can live his life without arms . . . just as one of his many victims does." She stood and visibly resisted the impulse to deliver a sharp punt to the man's exposed scrotum. She bent the needle and laid the spent hypodermic on his chest. She noticed his flaccid, tattooed fingers and lifted them to the camera and said, "I guess Ol' RIP 'N' ROAR may still roar but he will rip no more."

Reggie turned the camera off and re-immersed the alley into the misty darkness that surrounded the diffuse circle of dirty, yellow light and its degenerate centerpiece.

Haley pulled two more sealed bags from her backpack. The first one contained a worn passport sealed in plastic. She kissed the picture lightly, tore open the bag and dumped the untouched passport near the dented, green Dumpster. A ticket stub fell partially from the little blue book. The concert ticket was for a group called Poetic Justice. The second bag contained a Pepsi can. She opened the plastic bag enough to expose the top of the can. She popped the top, spilled some on the ground and placed the can on the edge of the second step.

Reggie ejected the tape from the camera and placed the cartridge on top of Rip's body next to the hypodermic, being careful not to smudge Bridget's prints. She unfurled a copy of their mission statement beginning *Patriarchy of the World* and placed it on his chest.

Haley scanned the area. She bent over the body and pulled the fletched sliver from between his unfocused eyes and rubbed a dusty thumb over the tiny hole. She dropped the missile in a strewn beer can, crushed the can and started to drop it in the huge recycling bin. She decided to shove it in her pocket instead. She lifted her eyes toward the murky sky and flipped a conspiratorial thumbs-up.

They dragged Jazz to the car, talking to him as though he were a drunk for the benefit of anyone who might be on the street. With just a little difficulty they folded him into the space behind the front seat of the tiny Fiat.

Haley took her chanter and walked into the main entrance to the bar. Reggie drove the car down the block around the corner and parked in the fog.

She leaned over the seat and cooed to Jazz and winced over his bruised and swelling face.

In a few moments a jazzy version of "Oh Happy Day" piped out of the bar around the corner. The tune segued into a countermelody—familiar but elusive. The piano player picked up the melody and soon several older female voices rose in song. It was an anthem from a few years back. "We are gentle, angry women and we are fighting for our lives!" When the music stopped, a burst of applause and cheering preceded the staccato of running feet. The other woman slipped into the front seat clutching the chanter as Reggie eased away from the curb without lights.

"I told them to check the alley," the woman panted.

They were even with the south end of the alley now and could see and hear the milling crowd in the dim island of yellow light.

"Somebody call nine-one-one!" a voice shouted.

Reggie idled down the block and around a corner before she turned on the fog lights and gently gave the Fiat some gas.

Jazz, certain he was hallucinating, watched in awe as the woman pulled the device that simulated the harelip from her mouth and jammed the contraption, along with the dark wig and heavy, rimmed glasses, into a brown paper bag. She ruffled her halo of dark auburn hair and massaged the crease in her upper lip area.

Reggie noticed Jazz's expression in the mirror and said, "Jazz, say hello to Haley Baxter."

Jazz was conscious enough to tell them where he had parked the rental car. Reggie circled around. Haley retrieved the vehicle before the police arrived, and she fell in behind Reggie's little sports car.

The two cars wended their way to the freeway. As if by telepathy, both drivers worried aloud that something had been missed due to Jazz's interference. Neither could think of a thing.

They were heading south on Interstate Five when they saw the rotating lights of sheriffs' cars hastening north through the swirling fog.

To ease some of Jazz's pain, Reggie pulled into an all-night truck stop and bought a couple of chemical ice packs as well as a conventional one and filled it with some chipped ice from the soda dispenser.

A trash truck was compacting trash from the Dumpsters behind the building. Haley dropped the bag with the Bridget disguise in the next Dumpster. She watched from around the corner as the truck smashed the bag and its contents into all the other garbage of the day. She did a little Snoopy dance back to the car.

They drove back to Hillcrest and helped Jazz into the cottage, reenacting the drunken routine. Reggie had some Tylenol 3 with codeine. That helped. Jazz allowed Reggie to bathe him and clean his wounds.

Haley bought some medical supplies and they patched him together, wrapping his ribs as he told them the story of his involvement. He didn't mention Gillian and Rachel's tailing Belle.

"I'm not thrilled by your being here or knowing our plan," Haley sounded off. "But, so far there seems to be no harm done. You probably left enough DNA in the alley to convict a celebrity murderer, but Rip, a bartender and some tipsy patrons are the only witnesses to tie you to that crime scene." She contemplated the scene for a moment. "And the bar was dimly lit," she added.

Jazz removed all but a single traditionally positioned earring in case the bartender in Encinitas recalled his array. Nothing seemed broken except a rib or two, nor were any stitches required.

"Your nose is going to have more character than before," Reggie noted. "And the oversized aviator sunglasses are going to be of more use than you anticipated."

They had to wait until Monday night to fly out of the country. They could return the rental car tomorrow. After all, Haley's passport showed her arriving from Southeast Asia Monday morning. Reggie's was stamped arriving from Belgium on Monday, also. The manifest for their returning flights reflected their presence on those planes.

Jazz was feeling guilty that he hadn't told them about Gillian and Rachel. He began tentatively, "Ah, Reggie," he sighed, "there's more."

Chapter 43
The Sands of Cuyagua

Rachel selected the single engine prop plane flight from the Valencia International airport to Maracay. She thought they would be able to see more. That part was true. What they saw was green, more green and then a deeper green occasionally traversed by squiggly lines. The westward hop was a typical bumpy small plane ride, an endless roller coaster with no degree of certainty that the flight would end well. Then they banked north.

The sea. The sea was spectacular. The snowy-white sand of the sea floor, visible under fathoms of pale azure water, sparkled with a hint of green. The sight of it suspended Gillian's touch of vertigo and let her squelch a curmudgeonly streak enough to admit it was an awesome sight.

A nice smooth commuter flight with Rachel might have allowed them time to recapture some of the intimacy they had shared on the beach last Friday. Incidents and events had been coming at them at such a fast and furious pace it made that romantic interlude seem like a misty memory snagged in a dream catcher.

The rickety vehicle that took them from the small airport on a steep, circuitous trek up over and down the mountain was called a jitney. That jalopy fell somewhere between vintage comic strip character Gordo's old decrepit fringed bus and Smilin' Jack's spiffy mud-encrusted World War II Jeep. The tortuous mountain road was every bit as harrowing as the primitive air travel so Gillian maintained a calm decorum while clinging to the jitney's floorboards with clenched toes.

Not until wending down the switchback trail to the pretty little bay near Guyagua's beach did she feel far enough removed from the events of the weekend to relax her tangled nerves.

Belle, or East Coast Bridget, as Gillian had come to think of her, sat in the front seat with her right foot braced on the empty doorframe. She shouted with the driver in Spanish. Rachel interpreted things of interest for Gillian.

"He said he drove three North Americans down to the hotel yesterday—a man and two women. He was told that the young man was a boxer who lost a fight and needed to recuperate and relax."

The driver's dark eyes twinkled in the rearview mirror and he added a comment.

Rachel smiled and quoted verbatim, "'the boxer man seems a little . . . ah . . . light in his shoes . . . to be a fighter but, I know nothing of North American practices.'"

It seemed pointless to take offense. The man didn't seem judgmental, just observant, and it was Jazz after all.

The overgrown thatch of an abandoned coconut plantation crowded down the steep mountainside right up to the coast road. On the seaward side of the road stretched the low sprawling adobe Hacienda Inn. At the front desk the clerk told Rachel in Spanish, "The surf is supposed to be ideal this weekend." They chatted a bit. Rachel signed the register and the clerk gave her two keys. Rachel gave one to Gillian.

"Don't I have to sign something?" asked Gillian.

"Some surfers really needed the second room. We have to share one, is that okay?" Rachel joked.

"Er . . . sure," said Gillian. Her mouth went instantly dry and her tongue felt furry and too puffy. At the same time she felt a blush start at a point between her breasts and spread clear up to the smile in her eyes. They sent their bags to their room and went to meet the others.

Gillian and Rachel stopped in the lobby doorway taking in the picture postcard view. Two curved palm trees leaning into the Caribbean breeze framed the scene. The water flowing over the long seaward side of the inn's pool created the illusion that it and the sea were one: their waters shared the same clear sea-greenish blue with the cloudless sky. Lush vegetation surrounding the hotel grew right down to the sand and was stippled with brilliant tropical red, gold and purple flowers.

Haley had reserved all their rooms with double doors opening directly onto the patio. A semi-circle of ten padded redwood lounge chairs faced the pool and the sea beyond.

Haley and Reggie were sitting upright side-by-side on one lounge. Belle must have come straight to them without checking in. She sat opposite Haley holding her hand. Jazz was stretched out fast asleep on one shaded lounge. The three women were laughing and crying and talking simultaneously. Rachel and Gillian joined the group. Reggie introduced Haley to Gillian then Gillian introduced Rachel to them both. Then Belle shook Jazz, introduced herself and pulled him and all the women into a bear hug dance to the tune of jubilant emotions and chatter.

Haley had scoped out the secluded spot last summer. While areas of the cities in Venezuela could be dangerous for travelers, this remote little cove felt safe for the first gathering of the overt North American players of Poetic Justice. Bridget had amassed and inspired the cadre on the Internet. Fate and friendship had brought Gillian and Jazz into the group and Rachel Bracken had joined them as their newly contracted attorney, bringing with her the protection of attorney-client privilege if that ever became necessary. Bridget's work was far from done. But what a start!

They pored over yesterday's papers. The headlines read variously: Mysterious Death Exposes Religious Hoax; Miami Police Mystified; Holy Moly! Who was Marcus Hollister; and Poetic Justice. The stories all had the same information.

Miami Beach Police and San Diego County lawmen continue to be mystified by two crimes committed on opposite coasts, at virtually the same time, with physical evidence pointing toward the same perpetrator.

Fingerprints, forensic evidence, eyewitnesses, and videotape all positively identify the assailant in each case as Bridget Clemens, a survivor of The Enclave kidnappings which began in Kentucky 26 years ago.

The stories described Bridget's captivity and abuse at The Enclave, her bouts of depression and years of psychiatric treatment and commitment before her suicide. It mentioned her only known relatives, Belle McCreedy of New York and Haley Baxter of South Carolina, each widowed and on an extended trip together in Southeast Asia.

The motives for the death in Florida and the serious injury inflicted on a man in California seem rooted in revenge for sexual crimes against children. Documents left at the scene in Miami Beach led investigators to discover that the Marcus Hollister impostor was in all likelihood child molester Clovis Ransom. Although never found or punished, Ransom stood convicted in absentia of the sexual molestation of children in connection with The Enclave kidnappings of the early '70s.

Ransom was identified by a pattern of moles on his neck and a five-inch scar on his right buttock inflicted and described by a survivor in the 1977 Enclave trial. Exact cause of death has not yet been determined.

The English editions of Amsterdam's *de Volkskrant* and Reno, Nevada's *Gazette Journal* both featured stories under the headline, Poetic Justice. The subject was Dr. Josepha Sterling, an American scientist working in the Netherlands and another survivor of The Enclave kidnappings.

Her abuser was one of five-escaped members of The Enclave. That

*man was found severely injured last weekend in a Southern California
beach town alley.*

*Twenty-five years ago the recently released sex offender Billy Ray
Ripley, 48, molested an eleven-year-old captive of The Enclave. He also
caused her arms to be snake-bitten in a religious ceremony. The cult failed
to get her medical care.*

*The girl survived the poisonous snakebites but lost the use of her arms
below the elbow. Ripley's parole for good behavior came just over nine
years after his capture and conviction. Unable to secure a location that
would accept his parole, he had finished his time as a resident on the
grounds of the prison.*

*The chemical paralysis inflicted upon him was videotaped and a
group calling itself Poetic Justice has claimed responsibility for the act of
retribution.*

Sterling was unavailable for comment.

The jitney driver carried a small stack of newspapers to Haley.
He looked surprised to see his two sets of passengers of the last two
days sitting and talking together. He promised Haley to bring more
papers in a day or two.

True to the newspaper code of, "If it bleeds—it leads," the initial
news accounts of last Saturday all focused on the "crimes." But won-
der-of-wonders, every one of today's papers featured The Manifesto.
Their stories revealed that mainstream media around the globe were
actually talking about the outrageous worldwide epidemic of violence
against children and women and dealing with theories of causes and
possible solutions.

The group read the accounts and sat in silent awe of the reality of
their accomplishment. Besides relief, vindication, and whatever other
complex emotions each woman felt that sunny day on the beach
in South America, as a group they shared a sense of wonder about
Bridget Clemens. Clemens, a woman broken and abused—driven
to die by her own hand before the first battle was even waged—had
brought them all together. Her organization of concepts and actions

had enabled them to take back some of the power stripped from them by predators and the injustices of the legal system.

The reality of killing a man, no matter how dastardly the man, was just seeping into Gillian's consciousness. She relived the sequence of events again and again. The conclusion she was settling into was that if she had failed to act, Belle, Rachel and she herself would all be dead . . . and Clovis would be left to become even more dangerous. In her heart—or wherever she kept values like truth and honor—Gillian knew Clovis had had no intention of letting his captives leave that dimly lit hallway atop his unholy empire alive.

Belle and Haley, aka East and West Coast Bridget respectively, talked about their gentle sister and her talents, about the years before and after The Enclave, and her innate sweetness.

This sisterhood—plus Jazz, of course—bonded now by so much more than their so-called victim status, lifted fruity tropical drinks to toast VenusD who had thought it best with all the notoriety to remain in Amsterdam.

"I'm going to be joining her next week in Brussels," Reggie said. "We haven't seen each other face-to-face in twenty-two years."

Her companions smiled interest.

"One day at a time, sis," Jazz admonished with a grin.

"Yeah, well, I'm thinking K.I.S.S., smart guy."

"Kiss?" Haley asked.

"It means: Keep it Simple, Stupid." Reggie laughed. "The old girl who raised us was addicted to AA meetings. She wasn't an alkie—just loved the meetings. We were raised on the wisdom captured in AA slogans."

"There are certainly worse ways to be raised," Belle offered.

"Speaking of wisdom," Haley asked Belle, "why didn't you just shoot Clovis in the left hand with a treated dart? That way if the hand was real, he's dead . . . if not . . ." She trailed off.

"It was a flash decision," Belle said. "In that split instant I realized we should have somehow proven his hand was real . . . or not. I don't miss often but what if I did . . . and we were wrong? Now *that* I couldn't live with."

Jazz chimed in, "What the hell was all that passport shifting about?"

Belle laughed.

"I'll field that one," Haley said. "One of our sisters in Poetic Justice is an employee in the U.S. Mint—an engraver—and another is an appointed authority with National Security Agency. We were fuzzing up the trail. Need I say more?"

The gathering cheered.

"We don't even know their true names. They were called Mudgie and Duffer in our chat rooms," added Belle. "I'm sure they will surface with new names."

"Let's all have dinner here tonight," Haley suggested. "But right now, I need a nap."

"Think I'll check out the surf before it gets too gnarly for me to look cool," Jazz said.

"Cowabunga!" Belle enthused. "I'm with you, Jazzy Dude!"

"Count me in," said Reggie.

"Cool!" Jazz grinned. "See you at the boards in ten." He strode to his room for a strap he had bought to hold his aviator shades firmly above the zinc oxide on his nose.

Rachel's eyes smiled over her sunglasses at Gillian.

Yahoo! Gillian shouted in her head as she leaped off the ground and clicked her mental heels. Outwardly she stretched her arms over her head and opened her mouth wide. "What a wonderful idea." She pushed out the words on the tail end of a feigned yawn. "A South American siesta!"

Jazz stood in the patio doorway of his room. The beads that hung across the opening as a barrier to flies conjured a brief déjà vu of the bar in Encinitas. He shuddered.

The insights and recollections I've had since last weekend jarred my status quo. They let me see a bit of what Reggie has been dealing with all these years.

For a moment Jazz watched the band of women standing around

before parting. His expression grew lighter. He smiled. *Reggie looks more radiant than ever. I've grown so fond of Gillian and Belle and Haley are twin hoots. More than the feeling of anxiety about the past, something else is welling up, something that feels like pride. I am so proud to be part of this group. I paid my dues in The Enclave now I'm part of the solution.*

He beamed wider yet and with his arms spread open he strode into the gathering.

Publications from Spinsters Ink

P.O. Box 242
Midway, Florida 32343
Phone: 800-301-6860
www.spinstersink.com

ACROSS TIME by Linda Kay Silva. If you believe in soul mates, if you know you've had a past life, then join Jessie in the first of a series of adventures that takes her Across Time.

ISBN 978-1883523-91-6 $14.95

SELECTIVE MEMORY by Jennifer L. Jordan. A Kristin Ashe Mystery. A classical pianist, who is experiencing profound memory loss after a near-fatal accident, hires private investigator Kristin Ashe to reconstruct her life in the months leading up to the crash.

ISBN 978-1-883523-88-6 $14.95

HARD TIMES by Blayne Cooper. Together, Kellie and Lorna navigate through an oppressive, hidden world where lines between right and wrong blur, sexual passion is forbidden but explosive, and love is the biggest risk of all.   ISBN 978-1-883523-90-9 $14.95

THE KIND OF GIRL I AM by Julia Watts. Spanning decades, *The Kind of Girl I Am* humorously depicts an extraordinary woman's experiences of triumph, heartbreak, friendship and forbidden love.

ISBN 978-1-883523-89-3 $14.95

PIPER'S SOMEDAY by Ruth Perkinson. It seemed as though life couldn't get any worse for feisty, young Piper Leigh Cliff and her three-legged dog, Someday.   ISBN 978-1-883523-87-9 $14.95

MERMAID by Michelene Esposito. When May unearths a box in her missing sister's closet she is taken on a journey through her mother's past that leads her not only to Kate but to the choices and compromises, emptiness and fullness, the beauty and jagged pain of love that all women must face. ISBN 978-1-883523-85-5 $14.95

ASSISTED LIVING by Sheila Ortiz-Taylor. Violet March, an eighty-two-year-old resident of Casa de los Sueños, finally has the opportunity to put years of mystery reading to practical use. One by one her comrades, the Bingos, are dying. Is this natural attrition, or is there a sinister plot afoot? ISBN 978-1-883523-84-2 $14.95

NIGHT DIVING by Michelene Esposito. *Night Diving* is both a young woman's coming-out story and a thirty-something coming-of-age journey that proves you can go home again. ISBN 978-1-883523-52-7 $14.95

FURTHEST FROM THE GATE by Ann Roberts. *Furthest from the Gate* is a humorous chronicle of a woman's coming of age, her complicated relationship with her mother and the responsibilities to family that last a lifetime. ISBN 978-1-883523-81-7 $14.95

EYES OF GRAY by Dani O'Connor. Grayson Thomas was the typical college senior with typical friends, a typical job and typical insecurities about her future. One Sunday morning, Gray's life became a little less typical, she saw a man clad in black, and started doubting her own sanity. ISBN 978-1-883523-82-4 $14.95

ORDINARY FURIES by Linda Morgenstein. Tired of hiding, exhausted by her grief after her husband's death, Alexis Pope plunges into the refreshingly frantic world of restaurant resort cooking and dining in the funky chic town of Guerneville, California. ISBN 978-1-883523-83-1 $14.95

A POEM FOR WHAT'S HER NAME by Dani O'Connor. Professor Dani O'Connor had pretty much resigned herself to the fact that there was no such thing as a complete woman. Then out of nowhere, along comes a woman who blows Dani's theory right out of the water. ISBN 1-883523-78-8 $14.95